INSATIABLE

INFERNO GAMES

ELISE KNIGHT

1

PARAGON OF VIRTUE

FELIX

"Let me the fuck in, you shitty excuse for a human!"

I recoil at Anthura's words, waking me from a sleep I don't want to awaken from. The smell of donuts fills the air, reminding me once again of Rowena and the time she ate one off the floor. Despite myself, I smirk at the memory before the anger comes back with a vengeance. I don't need to be thinking about Rowena and... I can't even let myself complete the thought. Not that Anthura gives me a chance to complete it.

"I will break this fucking door down if you don't open it in the next five..."

I miss the last word as I pull the blanket over my ears, but it's immediately yanked back, leaving me staring into Anthura's wrathful gaze.

"Stop hiding like a fucking coward and get up. The introductory meeting starts in half an hour, and I want to go through our strategy before heading down there."

My throat feels like I've swallowed razor blades and

my head is pounding. "I thought you didn't get through?" I mumble as I drag my ass out of bed. 'Hoped' would have been a better word, but I'm not in Hell because I've ever done any fucking thing right in my whole miserable life or death and Anthura is obviously my punishment. "And for that matter, how the fuck did you get into my room?"

She holds her portal up. "You forget I have access to everywhere. I wanted to give you the courtesy of answering your door, but you're a lazy fuck."

"If I'd have known I'd be spending eternity with you, I'd have become a virginal choir boy in my youth," I grumble, eliciting a frown from Anthura. She looks impeccable, as always. Her black hair is brushed back and both her makeup and outfit are perfect, and red. In another life... or death, I'd have fucked her just to shut her mouth, but something's stopping me... and it isn't just hatred, even though I despise the sight of her now. An image of Rowena staring at me, her mouth open in shock, comes unbidden, though hardly unsurprisingly. It's the image I've been playing over and over again in my dreams all night.

"I'm sure you would have been a paragon of virtue," she smirks, twisting her face into something ugly. "And you think they can get rid of me? Just because that fraud bitch Noémi decided I should be a contestant, doesn't mean I should be treated like one. Hades agreed to let me back where I belong, running the games. He's got another asshole running this level, but this time I'll be part of the team, and that means," she sidles up to me and runs her finger under my chin in a way which I'm sure she thinks is sexy but in fact makes my stomach churn, "I can help you get through the trials to the next circle."

I bat her hand away. "I don't need your help, Anthura. I'm going to get through this by myself."

She cackles as I stride past her to my bathroom. "You can't do shit without me. You think Gluttony is all about food? No, it's about your deepest temptations, your greatest desires and being able to resist them. She grabs my crotch and squeezes. "And we both know you are a fucking weak piece of shit. Fucking that bitch Robert is proof of how pathetic you are and how you'll fuck anything."

I narrow my eyes as I feel my blood pressure rise, and not to the part of me it usually heads to when a beautiful woman touches my junk. "Get the fuck out of my room, Anthura... and if I catch you using your portal to get into my room again, I will tell Hades about your cheating and have you thrown out for good."

Her eyebrow lifts. "You're going to tell on me? Fucking hell, Felix. Is that the best you can do? I can have you fed to the demons and let me tell you, in this level, they are really fucking hungry."

"Goodbye, Anthura." I slam the bathroom door in her face and lock it for good measure.

As the lock clicks into place, I lean against the door, feeling the weight of exhaustion settle over me again. Anthura's presence always drains me, but her threats and her touch leave me feeling filthy. I turn on the shower, hoping the hot water will wash away the grime of her insinuations and my own lingering shame.

The steam fills the bathroom, and I step under the scalding spray, letting it burn away the remnants of sleep. My thoughts drift back to Rowena, her image a persistent ghost in my mind. The way she looked at me, the shock and betrayal in her eyes—those moments haunt me more than anything Anthura can throw at me. I clench my fists, trying to shake off the guilt and focus on the challenges ahead. Gluttony. Temptation. Desire.

There is one thing Anthura is right about. I have always been weak when it comes to women. When I was alive, I thought bedding the world's most famous supermodels was a strength, but now I see how pathetic it really was. An ego trip, just like flaunting my wealth.

None of that matters. I'm going to be a father.

"Fuck!" I hiss, my words getting lost in the hiss of the shower, so I punch the tile instead, cracking it and splitting the skin covering my knuckles.

Above the two previous tattoos on my wrist, another one has appeared. This time it's a pale blue circle. If I stay in these games long enough, I'm going to end up looking like some wannabe gangster with a collection of terrible jail tattoos. Tearing my eyes from the most recent monstrosity, I watch the blood from my cut knuckles swirl around in the water and into the drain. I shouldn't be able to bleed in Hell, but I've been shown that isn't true. Nothing I was told of Hell as a human is remotely accurate. Rowena shouldn't be able to get pregnant. It's like some kind of cosmic joke. All the women that were desperate for my babies when I was alive and I didn't want them. I thought having a child would shackle me and make me an easy target for gold diggers to siphon my money. Shame coils in my gut at the man I was... and the man I am now, because I'm going to be a father with a woman I hate... a woman I can't stop thinking about. I can't buy my way out this time... and I don't even know if I want to.

I shut the shower off and hear the sound of my portal

beeping in my bedroom. Pulling a towel round me I open the bathroom door, glad to see Anthura heeded my threat and fucked off somewhere—probably to simper to Hades or whoever the next leader of the games will be. Or maybe she's plotting my downfall. I'm surprised to find that I don't even care. My portal has my full attention. Tension pulls at me as I lift it and I'm surprised at how disappointed I am that the message isn't from Rowena but a group message to remind all the Inferno Games contestants to head to the lobby in ten minutes for the introductory meeting.

I don't want to talk to Rowena, but I'm pissed that she doesn't want to talk to me. I gave her the one thing she never thought she could have, and her greatest desire. Bitch could have at least had the decency to send me a message. We're linked now despite the fact that neither of us can stand each other. I slam the portal down on my bed and head to the wardrobe to pick out a suit to wear. I get a flashback to the time when Rowena punched me. I'd been wearing a suit. No shoes. I remember it all too well. I'd been seething with anger. Ready to... to what? I didn't even know then what I was going to do to her. I sure as shit didn't know I was going to kiss her.

I lick my lips without even thinking about it. I can still taste the ghost of her strawberry lip balm. I wipe my mouth as though that will do any good, and grab a suit to wear. I don't need any distractions in this circle. I'm already at a disadvantage because of what I said to Anthura. I don't need some bitch with a baby destroying my chances of getting out of here. Whatever madness took hold of me in the last circle is gone now and despite what Anthura said to get a rise out of me about temptation,

Gluttony cannot be worse than Lust. I was set up for what happened. It has nothing to do with weakness. At least that's what I tell myself as I head to the door.

2

JAZZ HANDS

ROWENA

My Hell Cell has been blowing up for hours and at least two people have hammered on my door, but I can't bring myself to drag myself out of bed.

I don't want to see anyone.

I don't want to see him...

The look of pure terror on Felix's face as everything turned to black when we left Lust is more than enough to tell me what he thinks of our situation. My situation, because there's no way in literal Hell I'm letting him be a part of this.

This... I can't even begin to think of it as what it is. A pregnancy. Half of me wishes Noémi was blustering and it was her huge final joke, but the other half is terrified that she's wrong. It's a miracle I never thought possible and now that it's happening, I've never been more scared in my life. Not even when a thug twice my size threatened to kill me, then actually went through with his threats.

"Ro, Girl. Come out. Quinn and I are in fits, worried about you."

I ignore Juliette's imploring plea from the other side of my door and take in a deep breath, closing my eyes and running my hand over my flat belly for the thousandth time this morning.

"The leader of Gluttony is waiting," Quinn shouts, "but he says he won't wait more than five minutes. If you don't get down there now, he's going to tell Hades and you'll be out of the games."

I rub my face, then haul my feet to the floor. Opening the door, I find Juliette and Quinn staring at me expectantly.

"Thank fuck, I thought we were going to have to break the door down and drag you out," Juliette quips, before adding, "You look like shit!" She ushers me inside my room to my walk-in wardrobe and pulls out a flowery dress that I made a literal lifetime ago.

"We got our own clothes back?" I murmur, taking the dress from her hands. In the last circle, our outfits barely covered anything. I'm still stuck in the skimpy Moulin Rouge costume I threw together for the ball. Now, staring at my reflection—ripped stockings, hair a tangled mess—I feel a wave of nausea. What was I even thinking?

I know what I was thinking, and it was insanity. I just don't want to admit it to myself. I was trying to impress Felix... or show him I was worth something... that I could be beautiful. Oh god. What am I doing?

A wrinkle appears between Juliette's eyebrows at my expression. "Just go in the bathroom and put it on and for all that is holy, run a brush through your hair, Ro. I'm starving and can you smell that delicious breakfast? Bacon, eggs, pancakes." She closes her eyes and inhales, her face a picture of bliss. "Gluttony! Can you imagine what the food is going to be like here?"

I sniff the air, but all I can smell is donuts over the lingering odor of sulfur before I quickly have to swallow to stop myself retching.

Quinn helps me into the dress, apparently in a rush. I suspect I'm not the only one risking my place in the games with my tardiness. They are risking it by coming to fetch me. "I know you'll want to talk about the... you know, but we have to make this meeting. Afterwards, come to my room and we'll talk properly.

I spin round to face her. "I don't think I can face seeing him," I admit. I've thought of nothing but the child that may or may not be growing inside of me for hours, but with those thoughts come the image of that asshole Barclay. Literally anyone would have been a better choice to impregnate me than him. One of the demons in the lower levels would have been a better choice and they probably eat babies for breakfast.

Quinn links her arms in mine. "I won't let him come near you."

"Too fucking right!" Juliette adds, linking my other arm in hers. I manage a queasy smile. My entire death might be the most fucked up thing and my stomach is curdling, both with the stink of sugary donuts and the memories that brings, but at least I have two of the best friends at my side.

The huge stained glass windows that wrap around each of the towers now show depictions of food. The vibrant colors dance across the glass, creating a mesmerizing display of culinary delights. It's enough to churn my stomach.

In one window, a bountiful harvest is depicted, with fruits and vegetables spilling out of baskets in a riot of color. The next window shows a lavish banquet, with tables laden with dishes of every kind, from roasted meats to decadent desserts. I glance over and notice Juliette eyeing it, her lips parting as if she can almost taste it all. But the display just stirs something uneasy in me, a sense of revulsion creeping up as I take it all in.

I don't want to hope it's morning sickness. I can't give myself any hope that this pregnancy isn't just some cruel joke made up by Noémi to stick the knife in one last time before she was carted away.

I turn to Juliette. "First Lust and now Gluttony. This must be heaven to you," I mutter.

"I can't say the sex was particularly great in a circle that calls itself Lust, but how can they fuck up so badly with Gluttony?" she says with glee as we step onto the platform that will take us down to the lower level. "I'm going to eat so much food!"

Quinn shakes her head at her lie. Juliette was fucking Noémi's huge bodyguards the entire last circle, and while they turned out to be gross little demons under their glamor, they were both amazingly hot before their glamor dropped. When the awful heaviness of reality recedes a bit and I feel like I can breathe, I remind myself to ask her exactly what was going on in Lust.

"We have approximately thirty seconds to get down to the meeting before they throw us out of the games and we'll be stuck in this circle for eternity," Quinn gripes, panic etched on her face.

Juliette takes another sniff. "If the food tastes as good as it smells, I can live with that... er, stay dead with that!"

It actually takes us a full minute and a half to join the meeting, but the four people standing at the front of the curved sofas don't seem to mind. My eyes scan them, if only to keep my eyes away from the sofas where I know

Felix will be sitting. Hades is there, his arm around Twila, who looks as gorgeous as always in a black corset dress that's a masterpiece of lace and velvet, its dark hues contrasting against her fair skin. A crown of dark roses sits perched atop her head and her eyes are lined with kohl.

Every time I see her, I'm reminded that I can't pull off such amazing looks as she can. I don't have the curves she has for a start. Not yet, I remind myself, then push the thought aside as I check out the person standing next to Hades. A man I can only describe as rotund stands with a welcoming grin on his face and open arms. He's dressed impeccably in a three-piece suit, the buttons of his jacket straining due to his vast size and a yellow stain of some description down his front. Probably mustard. He's closer to Twila's height and is dwarfed next to the towering Hades. In fact, he's almost as wide as he's tall. In his hand, he holds a leash that is tied to a huge dog. Of course, this being Hell, it's not a normal dog. It has three effing heads, all of them slobbering saliva. I love dogs, but I still have to fight the urge not to back away slowly. At least it's on a leash and looks somewhat calm despite all the slobber. In his other hand he holds what looks like a half eaten turkey leg. I'm not sure if it's for the dog or him.

"Welcome contestants!" His voice booms almost jollily as he gestures to the sofas. "I think that's all of us now. Time to begin the third round of the Inferno Games."

Juliette almost drags me to the sofa where I sit down with a thud. The smell of donuts is even more intense down here than upstairs, and it takes me a few moments to get used to it so I don't inadvertently throw up. My stomach doesn't stay settled for long as my eyes finally fall on the last person in the leadership lineup.

"How the fuck is Anthura here?" Quinn whispers in my ear.

I shake my head. I'd like to say I'm surprised, but I'm not. If there was any way the conniving cow could sneak her way through, Anthura would take it. Just behind her is Moloch. I'd not seen him before because he has a habit of merging into the background.

Out of the corner of my eye, I catch a glimpse of a massive black wing—Dade's. That's all I need to see, because I know exactly who else is here, and I'm not ready to face him. I lock my gaze on the new leader as he steps forward to speak, determined to keep my focus anywhere but there.

"Welcome to my world!" he booms, his voice filling the massive space almost as much as he does. "My name is Gorge, but I find that humans like to call me George." He snickers as though this is a joke. "I think my real name hits a little too close to home and that makes some people uncomfortable." He rubs his belly, adding a grease stain from the turkey leg to the mustard, and chortles again. "What can I say about myself? I love food, but that goes without saying." He waves the turkey leg around for good measure and two of the three dog heads follow its motion, slobbering even more. You'll all be used to the layout of the tower because it's much the same as the other towers and if you don't know your way round by now, I'm afraid I can't help you." He grins again and beside me I hear Juliette sigh.

"Hurry up and let's get to breakfast," she mutters under her breath. "My stomach is eating itself here."

George doesn't seem to hear her as he continues. "Most of you will know Hades, and beside him is his lover,

Twila. Neither are involved with the games except to watch over what I am doing with the challenges. To my left is Anthura, who half of you will know from previous circles. And this beauty..." He rubs his hand over one of the dogs heads, "is Cerby, my baby."

I don't know what makes my stomach lurch more. The mention of the word baby, or the massive amount of drool dribbling to the floor from all three of the dog's heads.

"As we have people from two towers coming together in this circle," he continues, "I think we should all take it in turn and introduce ourselves. Anthura, since many of the people here don't know you, why don't you start? Let's 'dish' out some introductions!"

Anthura looks like she'd rather chew wasps.

She plasters on a fake smile. "I'm Anthura from Purgatory. I'm sure many of you are wondering why I'm still here in this circle, but it's because I love the games so much. She holds her hands up to her heart and glances over at Hades. "Isn't that right Hades?"

Hades gives her a slight nod. I have no idea why he would let her be here, but everyone who's ever met her knows why she's chosen to be here. Just like the rest of us, she wants out of Hell, but unlike everyone else here, she's cheating her way through the circles under the guise of being in leadership.

"I hope we can all become friends over the coming weeks," she lies.

It's nothing like the first speech I heard from her in purgatory where she called us all idiots and hoped we'd all die horrible deaths in the games, if dying is what you do when you no longer exist in Hell. Maybe she's softened up in the last few weeks, or maybe she's had the hard word from Hades to behave herself. Probably the latter. Anthura is as soft as a diamond pickaxe.

"I'm Moloch," Moloch says, barely peeking past Anthura. He looks depressed to be here and I can't say I blame him. Maybe he was told he had to come because Anthura did. Who knows? "Nice to meet you all. I'm just a helper." He says no more, so all eyes fall on Juliette who is perched on the very edge of the sofa.

"I'm Juliette!" she announces with a confident wave, the kind that comes naturally when you've become famous in Lust, with hundreds of fans clamoring for your autograph. "I'm thrilled to be here because, well, I just love food." She glances at George and gives him a playful wink. "I'm like you in that way."

He returns her grin warmly. As always, Juliette is completely in her element. Honestly, is there anywhere she isn't? I have yet to see it.

"I'm excited to find out what our first challenge will be, but whatever it is, I know I'm up for it." She turns to me and I know then that I'll have to turn to face the people on the sofas.

My heart pounds as I try to keep my eyes on their feet instead of looking at them directly. But I'd know his shoes anywhere. Designer. Shined. I shift my eyes up to the people further along the sofa and try to concentrate on the new faces instead.

Next to Felix sits a striking woman, the kind who could easily pass for a supermodel. Her platinum blonde hair cascades in soft waves down her back, shimmering under the light. Her skin is porcelain, almost too flawless, and her high cheekbones give her an ethereal quality. She's wearing a sleek, form-fitting gown that clings to her figure, just like the women I used to see on Felix's arm in magazines—the kind who are everything I'm not. I hate how this complete stranger is making me feel uneasy in my own skin, like I'm somehow less just by being near her. No matter what I achieve, in life or death, I'll never be someone who looks effortlessly perfect the way she does. And the worst part? She sits there with such confidence, like she knows it, too.

Felix, on the other hand, seems unbothered, his usual calm demeanor in place. He catches my eye, his expression unreadable. I look away quickly, fixing my eyes on the man on the other side of the new woman. He's middle-aged, with a slight paunch and the kindest eyes I've ever seen. He stands out from the rest of the group—aside from Orlin, he's the only one who doesn't appear to be in his early twenties. There's something refreshing about his presence, a warmth that feels oddly out of place in this room full of youthful perfection.

My eyes flutter to the next person, but before I can take them in, Juliette gives me a sharp dig in the ribs. "Say something!"

"Oh, sorry. I'm Rowena," I muster. The last time we did this, I told the whole room I wanted to be a mother. Nausea creeps up my throat at how much I gave away of myself. This time I'm going to keep it short. "I'm just happy to have the chance to be in the games. That's all really."

I let out a long breath as Quinn begins telling everyone about herself. She's much more forthcoming than I am, but then again, everyone knows she's with Dade and she has nothing shameful to hide. Everyone from our tower knows I'm pregnant thanks to Noémi's outburst as she was dragged from the last circle for sabotaging the games. The rest of the people here don't know and no one except Quinn and Juliette knows who the father is... And Felix. He knows.

I'm so caught up in the horror of everything I barely register who speaks after Quinn and it's only when I hear Felix speak that I come back to the present. My throat tightens as he introduces himself. He sounds so cocksure of himself as he lists his accomplishments in the living world, such as he was Times man of the year. None of that means anything down here. Death is the great equalizer. But not even Hell can equalize how unfairly attractive he is or the exact timbre of his voice that can both make me shake in fury and send me into a puddle of lust... and want to throw up as he's doing now. I press my hand over my mouth, taking a deep breath in an attempt to push the nausea down. It doesn't really help, and by the time I've managed to collect myself, the beautiful blonde has started speaking. My eyes drift to Felix as she introduces herself. He's watching her, but to my surprise, his expression is one of bored indifference.

"Hi. I'm Tate," she says with a confident smile that brightens her whole face, revealing two dimples in her cheeks. "I won my spot in the games from Lust. When I was alive, I worked in the oldest profession. I'm hoping to get back to Earth... I died way too young. One of my clients had a thing for strangulation, and, well, I guess he went too far."

Her tone is disturbingly nonchalant, as if she's simply reciting a fact of life. I shrivel my nose. I don't want to hear about women being murdered. It cuts way too close to home. Next to her, the older man stands and gives everyone a brief nod. Beside me, Juliette stiffens.

"I'm Tomas," he introduces himself, his voice carrying a faint Southern accent. "I hail from Florida, but I share the same origins as the alluring Tate - Lust. That's what brought me to the Inferno Games - a search for something more, something elusive that I've finally found."

He glances in our direction, causing Juliette to instinctively lean back and partially shield herself from his gaze. Then it's on to the next person, but my mind drifts away from their introductions. I can't bear to hear any more fabricated stories or half-truths. We're not here to become friends; the Games will make sure of that.

My relief is palpable when Dade speaks up, signaling that he's the last one and this charade can be over. As expected, Dade says very little beyond introducing himself. It's only then that I realize Remy and Candice are no longer with us. They didn't get through. I didn't care for either of them, but it's still a shock to see that they aren't here. It's a gutting reminder that any one of us could not get through to the next circle and be stuck in Hell forever.

My gaze shifts back to George, who's watching us with a predatory grin, his eyes gleaming with a hunger that makes my skin crawl. There's no doubt in my mind—if we fail here, we could very well end up on his dinner plate. Despite the jolly act he's putting on, I can sense the dark undertones beneath his cheerful exterior. He probably has something twisted and horrifying planned for us.

"It's going to be wonderful!" George announces, practically beaming with excitement. "I'll let you all get settled in, and by this time next week, we'll announce the first trial."

"Next week?" Dade cuts in, raising an eyebrow. "They usually reveal it sooner."

George strides over to him, clapping him on the shoulder in what seems like a friendly gesture. But I can see Dade stiffen, his discomfort evident despite his stoic expression. Being touched by a demon would unsettle anyone, but Dade's always been one to keep people—especially creatures like George—at arm's length. He was never the type to make friends.

"I want you all to truly understand what it means to be part of my 'home' first," George explains with a sly smile. "Besides, Anthura and Moloch were unexpected additions to the team, so I'd like them to be fully informed before we embark on the three challenges. Let's ensure everyone is well-fed with information before moving forward."

As soon as it's clear that the meeting is over, Juliette practically drags me up from the sofa as Quinn rushes over to speak with Dade, leaving us alone for a brief moment.

I turn away, trying not to look, but the sight of them still lingers in my mind. Quinn and her... laughing, leaning into each other, completely lost in their own world, like nothing else exists. It hurts more than I want to admit, a brutal reminder that some people get to find "the one"—they get to feel that kind of happiness. And I know I'll never have it. Not in the way they do.

I'M HAPPY FOR QUINN, really, I am, but every glance, every smile between them cuts deeper, showing me how pathetic my own situation is. I've wound up here, wrapped in this mess, hoping for something I know I can't have. It's pitiful, a sad reminder that whatever it is I'm chasing doesn't come with a happy ending. And watching them, seeing what I'll never get? It just reminds me how empty I am. How empty I'll always be. I don't want to look anywhere else either, so I turn to Juliette. I was expecting an expression of thorough excitement on her face owing to the fact it's breakfast time and the only thing she likes more than breakfast is cock, but she looks strangely subdued.

"Let's go get breakfast," she says, her face lighting up a bit at the mention of her favorite meal. "I can't wait to see what smells so good."

My own enthusiasm doesn't quite match hers. The nausea gnaws at me, but maybe food will help. We weave through the group as they disperse, heading toward the dining area. Just as we round the back of the sofas, someone steps into our path. My stomach lurches for a different reason this time, sinking when I see who it is— Felix. As always, he looks infuriatingly perfect, like he's been sculpted by the gods themselves—impossibly handsome, every inch of him put together like some kind of untouchable deity. No flaws at all. Well, except for his disgusting personality. Let's not forget the transphobia, the bullying, and the fact that he's a complete and utter asshole. Oh, and the father of my unborn child. How could I forget that? "What do you want, Felix?" I snap, unable to keep the irritation from my voice. The effort to keep cool feels like it's draining every ounce of energy I have left.

He stares at me like I've just asked the most ridiculous question in the world. And maybe I have. It's obvious what he wants. Now that I'm pregnant with his child, he has even more ammunition to torment me with. My stomach tightens as I brace for his usual cruelty.

"I want to talk to you... about..." His gaze shifts down to

my stomach. Instinctively, I cover it with my hands, as if that could somehow shield me from his scrutiny.

"Sure, but can we make it a musical? I've been practicing my jazz hands!" I blurt out. Kill me now. Even at a time like this, I can't seem to get over my habit of using stupid humor to deflect.

Felix looks at me like I've gone completely insane, and maybe I have. Speaking to him used to be so easy, even fun in a twisted way. He'd call me a gross slur, I'd insult his intelligence, and then we'd walk away feeling like we'd both won some kind of strange battle. But it stopped being funny after... after we slept together. And apparently, I've stopped being funny too.

"I think we should talk about this," Felix presses. "Is it—"

"Stop right there!" Juliette commands, stepping in front of me with a hand raised, her voice sharp enough to cut the tension. Relief floods me. He was about to ask if the baby was his, and I've never been more grateful for Juliette's impeccable timing. "She said she didn't want to talk to you, so take a hike. We're going for breakfast."

Felix's jaw tightens, a muscle ticking as he tries to hold back whatever insult is on the tip of his tongue. "Actually, she said she'd talk to me, just in a fucking weird way. I just want to ask her something."

"I'm right here, Barclay," I snap, my frustration boiling over. "Stop talking about me like I'm not standing two feet away. I'm telling you I don't have anything to say, and I'm not answering any of your questions."

"But—"

"You heard the lady." A black blur cuts between us as Dade steps in, his massive wings flaring like a shield. Dade never gave a damn about anyone but himself—and maybe Quinn—before this moment, but I'm not about to question it. Not when I've never been more grateful for the interference. His wingspan blocks Felix completely, and without a word, Juliette and I take the opportunity to slip past.

We're halfway down the hall before Felix even realizes we're gone.

3

A BLAST FROM THE PAST

JULIETTE

"**F**inally!" I breathe out as I slide into one of the booths in the restaurant. I know Ro needs to talk about the pregnancy, but I won't be able to hear a word she says until I eat some of whatever that delicious smell is. I look around for a waiter but none appear like they usually do. My stomach growls impatiently. "I swear to God... or Satan, that if they don't appear with breakfast soon, I'm going to start eating this table." Just then, Orlin shuffles past with a clapboard, saying SINNERS—ALL OF YOU on it. How he got into this circle is beyond me. I know I wasn't sleeping with him, so how he was getting such high points in the challenges in Lust is a mystery.

"I'm sure they'll be here in a few minutes," Ro snaps.

I hold my hand out to her. "Sorry. I know we should talk. It's just this smell is driving me to distraction. It smells like the bacon is so close it's being cooked right under the table." I duck down to check, but of course there's nothing but Ro's and my legs.

"I don't smell anything but donuts. It's making me sick, to be honest."

She does look a bit pale, but then again, Ro always has. Just then, Quinn slips into the booth seat next to her.

"I thought you'd be catching up with Dade. Some morning rumpy-pumpy." I raise my eyebrows and flash her a grin. "He was super hot with his wings out like that."

She rolls her eyes. "I literally saw him last night... and I said I'd come up to his room later. I wanted to be here for Ro."

Ro gives her a small smile.

"Do me a favor and tell me if you can smell bacon. Ro can't smell it."

Quinn lifts her shoulders. "I've been smelling grilled cheese sandwiches with chilli sauce all morning." She huffs and gives a sad smile. "I used to eat them with Jenny all the time. They were our go to snack. I couldn't afford much else. Maybe this place smells different to the individual. It wouldn't surprise me. We all know how much you like bacon and what I can smell reminds me so much of Jenny that it can't be a coincidence. What about you, Ro? What do you smell?

Ro's cheeks flush a deep shade of pink. "It's nothing... Just some donuts," she mutters, avoiding my gaze. A story lies behind that, one I'll have to pry from her later.

"Well, they'd better have more than just donuts on the menu. Where is our waiter? Ah, there's George." I wave him over with a flick of my hand. Cerby follows, all its jowls wobbling. I recoil at the sight of it, but don't want to put George out, so I rearrange my features into a winning smile. Quinn, on the other hand, pulls one of its disgusting heads into a hug. It slobbers all over her, but she doesn't seem to mind. At least it isn't eating her, which is a plus.

"Ladies, are you enjoying your stay so far?"

"Not exactly, George," I pout. "Where are the waitstaff? You can't tantalize a girl with all these mouth-watering scents and not bring her the goods!"

"Tell me, what do you smell?" He looks positively delighted. "No, don't tell me. For you, New York cheese-cake. Hot dogs for the lovely Quinn, and..." he pauses as his eyes land on Ro. "Goulash?"

I roll my eyes. "Not quite. We were hoping for break-fast - piles of bacon, eggs, sausage, tomatoes, mushrooms, hash browns - maybe some pancakes on the side. And some mimosas to wash it down."

"Not for me!" Ro interrupts. "Just plain orange juice is fine."

Damn it, how could I forget?

George interlaces his fingers over his protruding belly.

"I hate to disappoint you ladies, but we don't serve food here."

My mouth falls open in disbelief and the very defini-tion of Hell unfolds around me. No food? "Excuse me?"

He shrugs nonchalantly. "We can't very well call ourselves Hell and give everyone what they want. This is Hell after all." He chuckles as though this is a joke. It has to be a joke. He gestures around the room. "In life, many of these people were gluttons who ate themselves to death."

I take a closer look at the other inhabitants in the canteen and finally notice that George is the only one with any meat on his bones. Everyone else is painfully thin, their ribcages visible beneath their clothes.

"They're practically walking skeletons!" I exclaim, my

mind racing. "You're telling me there's no food in Gluttony?"

George pats his belly with a smug grin. "We demons don't follow the same rules as you humans. We have access to food in our quarters two floors below us, but unfortunately for you, the elevators won't take you there."

"But if we don't eat, we'll die!" I wail, my panic rising uncontrollably. "I'll die!"

George's laughter booms through the room, making me clench my fists and struggle to keep from lunging at him—and his insufferable dog. "My dear, you're already dead." He pauses, noticing the rage in my eyes. "Well, technically speaking. Don't worry. Not eating won't harm you in the long run. Think of it as the easiest diet you'll ever go on."

I open my mouth to protest, but snap it shut in disbelief. This can't be real. "What about her?" I point frantically at Ro, who looks ashen and terrified. "She's pregnant! You can't just let a pregnant woman starve!"

George's laughter fills the room again, echoing with cruel amusement. "Oh, you can't kid a kidder, my dear. There's no such thing as pregnancy in Hell."

I stand up, or at least try to, straining to get closer to his face. "She's pregnant, and she needs to eat. Ask Anthura if you don't believe me, but get us some fucking food!"

For the first time, George's face turns into an expression of something other than joy.

"I shall ask Anthura, but that won't change my mind. If by some unknown chance, your friend here is pregnant, the baby will be undead, just like the rest of you. Which means it can't die. It will survive without food, just as you all will. I suggest if you don't like the way we run things here in Gluttony, you put your energy toward doing your best in the games."

My anger boils over as he turns and walks away, taking his slobbering monstrosity with him. I slump back to the bench and bury my head in my arms, trying to contain my frustration. Food was the only thing keeping me sane in this hellhole. Every day, the thought of breakfast was what motivated me to get out of bed. But now, with George's threat looming over us, even that comfort is taken away.

"Nooooo!" I cry out in despair.

"It won't be that bad," Quinn says reassuringly, placing a gentle hand on my shaking arm. It's still wet with helldog slobber.

"We'll all survive," Ro adds, her face drained of color as she takes my other hand. "You heard George."

"Yes, I did hear George," I reply bitterly. "I heard him tell us that he's going to starve us. In Lust they made us have more sex than we wanted. Surely it should be the same here, but with food?" I think of other ways I can get something in my mouth. Only one way springs to mind. "I wonder if spunk tastes different in this level?" I ask hopefully.

Ro dashes up, her hand covering her mouth. She mutters something about vomit, then rushes away, almost knocking Quinn over in her haste to escape.

Fuck. "Should I go and hold her hair back or fetch water or something?"

Quinn shakes her head, her glare fixed on something behind me. I follow her stare to see Felix, who is sitting in the main hall looking like he's having a slanging match with Anthura. "I'm sure she'd rather be alone right now, but when she gets back from the bathroom, we'll focus on her more. Just look at what she's dealing with."

My eyes narrow at Felix and a surge of anger boils within me. "At least he has Anthura to occupy him," I mutter bitterly. "Hopefully that asshole will be too preoccupied with her to bother Ro this Circle."

"I was planning to speak to Dade," Quinn interjects calmly. "He'll make sure Felix stays away."

I let out a frustrated sigh. "I guess having a giant winged hotty for a bodyguard can't hurt." Suddenly, an idea strikes me and I sit up straight in my chair, excitement coursing through me. "Dade can access the lower level!"

Quinn gives me a suspicious look. "You heard George. Demons lurk down there. It's dangerous."

I narrow my eyes."You don't know dangerous until you've seen me go without food for more than a few hours," I snap, my stomach growling in agreement. "I'll take on whatever hell monsters are down there and then some."

"If it hadn't been for Hades, I'd have died down there yesterday. I did die... kinda."

I want to be a supportive friend and ask what happened down there, but my stomach thinks my throat's been cut and I can't concentrate. I look at her pleadingly.

Quinn rolls her eyes and lets out a long breath. "Fine, I'll see if we can find some food. But I doubt Dade will let you go down with him."

I'm about to reach across the table to hug Quinn when I see a familiar figure heading our way. My stomach drops, instinct kicking in before I even process the thought—I duck under the table. Too late.

"Juliette?" Tomas's voice cuts through the room, and my heart sinks. I force myself to look up from under the table, offering him a weak, sarcastic smile. "Hi, Tomas.

Fancy meeting you here. Guess when I told you to go to Hell, you took me a little too literally."

Quinn raises an eyebrow at me, curiosity gleaming in her eyes, but I can't meet her gaze. All my focus is on Tomas, the man who shattered me a lifetime ago.

"Do you know what brought me here?" His voice is thick with regret, but I don't care.

"Herpes? One of your countless whores?" I snap, thinking of the bimbo sitting next to him in the atrium. The hunger gnawing at my insides fuels my anger, making it harder to hold back. Not that I care. /he deserves my venom.

He flinches but doesn't back down. "I entered the games, hoping I'd find you. I saw your name come up on my portal months ago. When you moved from Purgatory to Lust, I spent weeks searching for you, but you must've been in a different tower. That's when I knew you'd entered the Inferno Games."

Anger twists in my gut, a much-needed distraction from the relentless hunger. If rage alone could carry me through this circle, I'd be unstoppable. Anything to get away from this man.

"And the last time I saw you, I told you to never darken my door again," I say, my voice cold. "Maybe you should've thought about that before signing up for the games."

A thought strikes me, and suspicion creeps into my voice. "How did you even get in? Only people from Purgatory are allowed to enter. You can pass through the circles, but you can't enter from them."

Tomas shuffles his feet, and for a split second, I'm dragged back to the moment he confessed to cheating on me. Was it the first time? The second? The tenth? Who knows? He had the same guilty shuffle then, like he wasn't already planning to do it again.

"We had people from Purgatory in our tower. I asked Hades if I could enter the games, and he let me." He shrugs like Hades hands out entry passes as if it's nothing. "He let Tate in too."

I remember the gorgeous blonde woman he was sitting next to on the couch and pull my face into a grimace. "Hooker wasn't she? I see you keep similar company down here as you did up there."

Tomas spreads his arms, trying to defend himself. "That's not fair! I barely know Tate!"

Quinn finally breaks her silence, her confusion palpable. "Someone want to clue me in? I take it you two know each other?"

I exhale slowly, knowing there's no point in hiding it anymore. "Tomas, meet my good friend, Quinn. Quinn, meet Tomas, the two-timing, lowlife, cheating scumbag of a man who also happens to be my ex-husband."

Quinn's eyes widen, her mouth falling open in shock.

"Not ex," Tomas interjects, holding up his hand to show the ring I gave him eons ago, still sitting on his finger. "We're still married. Look."

For a moment, I almost feel sorry for the naïve bride I once was, the girl who thought love could fix anything. But that sadness gave way to resentment long ago—at least when it came to Tomas.

"I might not have filed for divorce in life, Tomas, but as you recall, our wedding vows said til death do us part and seeing as we are both dead, I think that trumps divorce papers. Our marriage was over the second your penis fell into another woman's vagina. And as for my wedding ring, I took it off years ago."

The asshole actually has the nerve to look sad. "I shouldn't have done that to you. You were the love of my life, the mother of my kids, the—"

"Sun to your moon?" I cut him off, rolling my eyes. "Yeah, I've heard it all before. Every time you cheated on me, in fact. Now, if you'll excuse me, the lack of food and your bullshit—which I had hoped death would free me from—are driving me insane. I'm going to my room."

I sidle past him, but not before spinning on my heels and jabbing a finger in his face. "And don't even think about following me!"

4

WE'RE ALREADY
DEAD, REMEMBER?

QUINN

"You will never guess what just happened," I say, eyes widening as Ro finally returns to the table, her face pale and drawn. I lean in closer, my voice dropping to a whisper. "Juliette's husband is here."

Ro's eyes widen in surprise. "Tomas?"

"How did you know? Did she tell you?"

Ro shakes her head, her expression grim. She mentioned having a husband years ago and how he constantly cheated on her until she finally kicked him out. When Tomas introduced himself at the meeting, she practically disappeared into her seat. It all clicked together for me. "Is she alright?" she asks with concern.

"She looked pretty pissed when she stormed off. The sad thing was that Tomas seemed genuinely remorseful for what he's done to her. He even joined the games because of her. Managed to speak to Hades and wrangle his way in."

Ro raises an eyebrow. "Well, that's fishy right off the

bat. When has Hades ever shown any signs of compassion when it comes to the games?"

"Exactly. I had the same thought. We'll have to ask Twila about it later. But enough about them. How are you feeling?"

She lets out a deep sigh, her hand instinctively coming up to rest against her stomach. "Like I'm in the right place. Hell is exactly how I feel," she confesses, looking overwhelmed.

I nod sympathetically. "I can't imagine what you're going through."

"I threw up the last thing we ate in Lust and now my stomach is completely empty," she continues. "How am I supposed to keep a baby alive if I can't even keep food down? I know what George said about not needing food, but it just doesn't seem possible."

"You having a baby at all isn't supposed to be possible," I remind her. "Do you really think you're pregnant?"

She's quiet for a moment. "I'll be the first to admit that I have no idea what pregnancy is supposed to feel like, but if aching breasts and severe nausea have anything to do with it, then Noémi wasn't joking."

"But if it's true, you've been pregnant like a week. Surely you wouldn't feel anything yet?"

Ro shrugs. "We're in Hell. Who knows what's possible and not possible. I shouldn't be pregnant, you shouldn't be fucking a man with a wingspan and horns and Juliette shouldn't have to come face to face with a man who she once described as the devil incarnate, but here we are."

I laugh lightly then sigh. "What a fucked up mess, but hey, we're closer to getting out of this place. I'm a circle closer to Jenny and you are going to have a baby. Forget the father for a minute. You're going to be a mom. How do you feel about that?"

It's then that she finally breaks down. Tears flow freely down her face and I curse myself for my lack of thought, but then beyond the tears and snot comes a smile.

"I'm going to be a mom, Quinn." She wipes her tears up the back of her hand, liberally snotting up her sleeve as she does. "I'm going to have a baby. A real baby of my own. I never dared hope..." She doesn't finish the sentence, but I know what she's going to say. My eyes dart to the sofa where Felix was sitting earlier. I know Ro would rather pull her own teeth out that have him witness this. Thankfully both he and Anthura have gone.

"Come on. Let's go back to our rooms. I promised Dade I'd head to his room and it looks like you need some thinking time." I don't mention that she needs to think about Felix. She already knows what I mean, because like it or not, Felix is going to be a bigger part of her death that she ever wanted.

Dade is sprawled out on his bed as I open his door. He's wearing nothing but some leather pants. His wings are unfurled and his hands are tucked behind his head, propping it up slightly. He is the epitome of dark beauty, my sexier than hell human with wings. I grin, knowing he's waiting for me.

"How long have you been posed like that waiting for me to come through your door?" I ask as I slip onto the bed beside him and run my hands over his naked chest. A shimmer of lust runs through me.

"Since the meeting. I didn't expect you to take so long."

"Juliette had an issue," I murmur, reaching for his belt and unbuckling it, desperate for something to take my mind from the horror of this place and feel something real.

"Oh yes? She couldn't find anyone she wanted to sleep with?"

I yank down his pants exposing his giant cock. "Actually she couldn't find anything to eat, but I don't think I'll have that problem." I take his already hard penis into my hand, running it lightly through my fingers to tease him. I can't help but grin as I lick my lips, putting on a show for him. I lean in and take him into my mouth, feeling his sigh more than hearing it as I tease the head of his cock with my tongue. His breath hitches, and his hands tremble slightly as they grasp my shoulders. I slowly take him deeper, feeling his pulsating cock grow harder in my mouth. I stroke his length with one hand while the other gently caresses his skin, sending shivers down his spine.

His hips thrust forward, meeting my lips, and I taste the saltiness on my tongue. He moans softly, the sound music to my ears. I'm in my element right now, reveling in the sensation of his cock filling my mouth, the warmth of his skin and the sound of his breath. He wraps his fingers around the back of my head, gently urging me deeper. I go willingly, wanting to give him every bit of pleasure I can.

As I work him with my mouth, I can feel his body tense, the anticipation building. I want this to last, to savor every moment, but I can tell that he's nearing his peak. I increase my pace, taking him in deeper and more rapidly, my hand stroking in sync with my mouth. His groans grow louder, and his hips buck, thrusting harder into my face. I can feel his muscles tighten in his thighs, his grip on the back of my head becoming more insistent. I know this is the moment he's been building to, and I want to taste his release. As he thrusts, I keep pace, taking him in deeper than ever before, my mouth swirling around his shaft as he nears the edge. His body shudders, and I know he's coming. He moans loudly, his voice echoing in the room, the sound of release filling the air. His cock twitches and spasms in my mouth, and I feel the first gush of his semen hit the back of my throat. I swallow it down before crawling up his body and melting into his arms. I'm swept away by the intensity of Dade's touch, his hands tracing fiery patterns on my skin. Every brush of his fingertips sends shivers down my spine, igniting a primal desire within me. As his lips meet mine in a fierce kiss, I feel a surge of electricity between us. One thing about Dade. He never lets me go wanting and he gives as good as he gets. Everyone else I've ever slept with has fallen asleep right after they've cum and its game over. Not with Dade. Dade ducks under the covers. As Dade's hot breath teases my thighs, a shiver runs down my spine. His hands trace the curves of my body, sending tingles of pleasure all over me. He is like an entity from another realm, almost a demon that crossed paths with mine, yet he evokes such human passions within me—desire, arousal, and a hunger so intense that it threatens to consume me.

His tongue flicks against my clit, eliciting soft moans from deep within me. Each lick is a new wave of pleasure, each one building upon the last. I arch my back, offering myself to him as he explores my most intimate parts. His tongue plunges inside me, tasting me, claiming me. I am his.

My fingers tangle in his hair, pulling him closer, guiding him deeper, urging him on. Dade's fingers find their way inside me, sliding effortlessly against the wet folds of my core. With every thrust, a new wave of plea-sure washes over me, building up higher and higher like the crest of a never-ending wave. My breaths become shallow, my legs shake uncontrollably. My arousal reaches its peak before I shatter into a thousand pieces again and again.

Dade appears from under the covers with a satisfied smirk on his face. He wraps a giant wing around me like a blanket and it feels like home. If it wasn't for Jenny, I'd be more than happy to stay in Hell with Dade for all eternity if all my days were taken up like this. My body feels heavy after all the orgasms. Comfortable. I could never have guessed all those months ago when I came to Hell and had to work with Dade that we'd end up like this. I murmur words to that effect, but only a contented sigh escapes.

Eventually when the post sex euphoria wears off, I turn and look up at Dade. "Juliette has asked us to bring her some food up from the lower level when we next go down."

Dade shifts slightly, pulling his wing out from under him. He sits up on the bed and my moment of post sex bliss vanishes when I take a look at the stern expression on his face.

"What's wrong?" I ask, a knot of dread forming in my stomach.

"I can't shake this feeling that something isn't right. Last time we went down to the lower level, you were almost killed. And with everything happening in the Games, I don't trust that we're safe anymore."

I scoff, trying to brush off his concerns. "We're already dead, remember? We haven't been safe since we arrived in Hell. Look at what we've endured so far - poisonings, burns, nearly drowning."

His face darkens, but I don't need that kind of tell with

Dade. His aura does the talking for him and right now it's dark and suffocating. "That's not what I'm talking about. There's something bigger going on here and we're only seeing bits and pieces of it. I can't shake the feeling that we're just pawns in some twisted game."

"The Inferno Games?" I remind him, suddenly feeling sick to my stomach.

He shakes his head. "More than that."

"Noémi was a demon," he corrects sharply. "Lying, cheating, hurting people—that's what they do. Just look at Anthura. Hell, look at all of them. They act nice, accommodating even, but don't be fooled. Every last one would tear us apart if they thought it would bring them more entertainment. Noémi reveled in our suffering. And Anthura? She gets off on creating ways to punish and humiliate us."

I close my eyes, swallowing the lump in my throat. "But they're not all like that. Look at Hades."

"Hades?" He lets out a hollow laugh. "You really believe he's any different?" Dade shakes his head. "Hades is one of the worst. Don't let his love of the games confuse you into thinking he has a love for humans. He's taking his own pleasure from our pain. Why else concoct the Inferno Games in the first place? And remember the Labyrinth we all went through at the very start. The burning plants and trees, the flesh eating monsters. Don't let's forget who made that up."

I try not to think about it, especially since one of my friends is literally dating him. "What about Moloch?" I finally say, clutching at straws, my fingers gripping the sheets.

Dade's jaw tightens, and he crosses his arms. "Moloch

is afraid of Anthura. That's all. If he ever dared to step out of her shadow, he'd be as bad as the rest."

"It's not all bad," I say, my voice softer.

He looks me directly in the eyes, his dark gaze intense and searching. "Why are you defending this place?"

I take a deep breath, feeling the weight of his stare. "Honestly? Because I feel like you're about to say something I don't want to hear." I look away, blinking back the sudden sting of tears. "If it wasn't for this place, I would never have met you, and that's worth dealing with all those things you mentioned."

His expression softens and leans forward to kiss me. I can taste myself on his lips.

Suddenly, I realize the storm in his eyes isn't anger after all, but fear. It's palpable and suffocating and more than anything, bleak. "I watched you almost get reduced to ash yesterday. If Hades hadn't been there, you'd be gone."

"You're going to tell me that you don't want to go down to the lower levels again." My voice is hollow, like I've already resigned myself to what's coming. I cross my arms over my chest, trying to protect myself from the inevitable blow. Dade would never lay a hand on me, but if he says the words I'm dreading, it'll be worse than any physical pain. It'll be like he's ripping my heart out with his bare hands. We'll never make it through the games, and finding Jenny will be nothing more than a dead dream

Dade's features darken, like a maelstrom is about to turn loose. "It's dangerous. How many times have we barely made it out alive down there? Last night, when I thought you were... really gone, it shattered me. I can't go through that again." Dade's shoulders slump, his face a mask of despair. He leans closer, his hands trembling as they reach for me but hesitate, stopping just short of touching. "Valentine... I can't keep putting you in that kind of danger. If something happened to you..." His voice falters, cracking with emotion. "I don't think I could survive it."

Tears sting my eyes, blurring my vision as I shake my head. "What about Jenny? What about Emily? We've fought so hard for them. We can't just stop now."

"We still have the games. We've made it this far," he says, but the words are hollow, empty. They're nothing more than a desperate attempt to cling to something that's slipping away.

"The games?" My voice is sharp, edged with bitterness as I stumble out of bed, yanking on my discarded clothes with trembling hands. "The same games run by demons you said we can't trust?"

The room feels suffocating, and I need to get out. It's like everything is closing in on me—Dade, the walls, the oppressive weight of our situation. I pull my shirt over my head, barely holding back the sobs that threaten to tear from my throat. "You know what?" I say, my voice thick with pain. "Just five minutes ago, I thought maybe I could stay here. In Hell. With you. I pictured spending eternity at your side because, somehow, that seemed like the only thing that mattered. But in that fantasy, Jenny was safe. Emily was happy."

"Maybe Jenny is safe. Maybe Emily grew up to be the woman I always hoped she'd be."

I laugh, but it's bitter, cold. My hands are shaking as I grab my shoes, clutching them like they're my lifeline. "Maybe you're right about Emily. I hope, for your sake, she lived a perfect life. But after everything you've told me about these demons, how can you expect me to believe Jenny is being 'cared for' in the Seventh Circle?"

The door looms ahead of me, and with every step, I feel the weight of our unraveling. "I won't stay here and pretend I can live this eternity if it means losing the people I love." I clutch my shoes tighter, the tremble in my voice betraying the fear gripping me. "I have to find her." I don't wait for his response. My hand is already on the doorknob. "If you won't go to the lower level, that's your choice. But if you think for one second I'm going to stop looking for my sister, you don't know me at all." I leave his room, feeling a crushing weight of sadness. Dade has always been fearless, but now he's letting fear hold him back. As I head to my room and pass Felix on the stairs, it hits me—Dade has the marble key. Without it, I won't be able to access the lower level anyway.

5

TOXIC TOGETHER

ROWENA

I t doesn't matter how much I try to avoid Felix, he's always there and, worst still, Anthura is never far behind. I'd like to say I'm surprised about the pair of them hooking up again. But I'm world weary about anything when it comes to both of them. They deserve each other. I try to ignore the pang I feel when I think about them, but it doesn't take long for the pang of... regret... to turn back into the blazing anger I've felt at Felix since pretty much the first second I met him.

When there's a knock on my door much later, I already know it's him. Juliette always knocks quickly as though she's in a rush and Quinn has a habit of calling out as though I'm screening guests, which, to be honest, most of the time I am. Felix's knock is so typically Felix—curt and to the point. Two knocks, that's it.

I'm half inclined to ignore it, but he's been trying to talk to me all day, and I know he'll continue to bug me for the rest of my death if I don't let him in. Besides, I need something to take my mind away from the gnawing hunger and nausea.

I pull on a dressing gown over my nightdress and open the door, leaning on the door frame. "Barclay."

I have one hand on the door, ready to duck back in and slam it in his face.

"Can I come in?"

"Nope."

His face scrunches up for a second. "You infuriating bi..." He stops talking before saying whatever slur was about to come out of his mouth, which is an improvement.

It's almost fascinating watching Felix lose his composure and then scramble to regain it. He should be a politician, with all his lies and slander.

"I don't think you want what I have to say to be overheard," he says. As if on cue, the gorgeous blonde walks past, giving us a curious look before heading down the stairs. I hate when Felix has a valid point.

With a sigh, I open the door to let him pass, holding my breath as his shoulder brushes against mine, sending a shiver through my treacherous body.

"Five minutes," I warn him, my voice edged with steel. I need to remain composed. "Five minutes, then you'll leave this room and never have another conversation with me unless it's absolutely necessary for the games. Do you understand?"

"Is the baby mine?" he asks, his tone unreadable.

I knew the question was coming. I've known all day that's what he wanted to know, but it still hits me like a sucker punch to the chest. I don't sleep around. His question makes me feel dirty and cheap.

I glare at him. "You took my virginity and you know that."

"Yeah..." he falters.

"But you thought that after losing my virginity to you a whole week ago, I suddenly decided to sleep with every man in Lust. Is that it?"

He sucks in a breath and I wonder, not for the first time if he is going to kiss me or punch me. With Felix, it could be either. I ready myself for both but he just stands there.

"The baby is mine, Barclay," I reply firmly. "That's all you need to know."

His eyes drop to my stomach, prompting me to tighten my dressing gown belt further around it. "So you're really pregnant, then? How is that even possible?"

"You know it's not possible," I snap. "I know it's not possible. But it's happened and it's real. I've had morning sickness all day." I leave out the part about my tender breasts; the last thing I want is Felix thinking about my body.

"We... we slept together."

As if I could forget. It's been at the very forefront of my mind since the second it happened. "Yes, and I'd rather masturbate with a cheese grater than repeat the action."

I turn away so he can't see my eyes. I guess he's not the only liar in the room. He's just better at concealing it than I am.

"If the baby is mine, I want to help."

It's rare that Felix catches me off guard, but this is one of those moments. He's so close I can feel the heat radiating off him, his presence overwhelming, suffocating. The space between us is nonexistent, and it takes everything in me not to reach out, not to close that gap. Hating him is hard enough. Wanting him? That's pure agony.

It takes everything in my soul to keep my features impartial. "You come in here, insinuate that I sleep around and now you want to help me? Pray tell, Felix Barclay, what can you offer me? You have no fortune in here and I doubt your fathering skills are up to much. I've read up about what you did."

And just like that, he surprises me again. It's not the fact that he has skeletons in his closet. His walk in wardrobe is probably an elephant graveyard, but it's the fact that he looks scared that's intriguing. Barclay never looks scared. He's got an ego the size of a zeppelin and is as full of hot air.

His face falls and he runs his hands through his hair. "I fucking regretted it, alright. There's not a day that hasn't passed since my decision that day hasn't plagued me. That's why I didn't want to repeat the mistakes of my past. He falls to my bed and lowers his head to his hands.

I was talking about investing in a company that made baby milk and sold it to third world countries leading to mothers giving up on breastfeeding. The scandal happened before Felix was born but his company invested in that company anyway. Mostly it was all in the past when he invested and I was only bringing it up because I had nothing else to throw at him. But the way he is now tells me that whatever he thinks I've found out is far closer to home.

The desire to throw him out hasn't lessened, but a nagging voice in my head tells me to probe him. What on earth could the mighty Felix Barclay regret? He's certainly never shown any remorse for anything he's done in the past.

Begrudgingly, I sit next to him on the bed and ignore the flutters in my core. The last time I sat next to Felix Barclay on a bed, he took my virginity on it, and that's what led to this whole crapshow in the first place. I make sure there's enough distance between us so it doesn't look like I'm coming onto him.

"What did you do that has you worked up so badly?"

He looks up and turns his head to me, his eyes locking onto mine. For a second, I think he's going to kiss me, and holy hell, I'm not sure I want to stop him. But he doesn't. He speaks instead.

"You don't know? I thought you said... meant..." He stands up and runs his hands through his hair, his frustration evident. "Forget I said anything. Maybe you're right. You and me are fucking toxic together, and I don't even need this..."

Anger burns inside of me, quelling any ridiculous hint of want I have for this asshole. "I don't remember asking you for help. I don't remember asking you for anything. This... this..." I can't talk. I'm so angry and upset. "This baby..." I gesticulate to my belly, finally acknowledging it out loud. "You are nothing but a sperm donor. It has absolutely nothing to do with you."

The tears come before I can stop them, and I can taste the salt as they slip down to the corners of my lips. So much for keeping my composure, for pretending I could stay detached. So much for remaining impartial.

The bed shakes as he stands. "This has everything to do with me," he growls. I've seen many emotions in Felix, but this is something else entirely. It's raw, and it's overpowering. He turns and walks out the door, slamming it behind him.

It takes me ten minutes to compose myself to be able to do anything other than breathe, and even that is choky sob-filled gasps of air. I don't know what I expected from Felix and I don't know what he expects from me. Hell, I don't even know what I expect from myself. I've been given a gift that I could never have hoped to wish for in the past and yet now everything feels so messy. However much I hate to admit it, even to myself, there was a tiny part of me that hoped Felix would beg for forgiveness for everything he'd done, and doubly beg to be part of this baby's life.

He shouted at me. Screamed even. And maybe there was a shred of remorse for everything he'd done to me, but it isn't enough. It's not nearly enough. I lie back on the bed and press my hand gently to my belly. It's still flat. No real signs that this baby even exists yet. It could all be one last cruel joke by Noémi before they took her away. And yet I know it it's true. I know my child is growing inside of me. Felix's baby.

I huff and bring out my Hell Cell. If Felix isn't going to be forthcoming about his murky past, I'll have to find out myself.

The Hell Cell doesn't just have information about Hell. It has information about the living too. It's got a database of millions of articles and is up to date with current affairs on Earth, a fact I find sad and have ignored up until today. I type Felix Barclay into the search bar. His photo comes up immediately. Underneath it are the words FELIX BARCLAY. THIRD CIRCLE. CONTESTANT IN THE INFERNO GAMES. I don't bother to read his bio. I've already read it and can recite it word for word. Instead I click onto the earthly part of the Hell Cell. It takes me over four hours of searching to find it, and when I finally do, the breath leaves my body. Six years ago, Felix paid off a supermodel called Sylvia Rothwell to have an abortion, then buried the whole thing under a mountain of hush money. My chest tightens with every word of her story, the pain gripping me like a vice. She doesn't mention him by name—that's why it took me so long to uncover—but I recognize him instantly in the way she describes him. The arrogance, the charm, the manipulation. It's Felix, through and through.

And that's why it never hit the headlines. If anyone had known she was talking about Felix Barclay, it would have exploded. But instead, she vanished from the spotlight, left her modeling career behind, and used the blood money to start a ranch in Montana. Just... disappeared.

Suddenly, the memory of that task in the Lust Circle comes flooding back. The one where I conjured up a ranch house, and Felix shattered me, left me trembling on the floor. I didn't understand it then, but now I do. He wasn't just breaking me. He was remembering her— remembering what he did to her.

My hand drifts to my stomach, and I rub it slowly, the life growing inside me grounding me in the moment. A vow forms on my lips, one I should have made from the very beginning:

Felix Barclay will never come near this child. Not as long as I'm around to stop him.

6

A MEDIOCRE FUCK AT BEST

FELIX

"Open the fucking door, Anthura." I don't even know if this is still her room at the top of the tower, or if she's slinked off to the dungeons with all the other demons where she belongs.

She opens the door and narrows her eyes when she sees who it is.

"Look what the cat dragged up here. What do you want, Felix? A mercy fuck now your precious boyfriend has dumped you... He has dumped your pathetic ass?"

"Just let me in, you repugnant cunt. I need to talk to you." I push past her into her penthouse apartment. I'm surprised to see Moloch sitting on her sofa and for a second, I wonder if she's fucking him now. It's not like she's not fucked everyone else in this fleapit hellhole. Then I realize that, of all of us, Moloch probably has more sense. It's sobering thinking that Moloch might actually be better than me. Moloch the little mouse who's afraid of his own skin.

Anthura floats in behind me, leaving the door open. "Fuck off Moloch. Meeting's over."

Moloch slouches off the sofa, but as he passes me on his way out, I'm sure I see relief in his eyes.

I head to the kitchen and pull out a bottle of dragon-fire whisky. I unscrew the top and bring it to my lips as Anthura grabs it. "Just because you are a fucking waste of space doesn't mean you can't be civilized." She pulls out two glasses and drops a couple of ice cubes into each one before pouring us both a healthy measure of the amber liquid. I take a glass and down the whole lot in one. It goes down like battery acid, burning my throat, but that doesn't stop me pouring another one and retreating to the sofa where Moloch was sitting previously.

Anthura doesn't bother sitting down. Instead she hovers over me, grating my nerves.

"If you aren't here to give me the pitiful orgasms you usually offer, what is it you want, Felix?"

"You are now back in the Games committee. I want to win and I want you to help me."

She laughs. "And why the fuck would I want to do that? I thought you were going to do it by yourself without my help?"

I swallow bitterly, hating what I'm about to say, but needs must. "Come on Anthura. You and me. It's always been us."

She takes a sip of her drink then decides to finally sit down on a chair.

"You have been a mediocre fuck at best to me. The way I see it, Felix," she crosses her legs as she speaks letting her short red skirt ride up her thigh, "I have all the power here and apart from your pretty boy looks, you have nothing. Go and play happy families with your boy bitch and leave me alone."

Her turn of phrase riles me up and I know her well

enough to know she's trying to provoke me, but it wasn't that long ago I spoke about Rowena the way she is doing. I just smile and plaster on my business face.

"You want to get through these games as much as I do, Anthura. This was never about getting credit with the main man, or torturing humans for you."

"True," she muses, her red lip-sticked mouth curling up at the edges, "but torturing humans is a delightful byproduct."

"You want to win these games to get to Satan and plead your case. You want to go back to Earth," I say, my voice low, watching her carefully.

"I've never been to Earth," she spits out bitterly, her eyes narrowing with contempt.

"And you've never been human," I counter, the words sharp, cutting through her defenses. "That's what you want, isn't it? You despise us all because we've had something you never have, and you crave it. You can almost taste it, can't you, Anthura? Being human. Feeling it—living it. That's why you'll do anything to win. Because deep down, all you want is to be one of us."

She grimaces and slams her glass onto the coffee table between us. "So what if that's true. You can't help me in these games. You know nothing."

I sit back and relax a little. I didn't make my billions by taking shit and being a bad judge of character. First rule of business. Know your opponent, and especially know their weaknesses. Anthura likes to pretend she's strong, but underneath all her bullshit and red clothing, she's fucking terrified she won't get through this and will be stuck in Hell forever. The games are her only chance and if she fucks it up, back to Purgatory she'll go and will have to start the process all over again. And that's only if Hades lets her.

I lean forward, my voice low. "Say you do manage to appeal to the boss's better nature and somehow you get your heart's desire. Then what?"

She narrows her eyes. "What do you mean? Then I'll get to live out my life on Earth as a human, a luxury I was never afforded."

"You think you'll know how to fit in? You think you know how to be a convincing human?" I challenge, raising an eyebrow.

She smirks, crossing her arms. "I've been watching you fools for months. And before you, there were others. Thousands of humans. I've been studying your kind since humans first came here. I don't need your help." Her gaze flickers over me, cold and sharp. "Look at you. You're barely human yourself."

"I think you do need me and what's more, I think you know it. I might not be worth much in your eyes, but out there I was somebody. Fuck that. I was the person everyone wanted. I had it all, Anthura." I swig down the last of my dragonfire whisky. "Out there I was the shit. Do you want to ruin your one chance on Earth by being a complete nobody, scrounging for scraps like that pathetic snowflake Quinn or living in poverty with screaming kids like Juliette..." I hate myself for what I'm about to say and knowing I'm saying it for a reason doesn't make it any better. "...living like an outcast and ending up dead on a bar room floor because someone didn't like the way you looked like Rowena." My stomach clenches, but it seems to be getting through to her. "I can teach you how to not only survive in the big bad world, but to own it."

She raises a perfect eyebrow. "Color me intrigued. I've

yet to see any of this prowess you keep harping on about, but I suppose you did have a way of getting what you wanted on Earth."

And I'm going to get what I want now. "You help me through the three challenges in this Circle, and keep helping me if we manage to get through to the fourth circle, and I'll tell you everything you need to know to be a successful human being."

She sniffs, clearly aggravated, but she holds her hand out for me to shake. "Fine."

I shake her hand, letting go quickly. I forgot how hot her skin runs. "You'd better make this worth my time, Felix, because if I'm caught helping you, we'll both be out and not even you will be able to worm your way back in."

"I will," I promise, guilt gnawing at my stomach. "But before you tell me what the first trial is, you really need to get me access to some food. I'm fucking starving already."

She gives me a lifeless grin. "Follow me."

I stand and follow her to the kitchen. As far as I know, only the penthouses are full apartments with kitchens. The rest of us have a bedroom, bathroom and walk-in closet. She flings her cupboards open. I should be surprised when I see them stocked to the top with food, but I'm not. Of course the demons are eating. One look at George is enough to tell me they don't go without. I grab a ready-made sandwich from her fridge and bite into it. It tastes better than any food I've ever tasted in my life.

"The first trial is a banquet."

I raise my eyebrows as she sidles over to me.

"It's not just any banquet," she continues with a sly smile. "Everyone's favorite foods will be there. It'll be even more delicious than that sandwich you're holding."

"I don't get how that's a trial," I reply, puzzled.

"Because if anyone touches any of the food, or gets up out of their seat, they are immediately out of the games. The twenty that can resist the longest get to go through to the next trial. They also get the pleasure of eating the banquet when it's over while those that left the table or tried to eat are caged up and forced to watch what could have been theirs. Of course, no one will know that until all but twenty are left. But you know now." She sidles up to me, pressing her body against mine. "The question is, Felix. Will you be able to resist?" She licks her lips and runs her hand down to my crotch. I swallow the last of the sandwich as she squeezes lightly.

"That's right. Eat up. You'll need to get your strength up for what I have planned for you."

Reaching around her, I grab a box of cookies from the countertop.

"I'll help you when I get through the first trial," I say, hiding the cookies under my jacket. Annoyance fills her features as I back away from her, but I promised her help, not access to my cock. She can find cock somewhere else for all I care. I don't look round as I head back outside and start the long journey down the thousands of curved stairs to my room.

7

AT LEAST IN LUST THEY COULD FUCK LIKE BUNNIES...AND EAT

JULIETTE

Eight hours, thirty-seven minutes and twelve seconds since I was informed that I wouldn't be eating anything for the foreseeable future and I'm slowly going crazy. Ok, not so slowly. I'm sitting in the canteen, or what was a canteen in the other circles. I messaged Rowena and Quinn five minutes ago to meet me down here.

Rowena gets here first. "Don't bother complaining about food to me. I know we're friends, but if I even think about food, I'm going to throw up."

"I'm having hallucinations," I admit, finally dragging my eyes from the giant floating ice creams and chocolate cakes. Rowena follows my line of sight over her shoulder. "That's the big screen. They are showing food to mess with us. You're totally fine."

"Fine?" I grit out, frustration evident in my voice. "I've tried every diet there is—keto, Atkins, intermittent fasting, Weight Watchers. You name it, I've done it. And you know what happened after each of these diets?"

"I'm guessing it didn't result in you wearing a couple of dress sizes smaller?" she responds with a hint of sarcasm.

"No," I snap. "After just three days on each of them, I was ready to murder the first person who dared look my way and ended up binge-eating chocolate cake. Every diet I tried only made me go up a dress size. And now, the chocolate cakes are floating past my eyes. I can even smell the damn things. I wonder if I lick the screen, I'll be able to taste them."

"Hey," Quinn says as she sits next to Rowena, and I immediately realize my mistake. I should have sat where they are sitting, so I wouldn't be forced to watch the cakes. "What's going on?"

"I've spent the whole day with my head in the toilet," Ro explains, "and Juliette is about to murder someone."

"Anyone in particular, or can we nominate someone?" Quinn quips sullenly.

"You can have Felix," Rowena snaps, a venomous edge in her voice. "You can cannibalize him after you've murdered him if you like. At least I won't have to see his face again if you eat him."

"I'd rather eat mouse droppings, thanks," I shoot back, a grimace twisting my lips. "Oh fuck. That's going to be one of the trials, isn't it? We're going to have to eat one of the other contestants." I shrug, trying to shake off the rising dread. "I'd probably do it gladly by the time the first trial starts. Just not Felix," I add quickly. For starters, he's a prize douchebag, but mostly because Ro obviously has some bizarre hang-up on him, and who knows where that's going to lead.

I glance at my friends, and my heart sinks at the misery etched on their faces. Quinn's eyes are puffy and red, as if she's spent the entire day crying, while Rowena's skin has turned a sickly gray.

"Fuck Dade, who I'm assuming you're also offering up as a sacrifice and fuck Felix." I turn to Ro. "How are you throwing up? We've not eaten for over twenty-four hours."

Ro shrugs. "It's like magic. I think it might stop and then I'm rushing to the toilet again. Did you get morning sickness with your kids?"

It was such a long time ago that I was pregnant. I have grandkids now. "I did a bit, but that's because I ate. You know. Food!" I rub my eyes. "Let's change the subject. Quinn. What has His gorgeousness done now?"

Quinn looks around and lowers her voice. "He's refusing to go down to the demon level anymore. Says he's scared I'll get hurt."

Ro shrugs. "At least he gives a shit." She sits back in her seat and folds her arms, a grimace on her face. "Why are we talking about men... again!? We're like a group of complete losers that can only ever talk about men and how crap they are."

"Talking of crap men..." I nod towards George, who's just appeared from one of the elevators with a huge grin on his face and a giant cupcake in his hand. He nods cheerfully at a couple of skeletal people who nod back pitifully. Their eyes never leave the cupcake as he walks past shoveling the whole thing in his face, leaving pink buttercream smeared around his mouth. If he wasn't so repugnant, I'd fantasize about licking it off him.

"So we know it's possible to actually murder people in here." I say nodding toward George who's licking his lips, depriving me of even that pathetic fantasy. "Look at Lucia and whatshisface that died in the Purgatory. We just have to rip his head off, right? He might be built like a brick shithouse, but I'm fucking hungry and I know I can take him. I'm actually out of my seat before Rowena casually puts her hand on my arm to stop me.

"You kill the leader of the games and we're all stuck in here forever. Do you really want that? Imagine it. You'll never see a cupcake ever again."

The thought doesn't even bear thinking about so I sit down, cross my arms and pout instead. "I hate when you're right."

"Let's go and explore downstairs," Quinn suggests. "Who knows, that might be where George came from. I'm sure there was a cupcake store on the entertainment level in Purgatory."

My mind wanders. There *was* a cupcake store there. It was like heaven. I stand up and follow Ro and Quinn. "Why did we leave Purgatory again? It was heaven compared to this.

Ro presses the call elevator button and turns to face me. "We left because Quinn joined the games to find Jenny and we wanted to support her,"

"Hey, don't blame me!" Quinn retorts. "You both joined through your own volition. If I remember rightly, you were trying to get away from Barclay and you were trying to impress Hades."

Damn. Now *she's* right. "And look how that turned out."

"It turned out amazing," Ro said, linking her arms in mine as we step into the elevator. "Because despite everything being a gigantic pile of diseased dog poop, we're all still together."

I grimace. "I know that was your version of a rousing speech, but next time, wait until I have a cupcake in my mouth before you try to rouse me, eh?"

The elevator doors open. We step in and go down a level. Just like Purgatory and Lust, they open out into a kind of underground courtyard with the classrooms and the entrance to the Earthery to the right, Infernos night-club ahead and a parade of shops to the left. It becomes apparent very quickly that people don't come down here often like they did in the other circles. We're the only three here except for the people that I can see standing bored behind the counters in the stores.

"Is it me, or is this more depressing than upstairs?" I say, guiding my eyes along the storefronts, inwardly praying for a food store of some kind. Anything. I'd even eat a salad at this point and I really freaking hate salad. "Forget it. There are no food shops. Let's head into Infernos and get drunk. Maybe I can cope with the next few weeks if I'm inebriated the whole time."

A small spark of hope ignites within me as we walk into a dimly lit place that looks oddly familiar. The bar is empty, save for a demon bartender wiping glasses behind the counter. It's early, and the place has an eerie calm.

I sidle up to the bar, letting out a long breath of relief as I park my ass on one of the bar-height stools. I wave the barman over, eager for a taste of normalcy.

"Three Dragonfire whiskies, here we come!" I announce with a whoop, glancing at Rowena with a teasing grin. "Make that two Dragonfire whiskies and one virgin-whatever-you-have."

"It's been a long time since you were a virgin, ey?" I don't even bother to look toward the dark corner to know who is talking. I'd know that voice anywhere. It used to haunt me in my dreams. Now it only serves to annoy me. Tomas. No wonder he's here. He always did like the drink.

If heart disease hadn't killed him, cirrhosis would have. Or any number of STDs.

The barman plonks down three glasses: one tall cocktail glass and two shot glasses. Ignoring my ex husband's quip, I grin at Quinn and Rowena in anticipation. But as the barman upends a bottle into one of the shot glasses, nothing comes out. It's only when he pushes it toward me that I realize it's empty.

"It's empty!" I point out, frustration bubbling up. My voice is sharper than I intend, a mix of disappointment and anger simmering beneath the surface.

"And you're in Gluttony, the place for food addicts, alcoholics, drug addicts, and people who don't know when to say no," the barman retorts, his tone dripping with disdain.

"I could never say no to you, Jules," Tomas calls out. "Do you remember that? Irresistible you were. Want to come join us?"

I glance over at the dark corner briefly to see my stupid ex sitting in one of the booths with none other than Orlin Moss.

"Didn't you read up on this place before you came here?" continues the barman, so I look back and set my attention on him. "You're one of those Inferno Games contestants, aren't you? I can tell by the fact that there's still meat on your bones."

I can feel my cheeks flush with a mix of embarrassment and irritation. The barman's words cut deeper than they should, and I clench my fists, trying to keep my composure. Quinn and Rowena exchange uneasy glances.

"We didn't come here for a lecture," I snap back, unable to mask the edge in my voice. "I just want a fucking drink!"

"Let's go back upstairs," Ro suggests, but I'm angling for a fight and I'm not sure who I want to punch more. The nightmare of a bartender for not giving me what I want, my ex husband for giving everything to every woman he ever came in contact with or Orlin Moss for just being here and being his usual pathetic self. How the fuck did he even manage to get through to this circle, anyway? Oh, that's right. For some unfathomable reason, Orlin is a secret sex god who got more points than anyone in the last circle despite there being no one admitting to sleeping with him. I get the feeling he'd be surprised if someone pointed out he even had a cock, let alone him knowing what to do with it. "I still can't fathom how Orlin's still around," I mutter, "especially as Candice, the Hell slut, and Remy didn't make it through."

Ro elbows me in the stomach. "Don't slut shame just because you're hungry. It's gross how women are called sluts and men are called cads and studs for the same behavior. Besides, you're hardly a vestal virgin yourself."

"How did I not notice Remy wasn't here?" Quinn says aloud, her eyes widening. "I dated the guy, for Christ's sake."

At the other side of the bar, the bartender bristles with Quinn's choice of words.

Rowena shakes her head. "I'm going back upstairs. This is too depressing and I've been to some real dives in my time."

"Me too," Quinn adds. "I need to figure out how to change Dade's mind because if I don't, I'll have to go and find Jenny by myself. Juliette. You coming?"

I look back at Tomas and Orlin. They are probably the two people I'd least like to sit next to in a bar that serves air instead of alcohol, but sitting in my room twiddling my thumbs waiting for the first trial to start seems equally as depressing. At least hating on Tomas and Orlin will pass the time.

"You two go up." I wave them off. "I'll stay down here for a while."

They give me twin incredulous looks, but walk away leaving me at the bar alone. I pick up the empty shot glass in front of me because it feels like I should at least have a prop, and head over to the two men.

It's a hard push to decide who would be the worst to sit next to in the booth, but I remember that whoever I choose to sit next to, I'll have to stare at the other one... sober. Orlin's bad comb over and miserable face makes my mind up for me. I slide in next to him, which leaves me with the joy of spending the evening looking at my ex husband. He's thicker round the middle than he used to be, but he hasn't lost the boyish grin that captivated me back when he was a boy and I was a girl. The asshole was my first kiss, my first sexual experience and my first... and only broken heart. It irks me that he's still got it. No doubt he's still flinging it around.

"To old times, eh Jules?" He holds up his empty glass. Reluctantly, I clink his glass with my own but draw the line at pretending to drink from my glass like he does. He always was the pretender. Orlin stares into space as usual. I'm not even sure he knows we're here. Or he's here. His t-shirt reads 'Been to Hell and back—all I got was this lousy t-shirt!' It's surprisingly amusing for Orlin and reminds me of Maggie and Colin. They didn't make it through to this circle either, but something tells me that they'll be alright together. At least in Lust they can fuck like bunnies...and eat! I let out a sigh. I should have stayed there.

"Orlin, my man." Tomas starts, "What brings you to Hell?"

He's surely in here for chronic boringness, but I keep my mouth shut. Orlin is a man of few words, and I'm genuinely curious if he can articulate anything beyond his normal proclamations that we are all sinners. He doesn't get the chance to answer, because just then, one of the new girls... what's her name... Tate slides into the booth beside Tomas.

"Hi everyone. I hope you don't mind me joining you."

Tomas immediately turns on his charm despite the fact the girl must be half his age at least. "Of course not, Plenty of room."

Tate is exactly Tomas's type. All boobs and butt and skinny waist. Once upon a time I used to look just like her except without the white blonde hair. As soon as she sits, a sharp feeling of loathing overcomes me before I mentally check myself. I have nothing to be jealous of now. Tomas and I were over eons ago. He can fuck who he likes... and quite often does... or did. Judging by the way she sidles up to him and almost plants herself on his knee, they're probably already intimately acquainted with each other. She's young enough to be his daughter I think before I hear Rowena's voice mentally accusing me of being a hypocrite. It didn't count when I fucked younger men. I felt younger. I looked younger. I still look twenty four years old. Tomas doesn't. He might not have the sad ancient wrinkliness that Orlin possesses, but he looks like the middle aged man he was when he died. I guess Lust doesn't afford the youth that Purgatory did.

She gives me a wink then turns her attention to Tomas. "Hey Gorgeous," she purrs, just loud enough for me to hear.

"If you'll excuse me," I say, sliding away from Orlin before he gets any ideas. "I think I may have to go vomit."

I'm out the door and halfway to the elevators before Tomas catches up with me.

"Jules, come on. It wasn't what it looked like," he pleads, his voice full of desperation.

I stop and turn to face him, taking in his familiar features. A thousand painful memories crash down on me, suffocating me. The endless lies he's fed me over the years flood my mind. The man can't open his mouth without either lying or a woman's tongue going in.

"It looked like she was about to stick her tongue in your ear," I say, my voice icy.

"I don't even know her!" he protests, his eyes wide with feigned innocence. "I swear to god, I have no idea what that was about. She said she was a hooker. Maybe she's just soliciting business?"

"She called you gorgeous," I retort, incredulous. When he doesn't answer, I carry on. "Well, she came to the right place with you, didn't she? How much of our money did you throw away on hookers over the years so we couldn't afford to send the kids to university? You're a cheat, Tomas Perez." I say, prodding him in the chest. "You always were, and you always will be."

I turn on my heels and march toward the elevators, slamming my palm on the call button.

"I swear I don't know her," he calls out after me as I step into the elevator and pray for the doors to close quickly so he can't see the tears forming in my eyes. Tomas Perez is the only man that's ever made me cry, and he's had way too many of my tears in the past. Finally, the doors close. I wipe my eyes on the back of my hand and pull myself up straight. I will not let that man hurt me ever again.

8

THE FIRST TRIAL
ROWENA

Every morning this week, I've found two cookies carefully placed by my back door. Today, the morning of the first trial, however, I'm met with an entire box of them. I scoop it up, quickly shutting the door behind me, my heart racing with a mix of guilt and excitement. My curiosity gets the better of me, and I resist the urge to peek outside to see who's been leaving these unexpected gifts.

The first time I discovered the cookies, I accidentally stepped on one with my bare foot, crushing it into crumbs. But as I examined the second cookie more closely, I couldn't shake the thought—could these be from a mystery benefactor or a potential enemy trying to harm me? After extensive sniffing (which eventually turned into licking) and a hesitant bite, I concluded they were simply what they appeared to be—plain sugar cookies. Despite their lackluster taste, they provided some much-needed relief from my relentless morning sickness. Even as I devour a cookie from the box, my mind keeps wandering, pondering who could be behind this curious gesture. I know for a fact it's not Juliette, because every time I've seen her, she's complained about how hungry she is. Though I love her more than life itself and know that she loves me, I think she'd sell my soul to Satan himself for just one of these cookies. Quinn could have left them, but she hasn't mentioned it and hasn't managed to convince Dade to take her down to the lower levels yet. My mind wanders to Twila, who, in theory, could get us secret stashes of food, but I haven't seen her or Hades since the very first day. The thought twists in my gut that it's Felix doing this, but I throw the thought away. He's done everything he can to avoid me all week, which is fine by me. The few times I have seen him, he's been with Anthura and I've had to deal with the pair of them sniggering over some joke, no doubt to do with me. I honestly thought that Felix had the capacity to change, but as soon as his face healed, which it magically did at some point in the night between Lust and Gluttony, he's gone back to being the totally beautiful asshole he always was.

I sit on my bed and open the box, feeling guilty. I should be sharing these with my friends. Hell, I should have been sharing them with Juliette and Quinn right from the first morning they started appearing on my doorstep. If it wasn't for the baby, I would have shared them without a second thought, but the sheer terror of losing my only chance to be a mother has me putting my hand into the box and pulling out a handful of cookies. With them falls a folded piece of paper. I open it. There are five words in uppercase:

EAT ALL BEFORE FIRST TRIAL

It's written so perfectly that I have no hope of figuring out whose writing it is. I empty the box on the bed. There's no other note, but I count thirty-five cookies. I'm starving, but eating thirty-five cookies will have me spending the rest of the day with my head down the toilet. I pick one up and chew on it while doing what I should have done a week ago. I text Juliette and Quinn and tell them to get their asses to my room ASAP.

Less than a minute later, there's a knock at my door. I rush to open the door, finding Juliette and Quinn standing outside. Without uttering a word, I gesture for them to come in, closing the door behind them.

Juliette's eyes go immediately to the pile of cookies on my bed. She races over and grabs one. "Holy fuck. Where did you get these? No, don't tell me. Are they poisonous?" She takes a sniff and her eyes close. "Please tell me I can eat these."

"There are thirty-four. I counted. Twelve each for you. Ten for me. I already ate two."

Juliette looks as though she's just died and gone to heaven, which is ironic considering where we are. "They aren't poisonous. Go ahead."

With a whoop, she dives on the bed and starts shoveling cookies into her mouth three at a time.

"Rowena, what's going on?" Quinn asks hesitantly, her hand subconsciously resting on her stomach, most likely due to not having had anything in it for a week.

I take a deep breath, trying to gather my thoughts before speaking. "Someone has been leaving these cookies for me every morning. Today, there was a note inside the box," I explain, holding up the small piece of paper with the mysterious message.

Juliette and Quinn exchange a quick glance before turning their attention back to me. "What does it say?" Quinn asks eagerly, finally reaching for a cookie. I hand her the note.

"I was kinda hoping it was from one of you two."

"If I had cookies, I'd give them to you to your face, not leave them on your doorstep," Quinn says, her eyes scanning the note. Her brow furrows as she looks up at me, the weight of concern deepening the lines on her forehead. "I don't like this. We've both had awful notes sent to us before. What if they're from Anthura, just like the others were?"

"I thought Hades said Noémi sent the notes and that she's not here anymore," I reply, trying to dispel the growing unease.

Quinn folds the paper thoughtfully and I can see her mind racing. "Hades mentioned that she was responsible for everything that happened in Lust, but remember? She wasn't in Purgatory. I found notes like the ones we received in Anthura's drawer. I know it was her sending them."

I take the note from her hand, my fingers brushing over the unfamiliar handwriting. "This note is different. The handwriting is different. Besides, I've been eating the cookies all week, and nothing has happened." I attempt to reassure her, but a knot of doubt twists in my stomach.

"I love you both," mumbles Juliette, crumbs flying from her lips as she speaks, "but if someone had been leaving me cookies, I'd have devoured the whole lot without telling anyone. Sorry, babes."

I shake my head, laughter mingling with my anxiety. "I have been eating them myself," I admit, pressing a hand to my belly, mimicking Quinn's earlier gesture. "But I was only getting two a day. This box is a new development. It's obviously something to do with the first trial today."

Quinn pulls out her Hell Cell and looks at it. "I'm guessing we'll get a message soon. It's almost ten." She picks up one of the cookies on the bed. "If it's not Anthura trying to poison you, who do you think sent these to you?"

I shrug my shoulders. "As I said, I thought they were from you two. Who here has the ability to get cookies? It's not been anything else, just these cookies. I think we can assume the first trial is going to have something to do with food, so we should do what the note says."

Quinn looks uneasy. "I don't trust anything that's given to me by someone I don't know."

She's barely touched the cookie in her hands. Felix poisoned her in Purgatory with cookies. The thought forms like a knot in my stomach. This can't be Felix, I remind myself for the thousandth time this week. It's just a coincidence. Besides, I've established these aren't poisoned.

"I've been eating them all week and I'm fine," I reiterate. "I honestly think there's someone out there that wants to help me."

Just as predicted, all three of our Hell Cells begin to beep. I pull mine out and read the message.

GEORGE: PLEASE MEET DOWN IN THE EARTHERY IN FIFTEEN MINUTES SHARP FOR THE FIRST TRIAL.

"It's up to you," I say, looking up at Quinn. "You don't have to eat them, but if you don't make your mind up, there won't be any left to eat." We both turn our heads to Juliette, whose mouth and hands are full of cookies. "There better be enough left for us," I chide.

Between us, we finish off the box, miraculously managing to pry some away from Juliette. By the time we leave our room, I'm pleasantly full—something I haven't felt in a week. Even more amazingly, I haven't had the urge to throw all the cookies up. Nerves fill me as we gather outside of the Earthery. Not because it's the first trial in a new circle, although that's nerve-wracking enough, but because this will be the first time, I'll have to be close to Felix in over a week. As soon as the thought of him pops into my mind, I see him standing at the back. At least he's not with Anthura. She's at the front, standing next to George and Cerby. On the other side of George stands Twila, looking beautiful as always.

"Ladies and gentlemen," starts George. "So glad you could make it to the first trial. I'm sure all of you are familiar with the Earthery and what it can do. I don't want to give too much away because I don't want to spoil the surprise, but let's just say you are going to love this." He pats his round belly and gives us all a big smile, which none of us return. We've all been burned before, knowing what these demons think constitutes a good time.

It's only when we step into the Earthery that the source of my anxiety hits me like a tidal wave. The last time we were all in this room, chaos erupted—an explosion that left destruction in its wake and landed me and Felix in the hospital. I glance sideways at him, my breath hitching in my throat. Our eyes meet for a fleeting moment, and a shiver runs down my spine. I quickly drop my gaze, desperate to shield my thoughts and emotions from him. As soon as we're all in the Earthery, the darkness begins to recede, and we find ourselves in a huge banquet hall. In the middle of the hall is a long table with seats down each side and one seat at each end. I count quickly. There are seventeen seats down one side, which makes thirty-six altogether. Someone places their palm in my hand, and I realize it's Quinn standing next to me. Her other hand is holding Dade's, and he's looking as stoic as ever.

Reaching out with my spare hand, I grab Juliette's hand.

"Take a seat, take a seat!" George says, extending his hand excitedly towards the table. We do as he says, though not with quite the same enthusiasm he's showing. I think I can already guess what this trial is going to be. We choose to sit in the middle, not wanting to sit anywhere near George, who takes the seat on one end, and Hades, who takes the other. It might have been nice sitting close to Twila, who's sitting next to him, but Anthura and Moloch have taken up places right next to them. My heart pounds as Felix takes the seat opposite mine.

It's not until everyone is seated that George addresses us all. "For your first trial in the circle of Gluttony, you are required to partake in a grand feast," he announces with a wicked grin. His eyes glint with amusement as he continues, "However, there's a catch." My stomach clenches in apprehension, and I feel Felix's foot graze against mine under the table.

"Don't eat!" Before George has uttered the last syllable, the massive table begins to fill with food.

I say a silent thank you to my secret benefactor, doubling it as more food appears in front of us. The feast laid out before us is almost mocking in its extravagance: roasted meats dripping with juices, freshly baked bread steaming in the cool air, and bowls of stews and curries and goodness knows what else. The scents waft around me, making my stomach clench painfully with hunger.

"You've got to be fucking kidding me," Juliette hisses under her breath. I squeeze her hand tighter, if only to stop her from jumping on the table and loading as much of the food into her mouth as humanly possible.

I can't tear my eyes away from the display in front of us. The aroma of the food is intoxicating, making my head spin with desire. I can feel the hunger gnawing at my insides, begging to be satisfied. But George's warning echoes in my mind.

As I glance around the table, I can see the varying degrees of struggle on the other competitors' faces. Tate looks pale, beads of sweat forming on her forehead as she stares longingly at the spread. Juliette's eyes dart from one dish to another, a fierce battle raging within her. I tighten my hold on her hand. I only wish I could hold her other hand too, but when I look down, I see that someone has beaten me to it. On Juliette's other side sits Tomas. I'm surprised. I thought she hated him, but as I look closer, I spot that she's doing everything in her power to rip her hand from Tomas, who is gripping onto her like a dog with a bone. Her long fingernails are pressing down into his flesh so hard that blood is weeping from his fingers. She's not doing that to my hand, and I'm not gripping half as tightly, so I can assume they didn't kiss and make up after Quinn and I left them at Infernos last week. I should have asked her about that, but with the baby and constant hunger, it had slipped my mind.

At least he's preventing her from doing what she clearly wants to do. I turn my eyes to the end of the table. George is filling his plate cheerfully. I hold my breath as he takes a huge mouthful of something that looks like stew, but nothing happens besides my stomach rumbling harder and Juliette growling under her breath. On the other end, Hades and Anthura are cheerfully eating away too, but between them, looking sad, Twila has left her plate empty. She looks like a girl who'd rather be anywhere than here, and I know the feeling well. She gives me a sad smile and a slight nod, which fuels my resolve further. Twila is allowed to eat. There will be no consequences for her in her position as Hades' girlfriend. She's not eating out of solidarity with us, her friends. I've never been more grateful to have a belly full of cookies, but when an anchovy pizza with pickles and strawberry ice cream materializes in front of me, I can't take it anymore. I've heard of weird pregnancy cravings, but before now, I didn't have the first clue as to how strong they were. My stomach grumbles as I try to resist the urge to reach out and take a slice.

I look over the pizza as Felix catches my attention. His expression is unreadable as he gazes at the feast. There's a steely determination in his eyes, a resolve that sends a shiver down my spine. He's eaten before this. Everyone else is drooling at the food, and he's maddeningly unnerved by the whole thing. His eyes shoot up, and I don't have time to look away as his lock onto mine. The anchovy ice cream pizza is forgotten in an instant as it hits me. He *was* the one that left the cookies. He's helping me. My stomach tightens, emotions swirling in a chaotic mess —anger, confusion, disbelief. How can this be the same man who's made my life hell? And yet, behind all the torment, there's this... act of kindness. I can't make sense of it. I already don't know how to feel about him—half of me hates him, the other half... I don't even know. And now he does this. I don't know whether to laugh or cry.

My thoughts are shattered a moment later as a scream rends through the air. I swivel to my right to find one of the contestants that had a moment ago been eyeing a piece of pie, is now hanging in a cage ten feet above his seat.

I make to stand, more in shock than anything else, but

a sharp pain in my shin stops me. I glance up and see Felix staring at me. Almost imperceptibly, he shakes his head. He knows something. He knows something the rest of us don't. While it's not entirely unlike Felix to cheat in these trials, it's a surprise he's cluing me in on his cheating. I look down the table to where Anthura is helping herself to cheesecake. If Felix knows that standing up will be a problem, then there's only one person he could have gotten that information from.

I don't know whether to feel angry that he's cheating, angry that he's cozying up to Anthura... again, or relieved that I have a modicum of the upper hand in this trial. No eating and no standing up. Got it. I relay the information quietly to Quinn and Juliette. Quinn immediately whispers it to Dade beside her, but Juliette just pouts, saying nothing to Tomas, who still has her in his grip.

I steal another glance at Felix. He's staring at the plate in front of him, his expression a mask of indifference, but I wish I could see what's going on behind those unreadable eyes. The fact that he's helping me is undeniable now. The kick wasn't random; it was a warning. But the question gnaws at me—why is he helping me? Felix, of all people? I've never trusted the motives of men, especially not his, yet here I am, wanting to believe that his actions are genuine. It makes me feel weak, pathetic even, this need to cling to the idea that maybe, just maybe, he's doing something good. Urgh. I hate that I'm second-guessing myself, questioning his intentions while my defenses keep crumbling every time our paths cross. The more I think about it, the more disgusted I feel with myself, for wanting to believe in Felix of all people. Do people really change? I didn't used to think so. I look down at the food and concentrate on something that is in my power. I need to get through this trial. I need to feed this life growing inside me and that means gathering all the strength and willpower I posses.

The "feast" lasts for hours, and the food on the table doesn't remain static. As some courses disappear, other fresh courses appear in front of us. All the while, George continues eating as though he's the one who hasn't eaten for a week and not the rest of us. This circle is truly wretched, but I'm in Hell. I didn't expect a walk in the park. Thanks to the cookies filling my belly, I'm able to resist the weirder and weirder food that keeps appearing in front of me. I'm the only one getting meals like tuna fish and chocolate milk and chicken with horseradish, but I'm the only one that's pregnant.

One by one, the contestants ascend into the air as they can't resist the temptation any longer or they make the mistake of standing up. Each one hangs pitifully in cages above where they were seated. Finally, after what feels like a month but in reality is probably five or six hours, George stands.

"By my count, there are twenty of you left. The trial is over." He looks up to where ten people hang above the table. "You ten are out of the Games. Your punishment will be to stay in Gluttony forever. Well done to those who resisted food made by my finest chefs. Your reward is to eat the feast... for real."

I glance over at Felix, who picks up a chicken drumstick. He doesn't look directly at me, but for the briefest of seconds, I think I see his eyes flicker to mine. The food is safe to eat. I finally let go of Juliette's clammy hand. Within half a second, she's grabbing at the pile of hotdogs in front of her and shoving one in an unladylike manner into her mouth. I reach out and take a slice of the pizza that has been haunting me for hours and take a bite. The salty taste of the tuna mixes surprisingly well with the strawberry ice cream.

After the best meal I've ever had, we all make our way out of the Earthery. I hang back until I see Felix. Making sure Anthura isn't with him, I pull him aside.

"You knew what was going to happen in this trial, didn't you? You are the one who left cookies for me."

He gives me a look that I can't read and I hate it. "I don't know what you're talking about."

Just then, Anthura does appear and Felix is by her side in a second like a pathetic lap dog. I know he's lying. Maybe I was wrong about the cookies, but it was him kicking my shin that stopped me from getting out of my seat and therefore being disqualified from the games. Now I just have to figure out if he's helping me for my sake or if this is all part of a game thought up between him and Anthura and I'm merely the pawn.

9

DAMN IT ROWENA

FELIX

"What were you two talking about?" Anthura has been silent the whole ride up to the penthouse and now her voice grates on my nerves.

"Who two?" I ask as she steps off the platform to her door.

"You and him. Robert. I saw the two of you whispering when we left the Earthery."

"I left the Earthery five seconds before you did. What do you think we were talking about? An in-depth conversation about Shakespeare's best plays?"

"Don't be facetious," she snarls. "Are you coming in or not?"

I don't want to come in. I want to go to my room and sleep and maybe think about what the fuck I'm doing without Anthura constantly up in my grill, but to say no would make her suspicious and I need to get Rowena out of this circle, if only for the sake of the baby. I'm not having a son or daughter of mine spending their days watching George stuff his face while he or she withers away to nothing. It's a fucking baby, for fuck's sake. I step out onto the ledge next to Anthura. She gives me a curt smile, then opens the door.

I make to follow, but she's turned and is blocking the doorway. "If I thought for a second you were thinking of fucking that freak and are using me to help him, I'll send you into the fiery pits of Hell where you belong."

"I'm so confused," I deadpan, not confused at all. "I thought we already were in the fiery pits of Hell."

Anthura's faces turns down into a scowl. "I'll take you all the way to Satan himself and then don't beg for my mercy."

I put my hand to the doorframe and step closer to her. "Anthura. That's exactly what we're trying to do. Get to Satan, or have you forgotten? You can't get to Satan any more than I can without going through these bullshit games, so just cut the crap and let me in. I push past her and she doesn't try to stop me. If she didn't want me in her apartment, she'd have pushed me off the moving platform when it went past my floor. She just likes to think she's winning these little fucked up games of hers. I stride right over to the kitchen and grab a couple of cookies which I pocket for Rowena's breakfast tomorrow morning, then I pour myself a healthy measure of Dragonfire whisky.

Anthura sidles up next to me and wrenches the glass out of my hand.

"I was drinking that."

Anthura smirks, her eyes glinting. "You're not afraid of me, are you Felix?" she murmurs, her voice low and seductive. She holds the glass to her lips and downs the whole thing.

I'm not afraid of what Anthura can do to me. She's full of shit about taking me to Satan, but if she thought for a second there was anything going on between me and Rowena, she'd have her out of the games and there wouldn't be a thing I could do about it. I glare at her, wondering where she's going with this.

"You know what, Anthura? I'm done. I've eaten like a pig and my stomach feels like it's about to burst. Maybe I should go sleep it off." I take the empty glass from her hand and place it on the counter. "Maybe you should too."

I turn to leave, but she grabs my sleeve. "It wasn't sleeping I had in mind." As though she hasn't tried this move a thousand times, her hand travels up my arm, then down my body to my very unwilling cock.

She arches an eyebrow as she cups me through the fabric of my pants. "Looks like you might need a little encouragement." She bends down to her knees, then starts to unzip my fly. I pull back before she gets the zip half way.

Her look of surprise turns very quickly into anger.

"You never say no, Felix. Don't tell me you were arranging to meet up with that freak?"

I pull the zip of my fly to the top. "I'm not in the mood, Anthura. I've just eaten my own body weight in food. I can hardly move.

She licks her lips, then stands. "You've not been in the mood since we got to Gluttony. Let me make one thing clear, Felix. I don't like playing second fiddle and I won't do it to that freak. If I see you as much as look at him, I'll have you both out of the games. I won't need Satan. Hades will do it."

"I don't doubt it, Anthura, but I'm not seeing Row... Robert." I cringe inwardly. "I'll see you tomorrow."

This time when I try to walk away, she lets me. I let out a long sigh as I press the button to call the moving platform. Anthura might be full of shit, but some of what she's said is true. She could have both me and Rowena thrown out of the games and she will if she suspects us. I leave the cookies on Rowena's doorstep like I've done for a week then head back upstairs to my room where I lock the door behind me, then pull the night stand in front of it in case Anthura decides my excuse to not fuck her wasn't good enough and she uses her Portal to try to get inside.

I sit on the edge of my bed, fists clenched, a mixture of frustration and longing swirling inside me. All I can think about is Rowena and how desperately I want her.

I can almost feel her warmth against my skin, the way her laughter dances in the air, wrapping around me like a spell. Her eyes, full of mischief and something deeper, tug at something primal within me. I run a hand through my hair, trying to dispel the heat rising in my core, but it's no use. The ache for her is undeniable, intoxicating.

To go to her would be madness. I lean back, letting my head fall against the pillows, but it does nothing to ease the storm inside me. The more I think about her—her laughter, that fierce spirit of hers—the more I want to lose control. I let my hand drift down, the anger mixing with desire. Images flash through my mind, raw and vivid: Rowena standing before me, defiant and unapologetic, her hair cascading around her shoulders. I can almost hear her voice, the way she challenges me, pushing all my buttons. It fuels something dark and primal within me. I can't help it—I need her. My fingers wrap around myself, and I start to stroke, each motion filled with a desperate hunger that matches the ache in my chest. I envision pressing her against the wall, pinning her there, claiming her. The thought of her gasping, wanting me as much as I want her, drives me further into madness. "Rowena…" I growl her name, my frustration spilling over. I imagine her biting her lip, the way she teases me with that look in her eyes, and it ignites a new wave of anger. And I've only got myself to blame. My hand moves faster, each stroke pushing me closer to the brink, but the anger only intensifies my desire. I picture her beneath me, her body arching, her breath hitching as I take control. My heart races as I imagine her surrendering to me, and the tension coils tighter within. Rowena will never surrender to me, and that's probably what makes her irresistible. I've always gotten my own way, gotten what I want... until now. With every stroke, I push against the frustration, the need to make her mine, to show her who she truly belongs to. I'm lost in my thoughts of Rowena, the images blurring as the anger surges, fueling me until I can't hold back any longer. "Damn it, Rowena!" I shout, the tension snapping, pleasure crashing over me like a wave.

10

THE HELLBEAST

QUINN

Sitting next to Dade at the banquet had my nerves in a knot. He'd held my hand the whole time, even though I haven't spoken to him for almost a week. He's still holding my hand as we exit the Earthery. It feels like everything is normal but it isn't. It can't be. He doesn't want me to go to the lower level and I don't want to be without Jenny. We are at an impasse and it feels like everything I had been clinging onto is falling away, even as I still cling onto Dade's hand.

"If I'd eaten one more thing, I'd be waddling," I say to Dade, trying to lighten the mood as we step into the elevator. I'm still unsure of what to say if he asks me to go to his room. I've missed him this week more than I care to admit. It's weird how dark my life has felt without my dark king bringing me light.

I reach for the up button, but Dade's hand closes around mine, halting me. My breath catches in my throat as he turns to face me, his gaze intense and piercing. His eyes lock onto mine with a heat that makes my insides melt. Everything about Dade is overwhelming, but it's this look—this electrifying intensity—that leaves me breathless and off-kilter. Every. Single. Time.

He slowly pulls a marble from his pocket, the key to accessing the lower levels, and holds it up for me to see.

"You've changed your mind?" I ask, hardly daring to feel hopeful. I spent the last week trying to figure out how to get to the lower levels without him or the marble. The only thing that stopped me from stealing it when he slept was the fact that I couldn't do that to him. I need to get to Jenny, but the thought of going down into the bowels of Hell without Dade is a thought that terrifies me more than anything. It's not the demons that might attack or all the untold horrors that I might find, but the hole in my heart I'd create if I left him. And now, I can hardly believe it, but he's changed his mind.

"Seeing those people swinging there, watching us eat while they starved, reminded me that this is not a place I want to end up," he growls, his voice low and rough. His black eyes lock onto mine, burning with intensity. "But more importantly, it's not a place I want you to end up."

He shoves the marble into the hole next to the button on the elevator, his movements sharp, then cups my face in his hands. His grip is firm, almost desperate, as if he's holding on to something slipping away. I look up into those haunted, beautiful eyes of his, and it's like falling in love with him all over again—only harder, deeper.

"I don't want to be with you knowing your heart is still broken over Jenny," he whispers roughly. "I want you to feel whole, and that will never happen unless we find her."

I kiss him, flinging my arms around him in a surge of raw emotion just as the elevator begins its descent. The heat between us is undeniable, but beneath it, a wave of panic begins to swell. Juliette and Rowena flash in my mind—what if we actually make it out? What if we leave them behind?

My thoughts spiral as the elevator hurtles downward, the tension tightening in my chest. Then the soft ping of the elevator doors pulls me back to the present, and my stomach drops. Fear courses through me, sharp and cold, as the doors slide open to reveal whatever awaits us.

Dade takes my hand and the marble that has popped back out of the hole and together we step out into the corridor. It's ominously quiet, which should be a blessing, but the memories of all the things that have happened to us down here, the most recent only being last week, haunt me still.

"We know the way to the main elevator," he says, pulling off his black shirt that I know covers the tattooed map of the underbelly of Hell. My fear has always been that each tower is built differently and the map I tattooed on Dade's back will become useless, but as we begin to walk, a sense of familiarity washes over me. I know most of the way by memory without having to look at the map, but it doesn't stop me running my fingers over the black ink on his skin. The corridors leading through the lower levels are eerily quiet, a stark contrast to the hustle and bustle of the upper levels. Dade and I move swiftly, his tattooed back guiding us through the maze of passageways. As we delve deeper into the bowels of Hell, the air thickens with a sense of foreboding. I clutch Dade's hand tightly, drawing strength from him. We walk for hours, stopping every so often to consult the map. I'm tired and bloated from eating so much food. "We probably should have done this tomorrow morning," I sigh, leaning against one of the gray walls. Suddenly, a low, guttural growl echoes through the corridor, causing us both to freeze in our tracks. Dade's grip on my hand tightens as he scans our surroundings, his eyes narrowing with focus. Without a word, he steers us down a narrow side passage. We emerge into a vast chamber bathed in an otherworldly glow. The source of the glow becomes apparent as we step further into the chamber. Luminous crystals jut out from the walls, casting an ethereal light that illuminates the cavernous space with a mesmerizing shimmer. Dade's eyes widen in awe, his usual stoic demeanor momentarily faltering at the sight before us. But our moment of wonderment is short-lived as a hulking figure stirs in the shadows across the chamber. A massive creature, its form twisted and contorted, slowly emerges into the light. Its eyes gleam with a malevolent intelligence, locking onto us with a predatory gaze. Dade positions himself in front of me, shielding me from the creature's advancing presence. The creature lets out a primal roar, sending shockwaves through the chamber as it charges towards us. Dade braces himself, his stance solid and unwavering. I try to pull him back, but he remains steadfast. He's lost it! The monster is at least twice his size. My panic increases as the creature's monstrous form looms closer, its massive claws scraping against the stone floor with a menacing growl. Its eyes, filled with a malevolent intelligence, never waver from us, fixating on Dade and me with a predatory intensity. I can feel the heat of its breath, thick with malice, as it closes the distance between us. With a thunderous roar, the creature launches itself forward, its massive frame hurtling through the air with terrifying speed. Dade's reflexes are swift, as he ducks in front of me, shielding me from the monstrous beast. I use the opportunity to grab one of Dade's wings and pull him back out into the corridor as the beast is hurled back because of the chains holding him to the far wall.

"What the hell was that thing?" I heave out, my heart pounding with each breath.

Dade shakes his head, his expression grim. "Did you see the door behind it? That's the way out."

I stare at the creature, still straining against its chains, then at the wall behind it. I hope Dade is wrong, but of course, he's not. Right behind the monstrous figure is a door.

"There wasn't a door like this in Lust," I say, my voice tinged with disbelief.

"There wasn't a monster like this either," Dade replies, his gaze steady. "But it tells us one thing."

"What's that?" I ask, a shiver running down my spine.

"It tells us that they are on to us. From now on we can expect to have our every move watched. If they don't know how we get down here now, we can assume they'll find out. We need to figure out how to fight it sooner rather than later."

Fear grips my heart. Jenny is down here somewhere. All the times we've been down in the underbelly of the towers, it felt terrifying, but I always had hope that we'd find her. When we found the elevator in the last tower, I could almost taste freedom, but now, if Dade is right and this monster is here just for us, then we'll never find her... not unless we win the games and get through the next three circles. I pull out my Hell Cell and snap a photo of the massive growling beast.

Dade raises an eyebrow. "What are you doing?"

"I'm not risking your life just to get to a door. If you're right and that... whatever it is, was put here just for our benefit, I think it's safe to assume it likes to eat humans.

"Giving up, Valentine?"

I shake my head, the determination in my chest burning hotter. "Never. But I'm giving up for today. I have a plan. One that won't have us ending up as monster food." I tug at his arm, pulling him back from the edge. "Come on."

I take Dade's hand in mine and guide my reluctant hero from the chamber. We sneak back through the corridors, but there's no need for our stealth. No other monsters or demons jump out at us. I guess the demons thought one monster was enough.

Once upstairs, I say a swift goodbye to Dade and head to the canteen. The giant window is projecting images of milkshakes which would usually have my stomach grumbling if not for the fact I've just eaten half my weight in food. I need to speak to Twila. I have no idea where Twila and Hades sleep, but I'm guessing they have a room down in the dungeon somewhere. They both know we can get down there thanks to Hades saving us last time, but I have no wish to roam the corridors looking for them. Luckily, I spot them straight away, sitting at one of the tables. In front of each of them is an elaborate milkshake, similar to the ones on the big screen. One of the emaciated residents of this circle sits at the next table, not hiding the desperate desire for a sip of their milkshakes. It's perverse and sick and I can't watch his drooling, so I turn my eyes back to Twila, hating myself for ignoring the man nearby after eating such a scrumptious meal. My stomach rumbles in agreement.

"Hey Quinn, What's up?"

Twila looks as ravishing as ever. Being in Hell has never suited anyone like it does her. She's wearing a tightly boned black corset which hoists her boobs right up and, looking down, it seems she's gone for tight leather pants instead of her usual black lacy skirts.

"Nothing really," I finally answer, trying to think of a way to start a conversation. Then I remember Juliette begging me to get her food from the demon levels—which I didn't. Not that Hades would care about Juliette's hunger. He might care about Ro's, though. I pull a conversation starter from my tired brain. "I'm just glad to have got through to the next trial. I was wondering if I could ask you both something?"

"We can't tell you anything about the next trial, Quinn," Hades cautions.

I shake my head. "It's not about that. I was wondering if either of you know what happened to Noémi? I mean. She was the person that tried bringing down the games, right?"

Hades eyes me suspiciously. "She was dealt with by his highest majesty, Satan. You will not have to worry about her any longer."

This is interesting information. She sabotaged the games which took her right where she wanted to be, where we all want to—it gave her an audience with Satan himself. However much the thought of that sends shivers down my spine, we all must pass him if we ever want to get out of here, and Noémi somehow managed to fast track her way there.

I'm learning a lot though I'm not sure how helpful this information is. Sure, Noémi probably got an audience with Satan, but he probably reduced her to ash, or whatever it is that infernal deities do to demons that go against him. Now that I have Hades' attention, another question pops into my head.

"You know that Noémi made Rowena pregnant, right?"

Hades quirks a brow. "I believe that was actually another of your ranks. Mr. Felix Barclay if I'm not mistaken." He glances across at Twila, who nods her head in affirmation.

"Yeah, well Felix and her definitely bumped uglies, but that's not my point. She's pregnant."

"I can't break the rules, Quinn. I already know what you are about to ask me," he says sternly. "The baby is unlike anything I've known in Hell," he adds with a deep sigh, looking weary and troubled.

"Don't demons get pregnant?" I ask, trying to understand. "I mean, you all sure seem to fuck a lot."

Next to me, Twila can't contain her laughter at my blunt question.

"Demons don't procreate," Hades states matter-of-factly. "Sex is for carnal pleasure alone. Demons can't get pregnant."

I furrow my brow, processing this new information. "So, where do demons come from?" I lift my hands up into a half shrug. "I mean, there are so many of them. I know they can die, or at least stop existing, but they must come from somewhere in the first place."

Hades answers with a hint of bitterness in his voice, "They are brought into being by His highest majesty, Satan. Only he can produce life in this place of death." He pauses, considering his words carefully. "Everyone you see here that didn't start off as a human was created by Satan and put to work."

I ponder Hades' words, trying to wrap my mind around the concept of Satan creating life in Hell. It seems so contradictory, life springing forth in a realm defined by death and suffering. But then again, everything about this place defies the natural order.

"So Satan just... conjures demons out of thin air?" I ask, still grappling with the idea.

Hades chuckles darkly. "You have no idea the extent of his powers, Quinn. Creating life, even demonic life, is child's play for him. But enough about that—I already told you I cannot break the rules, not even for your pregnant friend."

I clench my fists in frustration. Rowena is counting on me. I can't let her and her unborn baby starve. On the other hand, asking him for food is probably counted as cheating, even if he is the head of the games. I know I can't appeal to George's better nature seeing as he doesn't have one and Anthura... well, she'd relish the idea of a baby suffering. She'd probably be first in line to buy tickets if suffering was an Olympic event. Then I remember the real reason I was here talking to them.

"Fair enough. I get it. I was wondering if I could borrow your girlfriend for half an hour or so? I know we can't have a coffee together, but I was hoping we could have a catch up?"

"I am not Twila's keeper," Hades mutters, dismissing us with a wave of his giant hand.

A minute later, we're sitting on one of the canteen benches near the large window screen displaying floating milkshakes, now slightly nauseating to watch after my massive meal earlier. Twila shakes her head as she speaks, her dark hair falling over one eye.

"Seriously, Quinn," she says, exasperated. "Just because he's a demon doesn't mean I'm his slave. I can't believe you asked for his permission to speak to me alone. Where's your feminist spirit?"

"Sorry," I reply sheepishly. "He just doesn't strike me as the feminist type."

Twila rolls her eyes. "You know I can't help you either. I cheated once. I can't do it again."

"I'm not asking you to cheat... sort of," I clarify quickly. "I do want your help, though. I was down in the lower levels earlier, and there's a new area. A kind of chamber with a monster in it." I show her the picture I snapped on my Hell Cell.

She looks surprised for a moment before composing herself. "I can't believe you're still going down there. You'll get caught, and next time Hades might not be around to save you."

"I know, but I need a backup plan if I don't make it through the games," I explain earnestly. "I only need to go a few more levels down. We were so close last time."

Twila shifts uncomfortably in her seat. "You think you were close? How do you know?"

"There was an elevator," I reveal with excitement. "I even have a map of how to get to it."

"How did you get a map?" Twila asks, shaking her head in disbelief. "Never mind, I don't want to know. Just because you found an elevator doesn't mean it goes where you want it to go. Satan is a trickster, it could have been a decoy."

I consider this for a moment before responding. "It could be, but I don't think so. It was too hard to find and too heavily guarded. I doubt Satan would go to such lengths just to protect a decoy... which brings me to the favor I want."

"I want to help you, Quinn," Twila assures me. "Believe me, nothing would make me happier than you finding Jenny, but what can I do?"

"I need to know how to get past the monster guarding the door."

Twila sighs. "I have no idea how to do that. My knowledge of Hell extends only to Satan and Hades. Satan is a tricky customer, as I've already told you, and you won't get anything past him. And Hades... well, let's just say he's amazing in bed, but that information won't help you here. I know nothing about hell monsters."

"But you could find out," I persist. "Maybe ask Hades for a romantic stroll around the corridors."

Her face softens a bit. "Seriously, Quinn. Be careful. Hades might enjoy the chaos of these games, but Satan? He won't hesitate to crush you if he feels threatened."

"I know," I murmur, glancing at the screen. "But I can't stop. I need to get Jenny back, Twila. She's the only family I have left." My voice cracks, and I quickly clear my throat, hoping Twila didn't notice.

Twila ponders this for a moment, her lips curling into a sly smile. "Hades isn't one for nighttime walks, but I suppose I could convince him by saying I'd like to try something new in bed. Maybe doing it in front of a monster could be fun." She wiggles her eyebrows suggestively.

I can't help but laugh at her audacity. "Twila, you are wild, weird, and kind of gross, but I love you."

"Don't let Hades hear you say that," Twila warns with a smirk. "He might drag you in for a threesome."

11

HARDLY A VESTAL VIRGIN
JULIETTE

A week has passed since the first trial and though I ate enough food to fill the entire army, navy and air force, the hunger pangs are back with a vengeance. I'm starving, miserable and ready to bite the head off the next person that crosses me. As if he heard my thoughts, I hear the familiar voice of my ex-husband behind me. My heart flutters involuntarily, betraying my attempts at keeping a distance which I've managed all week, mainly by staying in my room and saying no to Rowena's many offers of starting up night classes again. "There you are, my love," Tomas says, taking a seat on the bench opposite me.

"You never did respect boundaries," I mutter, feeling irritated by his presence. "I'm waiting for my friends."

"Oh? Breakfast with them?" he asks, his tone dripping with feigned innocence. Even with his slight paunch and thinning hair, he remains the most attractive man I've ever known. He doesn't possess Hades' god-like allure or Felix's billionaire charm, but there's a warmth and a twinkle in his eye that nobody else can quite pull off. It's infuriating.

"Clearly not in this circle," I retort, irritation bubbling beneath the surface. "We were supposed to discuss the next trial."

"They're not here yet," Tomas points out, a smug grin spreading across his face. "Why not talk to me instead?"

My frustration mounts. "Are you intentionally trying to get under my skin, Tomas? Why don't you go back to your new little slut?"

Rowena joins us on the bench, sliding in next to Tomas and nudging him over. "Who are you slut-shaming now?" she challenges, arching an eyebrow.

I stifle a groan, knowing Rowena will undoubtedly lecture me on my choice of words. "Tomas has a new girl-friend who's younger than our own daughter."

"That's not true!" Tomas bursts out defensively. "She just sat next to me once. That's it—totally innocent!"

"And proceeded to drape herself all over you and call you gorgeous," I retort bitterly, remembering how Tate's long silvery white hair cascaded over his shoulder as she leaned into him. "Innocent, my ass."

Rowena lifts an eyebrow in disbelief and I can almost see a smirk forming on her lips. Traitor!

"Aren't you going to lecture me for slut shaming?" I snap, irritated with the pair of them, which is exacerbated by the lack of food.

"You already know my thoughts on that, but," she turns to Tomas, "I am intrigued as to who your new girl-friend is. We've only been in this circle a couple of weeks. You worked fast."

"He always did." I grumble.

Tomas gives me a look that has my heart squeezing. "If you don't mind, Rowena, I just remembered something."

Rowena steps out of the bench seat to allow Tomas to pass her.

"What's the deal with you two?" she asks when he's out of earshot.

I sigh. "He's only been here two weeks and already he's fucking some young sl... woman. It's gross! And have you seen her? Every time I've seen her, she's wearing a low cut top with her tits nearly hanging out."

Rowena raises an eyebrow and casts her eyes down to my own low cut top.

Annoyed, I pull my top up and cross my arms. "It's different on me. That's décolletage. It's tasteful."

Rowena sits back. "Why do you care? It's been years. You've had other lives since the two of you were married. Hell, you've had whole deaths and, let's be honest, you've hardly been a vestal virgin yourself."

"That's different," I say, pouting. "I was single when I got my fun times with other men."

Rowena shrugs. "And isn't Tomas single now?"

"I hate when you throw logic at me when I want to rant. You usually love a good rant about men and here I am, giving you the perfect opportunity."

"And you usually love to tell me how amazing they are. This is different. It's personal. If I didn't know you so well, I'd think that you still have a thing for Tomas." She raises an eyebrow as if she's challenging me to deny it.

Damn her and her logic and the fact she *does* know me well.

"Tomas Perez was the love of my life," I admit with a sigh. "He's also the biggest asshole, cheating liar, that I've ever met. I'd rather stick a fork in my eyeballs than do anything with that man ever again!"

Both our Hell Cells beep before she has a chance to

hit me with another grain of truth that I don't want to hear.

My heart drops when I read the message from George

SURPRISE! YOU ARE ALL INVITED TO A MANDA-TORY PARTY. MEET UP IN THE DOWNSTAIRS CLASSROOM AREA IN TEN MINUTES.

Normally, the word "party" would fill me with excitement, but I sense that George doesn't quite grasp the idea that parties should be enjoyable for everyone—not just himself. Still, a flicker of hope ignites within me that he'll whip up some delicious food again.

Rowena lets out a long sigh. "Come on, let's get this over with."

We make our way to the elevator, where we find Quinn waiting for us. George, Anthura, and Moloch are already gathered in classroom one. In the corner, Cerby, the three-headed hound, lounges lazily, its three sets of lips eerily synchronized as it laps at the air. Quinn, unfazed by the disgusting thing, immediately runs over to pat each of the heads.

Anthura leans in, whispering something to George. Her cold, flickering gaze lands on us, her lips curving into a smile that doesn't reach her eyes. "Welcome. Come and take a seat while we wait for the others," she says, her voice sickly sweet. But I can sense the malice lurking beneath it, like poison dipped in honey.

The room is laid out with rows of small tables, each with a single chair on either side. The sight of the empty tables makes my stomach clench—no food, not even a crumb. Something feels off, but I can't put my finger on it. I start to sit opposite Rowena, but Anthura's sharp voice cuts through the air, freezing me in my tracks.

"You," she says, her eyes boring into mine. "Sit at a table on your own. I don't want any of you three together."

Her words hang in the air like a commandment, and the temperature in the room seems to drop. I glance at Rowena, who gives me a tight nod, before reluctantly moving to a table on her own.

"Some party!" I mumble under my breath, frustration bubbling up as I plop down at the next table over. My gaze flickers to Rowena, and I see the same irritation mirrored in her eyes.

Dade comes in next, his presence like a dark storm cloud. He moves straight towards Quinn, but Anthura intercepts him with a sly smile, guiding him to a table at the other side of the room. I can practically feel the annoyance radiating off of him.

My heart sinks further when Tate walks through the door looking the exact definition of perfection. I've not said two words to the woman since meeting her, but something about her fills me with hate. Maybe it's because she's a little too perfect, a little too much like the women Tomas would go for. She's alone, but the mere sight of her makes me clench my fists. Anthura points her to the chair opposite Dade, eliciting a raised eyebrow from Quinn. I stifle a groan, knowing exactly what Anthura is up to.

Tomas saunters in next, and my heart lurches. So soon after Tate? I don't want my mind to go there, but the thought gnaws at me. He gives me a cheery smile, and I feel a wave of disgust wash over me. Anthura must have caught my expression because she guides him right to my table. Of course she does. This is Anthura we're talking about, always putting people who don't get along together. And in Tate's case, pairing her with Dade to irritate

Quinn. Not that Quinn looks particularly irritated, which surprises me. Dade is fiercely into Quinn, but Tate is the type of woman that won't care and would try her luck, anyway. And Dade, well, he's a man at the end of the day. Tate is good looking enough to turn any man's head.

When Felix walks in, I half-expect her to send him straight to Rowena. Instead, she places him near Dade and Tate. I sit back in my chair with folded arms, ignoring the grin that I know is plastered on Tomas's face. Despite the years and years without seeing him, I know him so well. That fact alone irritates me to no end.

"I think that's everyone?" George flicks his eyes to Anthura who nods her head. She has a sly smile on her face telling me that whatever this "party" is about, it's not going to be anything good.

"Wonderful. Welcome everyone. I hope you're all doing well. Thank you for coming to my party at such short notice. So this isn't a party like you are used to."

"No shit," I whisper. Opposite me, Tomas snorts, sending the eyes of the contest leaders our way.

"Sorry," Tomas musters. "Cough."

The corners of my mouth turn up almost automatically and I hate myself for it.

Anthura sneers, but doesn't say anything, allowing George to continue. "This party is for talking. I want you to get to know the person in front of you."

I flick my eyes over at Tomas to find him staring back at me. We both know each other a little too well. This is going to be a pointless task.

"Moloch is going to hand out some sheets of paper with some questions on it for you. I'd like you to look into the eyes of the person you are sitting with and ask them the questions."

Well, shit!

Moloch ambles around the tables slowly, depositing the questions. It's like being back at middle school. Ironically, middle school is where I first met Tomas. For a second I wonder if this isn't a ploy to take us back to our pasts, but then remember, I didn't meet any of the others in school. It's just bad luck that this task brings back so many memories. Great memories, damn it. I wish I could remember the bad things Tomas did while we were at school together, but he was amazing back then. He was the handsomest boy in school and a bit of a bad boy, which, of course, appealed to me. By high school we were ditching lessons together to make out or drink the vodka he'd stolen from his parents' liquor cabinet. They were amazing times. It's such a shame he turned into such a toad.

"Jules!" Tomas stares at me as though he's waiting for something. He holds up the piece of paper that Moloch has just deposited on our desk and reads the first question aloud. "What's your favorite food? No, don't tell me. Bacon!"

"No, actually," I lie, crossing my arms and trying to sound indifferent. "My tastes have become far more refined since you left me."

His expression hardens. "You left me," he corrects, his voice tight.

"Only because you were cheating on me... again," I shoot back, my words laced with bitterness.

George walks past, chortling, and scribbles something on a pad of paper he's holding. I narrow my eyes at him, irritation bubbling up, but he's already jotting down something that Quinn has said to Orlin, who she's been sat with.

"What is your favorite food?" I say through gritted teeth, already knowing the answer but needing to fill the silence.

"Key lime pie," Tomas replies, his voice tinged with nostalgia.

Another core memory unlocks, making me hate him even more. I used to make him key lime pie every Friday. One Friday, he didn't come home. He was fucking some hussy and forgot the time. Then I remember where that particular pie ended up—right in his face. It was quite amusing, actually.

A smirk tugs at my lips despite myself. I was so angry at the time, but now the memory of the pie filling dripping down his nose is funny. God, we used to hurt one another. The thought is bittersweet, a sharp pang of the love and betrayal that used to define us.

Tomas looks at me, confusion flickering in his eyes as he notices my smile. "What's so funny?"

"Just remembering something," I say, the smirk widening. "Like the time you wore a key lime pie."

He chuckles, the sound surprisingly warm. "I deserved that."

"You deserved worse," I snap, but there's no real venom in my voice. Just a weary resignation.

"Maybe," he agrees, looking down at the table. "But I'm trying to make things right."

We carry on asking each other questions about food, which is excruciating.

Tomas tries to keep the conversation going, his voice soft and careful. "Do you remember that chocolate lava cake you made for my birthday?"

I glare at him, but the memory slips through the

cracks of my anger. "Yeah. You almost burned down the kitchen trying to make it yourself."

He laughs, a genuine sound that catches me off guard. "True. You saved it, though. Best cake I've ever had."

"Doesn't mean anything now," I retort, but there's less bite in my words.

"Maybe not," he says, his eyes meeting mine. "But I still remember it."

We continue the questions, the air between us thick with unresolved tension. Each answer is a reminder of what we had and what we lost. My stomach growls loudly, and I can hear similar sounds from the others. It's almost comical, the way we're all sitting here, starving and talking about food.

"Trust demons to come up with a party where we talk about food after not eating for seven days," I mutter under my breath.

Tomas smirks, the corners of his mouth twitching. "You know, for what it's worth, I'm sorry."

I stare at him, the words hanging in the air. "Sorry doesn't change anything."

"I know," he replies, his voice barely above a whisper. "But it's a start."

I shake my head, trying to keep the walls around my heart intact. I've heard him say he's sorry countless times in the past. The word has become meaningless when he says it. "Let's just get through this."

"Okay!" George claps his hands as his huge voice fills the room. "I want to mix you up a bit." He points at Tate. "You come here and take the place of... er... Tomas. Tomas, you can sit with Quinn, Orlin, can you sit with Dade?"

The sound of chair legs being pulled across the floor fills the air as everyone moves around to George's satisfaction. He moves a few more before deciding he's happy with his choices. Rowena looks bereft as Felix is forced to sit at her table. The only good point is that Anthura also looks pissed off with the situation. I have no idea if Felix and her are still fucking, but I've seen them arguing together more than once in the past week, so something is going on with them.

I turn my attention to the impossibly beautiful Tate. In Hell, I look the best I have in years, but I can't compete with Tate. She's stunning. Bitch!

I sit at the table, arms crossed, staring daggers at the woman across from me. Tate. Even her name sounds too perfect. She's sitting there, smiling like she hasn't a care in the world, while I'm practically vibrating with anger. She looks calm, cool—like nothing could ruffle her. God, I hate her already.

I force a smile, though it feels more like a grimace. "So, how long have you and Tomas been fucking?" If Tomas won't admit to screwing her, maybe she will.

Tate raises an eyebrow and glances at me. Her eyes, a startling shade of blue, flicker with something amused. "He's your ex husband, right?" Like she doesn't already know. "What happened between the two of you?"

"Tomas has a habit of finding new distractions when he gets bored."

Tate leans back in her chair, her gaze never leaving mine. There's something about the way she looks at me that makes me feel exposed, like she can see right through the mask I'm trying to keep in place. "I'm not one of his distractions," she says calmly. "Trust me, he's not my type."

"As a hooker, I doubt that, but I must warn you. He

doesn't have much money. Anything he did have when he died was left to our kids."

Her perfect face falters for just a second before she smiles again, flashing those dimples in her pink cheeks. "I like Tomas. He's a good guy. I think you're still in love with him."

God, she's a condescending cow. "I'm not in love with him," I snap, my voice coming out louder than intended. Across the room, George's eyes light up as he glances at me, furiously scribbling something down in his notepad.

"I'd believe that if you didn't shout it so loudly," she replies, her tone dripping with smugness.

"I'm not shouting," I mutter, quieter now, but the irritation is bubbling just beneath the surface. She's really starting to get under my skin, and I hate it. This is none of her damn business. "I was in love with him. I'm not now. I just don't like the thought of him with—"

"Me?" she interrupts, her eyes gleaming as if she's won some twisted little game. "Other women," I say, even though she's hit the nail on the head. It *is* her specifically. If Tomas had started dating Quinn or Ro or Twila, I'd be fine with it, or at least not as incensed as I am about him dating this woman. So what is it about her that riles me up? It's because she's exactly the type of woman I wanted to be and never was. She's the pin-up that graced Tomas's teenage wall, the supermodel that he drooled over in magazine spreads, the woman that always had it together as I was falling apart with three kids to look after. She's the woman that I always thought Tomas secretly wanted to be with. She's not got a single flaw and I hate her for it.

"What's your favorite food?" I ask through gritted teeth, my grip on the paper tightening until it crinkles beneath my fingers.

"I enjoy licking whipped cream off of..." she starts to say, but I quickly raise my hand to cut her off before she can finish with the word "cock."

It's a phrase that would normally make me laugh if one of my friends said it, but from her lips, it sounds disgusting and offensive. I struggle to maintain composure and hide the inner turmoil this conversation is causing me. As George steps forward to write in his book, I try to focus on anything but the gnawing irritation inside me. I need to keep my head clear and not let people like Tate get under my skin. But when I look down, instead of one piece of paper, there is a small pile of pieces on the table in front of me.

The next hour goes by in a blur as George swaps us around to ask the same stupid questions. Finally, he stops everyone with a clearing of his thick throat.

"Well done, everyone. I told you in my message this morning that I had a surprise. Well, this is actually the start of the second trial."

Murmurs fill the room, but I'm not even surprised. I sigh, feeling a familiar sense of dread settle in my stomach.

"Together, we will head to the Earthery now. Come, follow me," George announces with a smug smile.

I stand up, following George and everyone else out of the classroom and to the Earthery doors where we gather. The air feels thick with anticipation and anxiety.

"This trial is going to be surprisingly easy," George continues, his eyes twinkling with mischief. "I'm going to send you in pairs. You will find a delicious meal inside. Only one of you can eat it. If you share the meal, you will be disqualified. The person who chooses to eat the meal must eat the whole meal and leave nothing left."

A collective gasp ripples through the group. I glance at Rowena, her face pale and eyes wide. She looks at Felix, who gives her a reassuring nod. My stomach twists with unease.

"What kind of meal?" Quinn asks, her voice laced with skepticism.

"An exquisite, mouth-watering feast," George replies, almost licking his lips. "But remember, only one of you can eat it. Choose wisely."

I feel a knot tighten in my chest. This isn't just a test of willpower; it's a test of loyalty and trust. I steal a glance at Tomas, who looks back at me with an unreadable expression.

George starts calling out pairs, and the tension in the room heightens. "Quinn and Dade, you're first," he says, motioning for them to step forward.

Quinn exchanges a worried look with Dade, then they step through the Earthery doors together. My heart pounds as I watch them disappear inside.

"Juliette and Tomas," George calls next.

I swallow hard, my throat dry as sandpaper. Tomas steps up beside me, his presence both comforting and infuriating. We walk to the Earthery doors, the tension between us palpable.

As the doors close behind us, the sight of the feast laid out on the table hits me like a punch to the gut. One plate with a mountain of bacon and another with a key lime pie. My stomach growls loudly, betraying my hunger.

"Remember the rules," George's voice echoes through the room. "Only one can eat."

Tomas and I exchange a long, charged look. I can see the conflict in his eyes, mirroring my own. We both know what's at stake here.

12

THE SECOND TRIAL

ROWENA

It's hardly a surprise that George has picked Felix to go in with me. The tension between us in the classroom was palpable and it didn't help that Anthura hovered near us, listening to our every word. I glance over at her sour face as Felix and I line up to enter the Earthery. The memory of when this whole place crashed down around us, almost killing me hits me sharply until I remember who saved me last time. It was Felix who shielded my body from the rubble. If it wasn't for him, I'd be dead.

I close my eyes as we step into the darkness. When I open my eyes, I swallow thickly, I'd expected a table full of our combined favorite foods gleaned from the past hour in the classroom. What I didn't expect was to find myself in the same cottage where we'd spent the first trial in Lust. The same trial where I'd masturbated furiously on the kitchen floor while Felix had stared at me in horror and disgust. I can't look at Felix's face as I take a seat at the kitchen table. There in the middle, is not the foods that Felix and I mentioned at all, but instead, a perfectly cooked, deliciously smelling Beef Wellington. The same meal that I'd tried making before the weird magic they pumped through the Earthery had me doing unspeakable things.

Felix sits opposite me at the table. Neither of us speaks for a few minutes. The tension in the air could be cut with one of the knives laid out on the table.

"I shouldn't have said what I said," Felix finally breaks the silence, his voice low.

"You'll have to narrow it down," I reply flatly, my mind flashing back to the venomous words he used the last time we were in this kitchen.

"When we were here... I didn't understand."

"You called me a disgusting bitch, if memory serves," I remind him, my tone icy.

He takes a breath, then picks up a knife and fork. I watch in shock as he slices off a large portion of the beef wellington onto his plate, before heaping the plate with the butter vegetables and potatoes. Selfish bastard. He's not even asked if I'm hungry. He can keep the stupid meal. I hope he chokes on it.

I turn back to the window, trying to focus on the view —the plains stretching out endlessly, the mountains in the distance. It should have been calming, something to anchor me, but this place has twisted everything good into something unbearable. Even the air feels heavy, suffocating. The room, the food, Felix—none of it is what I want, not really.

"What are you doing?" Felix's voice cuts through my thoughts, jarring me back into the moment.

I spin around, half expecting him to say something biting, something to drag this out into another fight. But instead, my eyes fall on the table, where the untouched plate and glass sit in front of my seat.

"You're letting me eat?" I ask, disbelief dripping from my words. I was expecting him to push back, to make this harder.

"I'm letting the baby eat," he says, his voice so measured, it almost feels rehearsed.

A bitter laugh bubbles up inside me, but I swallow it down. Of course, it's about the baby. It should make me feel something—relief, maybe—but it feels hollow, like everything else when it comes to Felix. "Fine," I mutter, sliding back into my seat. "Wouldn't want to let the baby starve."

Felix watches me closely, like he's searching for something in my expression, but I don't give him anything. I pick up my fork and take a bite of the Beef Wellington, and damn it, it's good. Too good. It makes the ache in my stomach worse, not because I'm hungry, but because I don't want to enjoy it. Not here. Not with him sitting across from me, watching me.

"You've been eating up at Anthura's penthouse," I say, the suspicion twisting in my gut. It would explain a lot. Why he's not starving, why he's so calm about giving up his meal. He doesn't need this.

He looks at me, his expression unreadable. "That would be cheating."

"It would," I agree, eyeing him carefully. "Funny how you haven't actually answered me, though."

His silence stretches out, and I hate how much it bothers me. It shouldn't matter if he's been with her. It shouldn't matter if he's been eating better than me. But it does. I hate that it does.

"Does it matter?"

I want to say no, that I don't care what he does or who he's with. I want to pretend like he doesn't still have the power to hurt me, but the lie feels thick on my tongue. "No," I say, taking another bite, my eyes on the plate instead of him. The food is incredible, the best thing I've eaten in what feels like years, but even that's tainted by the tension hanging in the air.

"Rowena, I—" he starts, and I know what's coming. The apologies, the excuses, the same old cycle.

"Save it, Felix," I cut him off, my voice sharp enough to slice through the moment. "Just let me eat in peace."

He nods, but there's something in his eyes, something I can't place. Regret? Guilt? It doesn't matter. Not anymore.

The silence between us is thick, suffocating, filled with everything we're not saying. I focus on the meal, trying to lose myself in the flavors, but no matter how perfect the food is, it can't erase the weight of everything else. I hate that I feel guilt with each mouthful. He would have told me the truth if he wasn't cheating, so he can't be as hungry as everyone else, but with each rumble of his belly as he watches me eat, I begin to wonder if I'm wrong about the whole thing. Felix is a cheat for sure, but if he is telling the truth this time, this must be excruciating. I try not to look at him, but every time my eyes flicker up, I see a hint of desire in his eyes. Once upon a time, that desire was for me. Now he's practically drooling over the food, and I'm not sure if I'm disappointed or relieved. The Earthery can read my mind and knows how to twist my heart.

"Please stop groaning," Felix complains, his voice tense. "It's driving me to distraction."

Damn. I wasn't aware that I was. "You didn't complain about me groaning when you were eating me out, Felix."

His eyes darken with desire, fixated on me instead of

the meal. I know I've put my foot in it. "Forget I said that," I stammer, flustered. "Sorry about the groaning. I'll try to stop."

I cut myself a second slice of the beef wellington, eating it as quickly as I can. The quicker I finish this food, the quicker I can escape to my room and hide my mortification.

By the third and final slice, I'm beginning to feel uncomfortable. My belly has grown faster than a normal pregnancy, and there's already a hint of a bump that I've been hiding with my flowy dresses. But nothing can hide the way my stomach is expanding with the sheer amount of food I'm consuming. No doubt morning sickness will have me throwing up this whole meal in a couple of hours, anyway.

The sharp pain in my stomach intensifies, causing me to double over and clutch at my abdomen. Felix's eyes track my hand, concern etched across his face.

"Are you okay? Is it the baby?" he asks, his voice laced with genuine worry.

"Is that concern I see?" I retort, my tone dripping with bitterness.

"Yes. Fuck, Rowena. Of course I'm concerned. Why do you think I let you have the meal?" His words are filled with frustration and anger.

"I thought we had agreed that you were eating Anthura... 's food," I snap back, refusing to give him an inch. My pulse is racing, but I'm not about to let him win this one.

"Damn it, Rowena. You are one infuriating bitch," he growls, his jaw clenched tight.

I raise an eyebrow. "Didn't you just apologize for calling me a bitch the last time we were here?"

"Yes, but this time I mean it. I'm trying to help you," he bites out, his words sharp enough to cut.

I cross my arms, narrowing my eyes. "So last time you said it just for fun?"

Felix's jaw tightens and his fists clench at his sides, his frustration reaching its boiling point. "Last time I was an idiot. This time, I'm trying to make amends."

I look away, unable to process the mix of emotions swirling inside me. "Well, your concern is noted. But I can take care of myself."

"Evidently," he mutters. Once again I've pushed him too far, but Felix likes to hurt with his words, not his fists.

He says something, his face tight with anger, but I can't hear anything. My mind is swirling, pretty much like the food in my belly.

"Something's wrong," I cry out, holding my belly that now looks enormous. "I..." My stomach feels like it's full of snakes. Half a second before I black out, a terrible thought occurs to me. The food was poisoned... and Felix gave it to me willingly. He knew. The bastard knew. I can't get the words out before everything goes dark and I crash to the floor.

13

LUCIFER WAS AN ANGEL ONCE
QUINN

"**D**ade?" I cry out his name, running round to his side of the table where his face has slumped right into his food. As I pull him out of his dessert, his head lolls back, his eyes closed. "Dade!" I cry out again, giving him a shake. Bits of chocolate pudding drip from his face to the floor. "Someone help me!" I shout out desperately.

The room goes black and then the Earthery lights come back on. I stare through tears at the warehouse sized room. Dade isn't the only one on the floor. Looking around, I see one of each of the pairs is on the floor. Fuck. They were poisoned. Anger swirls in the pit of my stomach, hot and relentless, but I force myself to keep it under control. The panic is there too, clawing at the edges of my mind, threatening to spill over, but I bite down hard, refusing to let it show. I won't give the leadership team the satisfaction of seeing me unravel. Not here. Not now.

"You bastard!" someone shouts out as George steps into the Earthery.

George chuckles as though this is some kind of joke to

him. Beside him, Anthura looks smug as she surveys the giant room. Her eyes land on Felix, who is hovering over Rowena protectively. Her face hardens into a snarl. She clicks her fingers and a number of glamored demons come running in with stretchers.

George's voice echoes round the cavernous room. "I couldn't make the second trial too easy. I did plan to, but then I thought it was a bit boring. So one of you eats a meal. Big deal. This Circle is all about gluttony and I can say that either you left standing are more selfless than the average human or those on the ground are gluttons, just like everyone else in this place."

"What did you do to them, you monster?" I look over to see a distraught Tomas holding Juliette in his arms. She's unconscious, like the rest of them.

"I put a little something in their food. It may kill them, it may not. Only time will tell, but here's the good news for those of you left. You have all gotten through to the next trial."

I stare at him open mouthed. If those still standing are through to the next round, the implication is that those who ate are not... if they even survive. I let out a sob. This can't be happening. Two demons pull Dade from my arms and place him onto a stretcher. His huge wings scrape the floor beneath him. I don't even bother to ask where they are taking him. Wherever Dade is going, I'm going too. I follow them out to the elevators. Dade's wingspan is so huge and with them draped over the side of the stretcher, just the four of us can fit in the elevator. I'm so angry I can barely breathe, but beyond that, I'm scared. Right from the start I knew I'd get through this with Dade. Without him, I don't know if I can do it. I tuck his wings up as gently as I can onto the stretcher. After the elevator doors open, it becomes apparent where they are taking him. It's a place I've been more times than I care to think about. We are the first to arrive at the hospital wing. The demons hoist him onto a bed at the furthest end before leaving him alone.

A demon doctor comes over quickly with some of the magical apparatus I've come to recognize take the place of normal hospital equipment. It's clear she knew we were coming. As Juliette is placed on the bed next to Dade, another doctor runs out.

"He's been poisoned," I say, my voice tight with the memory of the burning sickness that comes with it. At least Dade is unconscious, his body slack, free from the pain for now.

"I know," the demon doctor confirms, not even glancing up from her notes. Her tone is as indifferent as her expression, and it sends a chill through me.

"Will he be alright?" I ask, urgency creeping into my voice.

She shrugs, her hands stilling. "The poison will either kill him or work its way out of his system," she states flatly, as if discussing the weather. "The first twenty-four hours are critical. If he survives that, recovery will take about a week."

I stare at her, disbelief twisting inside me. She turns to leave, but I step forward. "That's it? You've not even looked at him!" My voice cracks, anger bubbling beneath the surface.

She stops, turning slightly, her eyes bored and emotionless. "I don't need to look at him. I know what's wrong with him," she says with a dismissive wave. Then, without another word, she moves on to another patient.

Tears well up, blurring my vision as guilt gnaws at me.

If only I had taken the food when Dade insisted that I eat. But I'm headstrong and refused to eat it, so he would. I spent my life not being able to afford enough food and giving up most of what I had to feed Jenny. I'm used to feeling hungry. When I came into Hell I was incredibly skinny, but in the first two trials, I thickened out and my skinny body got curves and became more womanly. I know my body can handle being skinny again, but I couldn't bear that for Dade, so I forced him to eat. And in that small act, I will go on to the final trial and Dade won't. My heart grips when I think of the decision I'll have to make. If I go through the next trial and win, I'll be closer than ever to Jenny, but with every step I take toward finding my little sister, I'll take another step away from Dade.

Loud sobbing takes my attention away from Dade. With another jolt of my heart, I see my best friend lying on the bed next to his, her breathing shallow. The sobbing is coming, surprisingly from Tomas, who is clutching her hand in his. I'm surprised he's even bothered. From what Juliette told me of him, he didn't care about her. He cheated on her repeatedly, but I don't see that on his face now. My own despair is echoed in his face, but there's remorse too. Maybe he does love her.

"Juliette is a fighter," I say to him, placing a comforting hand on his arm.

"I know." He smirks mirthlessly through his tears. "She fought me all the time. Living with her was like going into the ring with Muhammad Ali, except wearing washing gloves instead of boxing gloves."

Despite everything, I smile at the image. I could imagine Juliette being hard to live with.

"She's a feisty woman. That's how I know she'll make it."

Tomas nods toward Dade, a curious gleam in his eyes. "Your chap looks like he's made of sterner stuff, too. Demon?"

"Not exactly," I reply, watching Dade out of the corner of my eye. "He's tried out for the Inferno Games before. Each time he competed and lost, then tried again, he became... more demon-like."

Tomas considers this, his brow furrowing. "So, all these people... they'll start to look like demons the longer they're here?"

I shrug. "It seems that way. The more you fail, the more you lose a part of yourself. You adapt, or you become one of them."

I hadn't considered it before, and it wasn't something I wanted to consider now. Dade was so close to becoming a full demon as it was. The only thing he didn't have was the red scaly skin and the hooves. Would that be next? "I'm hoping it only happens if you try out for the Inferno Games again, which I don't think they can do from this Circle. They only have that chance from Purgatory. I'm surprised they let you sign up from Lust to be honest. I thought only people from Purgatory could sign up for the games."

"I was surprised as anyone that I was let in."

It doesn't make sense, but I can see that he's telling the truth. Besides, nothing about Hell makes sense to me. It's full of liars and backstabbers and demons that consistently bend the rules to suit themselves.

My thoughts are interrupted by loud shouting coming from the other end of the hospital wing. I look up to see Rowena being wheeled in on a stretcher, her face

contorted with pain even though she appears to be unconscious. Felix is with her. Anthura and George follow
behind, their voices echoing off the walls.

"You fucking bastard!" Felix's enraged voice pierces
through the air as he confronts George. Surprisingly,
George just smirks in response to the outburst.

"She's pregnant!" Felix screams, his fists clenched at
his sides.

"Calm the fuck down," Anthura hisses, trying to
restrain Felix from attacking George.

"I will not calm down, Anthura! I'm sick of you always
telling me what to do!"

"Felix," she warns sternly.

"It doesn't even matter now."

"Yes, it does matter! Now get your ass outside before
you do something stupid that you'll regret."

"I'm already going to do that," he seethes, pulling his
arm back and delivering a powerful punch to George's
jaw. The force causes George's jaws to wobble before he
collapses onto the ground.

A cheer goes up amongst the contestants that remain
awake. As a team of demon doctors rush over to tend to
George, who definitely deserved the hit, Anthura quickly
drags Felix out of the room.

Everything I am wants to stay by Dade's bedside, but
there is nothing I can do for him sitting crying at his
bedside. I'll come back later, but first I need to see the
only person that can help me and Dade stay together
without me destroying my chance to get to Jenny.

I say a quick goodbye to Tomas and quietly slip
through the hospital wing. As I approach the door, I
catch the tail end of an argument between Felix and
Anthura. Normally, I wouldn't care less about their

drama, but after what Felix said to her, I decide to linger and listen.

"I fucking knew it. I knew you'd give her your food, you spineless wimp," Anthura snaps.

Felix's voice rises in response. "So you wanted me to eat it and stay back here, on death's door? If you knew I'd give her my food, maybe you should have tried harder to keep us out of the trial together. Then we'd both be okay."

"I didn't get a say in who went in with whom," she retorts, venom dripping from her words. "I don't give a shit that the knocked-up freak of yours is probably going to die. Without *it* around, you're free to move on to the next circle, and we can put all this shit behind us. Quite frankly, I'm sick of it."

I can't see Felix's face from where I'm standing, but I can hear the incandescent rage in his voice.

"Fuck you, Anthura. Fuck you and fuck all of this. I'm going to do what Twila did in the first circle and tell Hades I cheated and rescind my part in the games so Rowena can take my place."

"You fucking wouldn't dare."

"Watch me."

There's a scuffle and then, "You go to Hades and I'll make sure Rowena never wakes up. In fact, you'd better stay by her side because the second you look away, I'll make sure she never leaves this hospital. Her and that bastard freak of a child."

I'm almost knocked over by Felix barreling through the door and past me. He's so red in the face that I don't think he's even noticed I'm here. I wait for the click clack of Anthura's heels then slip through the door. So Felix has been cheating? What's new? The guy never once did anything that didn't suit him. Except stand up to Anthura for Rowena. If only he wasn't a cheating murdering child rapist, I might actually be impressed.

I don't have time to ponder Felix's behavior, I'm only glad he's going to keep Rowena safe... for tonight at least.

Anthura is already stepping through the door that will take her to the moving platform back to her penthouse when I get to the atrium. I scan the area, taking in the almost empty canteen as I search for Twila. She's not there, so I head into the elevator and head back down to the entertainment floor, hoping to catch her if she's with Hades.

When the elevator opens, I take a turn to the right and race down the classroom corridor to the first classroom. I barge in then wish I hadn't as I find her giving Hades a blow job on one of the tables.

"Er, sorry!"

I close my eyes at the sight of Hades' member which is so huge it's making my eyes water and I'm not the one trying to deep throat it.

It's like watching a car crash where you can't take your eyes away. If I wasn't going to have nightmares about this day already, I would now.

"Let's go outside," Twila says, extracting herself from Hades and guiding me back through the door behind me.

"I need an eye enema," I joke feebly as we make our way to Infernos. Twila orders two dragonfire whiskeys from the bartender, and when they arrive, they're more than just empty glasses—they're filled with the promise of oblivion.

"I shouldn't be drinking this," I remind her as we find a dark corner to sit in.

"I'm allowed to eat and drink, and after what happened in the second round, you deserve this."

I eye the glass of amber liquid suspiciously. To drink it would be cheating, and should I get caught, it could very likely have me thrown out of the games, no matter what Twila says. But then I remember that Dade is already out. With a quick, defiant breath, I down the whiskey in one go.

"This is going to give me a hell of a hangover on an empty stomach," I choke out, my eyes watering with the heat of it.

"I'm sorry about Dade. I knew about the trial, but I want you to know I didn't know that the food was poisoned. I would have warned you." Twila's voice trembles slightly, a hint of guilt seeping through.

I cover her hand with mine, squeezing it gently. "I'm not blaming you, but you are the only one that can help me now. Please tell me you asked Hades about the monster."

Twila shakes her head, then flicks her eyes around the bar to ensure we are out of earshot of anyone else. Her usual confidence seems to falter. "Before I tell you how to get past that monster, you must know its madness. You won't get to Jenny that way. The only way you'll get to her is by continuing through the games."

"Dade, Rowena, and Juliette are all out of the games. They can't stay here." Desperation edges my voice, and I can feel the weight of my words pressing down on both of us.

Twila casts her eyes downward, her shoulders slumping. "Trying to get down through Hell in the elevator is a death sentence."

"And the Inferno Games aren't?" I snap back, my voice laced with frustration. "They might die, Twila. And if by some miracle they all pull through, they'll be stuck here forever. Dade will never find out what happened to his daughter. Rowena will have her baby here. Can you imagine being born in a place where you can't eat? Her child will never know what it's like to taste food, and I don't even know how that's supposed to work. And Juliette —she's barely holding on. Without food, she's on the verge of a complete mental breakdown. She'll lose her mind."

Twila's eyes flash. "You think I don't know all that?" She sighs heavily. "It's not that I don't want to help; I'm just telling you the risks. When it was just you and Dade, it was insane. But now you want to bring Rowena and Juliette into this too?"

"Just tell me how to get past the monster," I demand, my voice steady even though my heart is pounding in my chest.

Twila slumps further, looking more defeated than ever. "I wish I could tell you it's easy, but it isn't."

"Since when has anything ever been easy in this place?" I retort.

"It's a hellbeast. "You can't lure it with food, you can't sneak past it, and trying to fight it would be suicide. The only thing hellbeasts fear are angels."

I blink at her, waiting for the punchline, but there isn't one. "Angels?" I repeat, incredulously. "You're telling me the only thing that can get past it is an angel?"

Twila shrugs helplessly.

I throw my hands up in exasperation. "Because angels are just so abundant in Hell! I'll just swing by the angel store and grab a couple, right?"

"Lucifer was an angel once," Twila says quietly. "He's the only one who can control these kinds of hellbeasts, and, of course..." She trails off, leaving the thought hanging.

I narrow my eyes at her, the pieces clicking into place. "We can't get to Lucifer unless we get past the hellbeast in the first place."

"That's about it," Twila says apologetically. "He must have brought it up himself at some point. Probably before the Games came down to this circle. I would imagine that he has many of them guarding the elevators in the other towers too, now that he's seen how close you and Dade got to the elevator in the last circle. You were never meant to find it in the first place. I'm guessing he's pretty pissed."

I lay my head on my arms and try to stop the spinning in my head, thanks to the dragonfire whisky. I've managed to piss off Satan himself. Just fan-fucking-tastic.

Either I forfeit my place in the games and stay in this circle with Dade, never finding Jenny, I go on without him, leaving him in this miserable hellhole, or we try to figure out a way to get past a monster that isn't get-pastable.

"I wish there was something else I could do."

I love Twila, but it's so easy for her. She likes Hell. She gets all the perks of being in this place without actually being a demon. It's like she was born for this world. Meanwhile, I'm stuck here, fighting for every inch, and this pull of jealousy I feel is starting to gnaw at me.

I sit up and look at her, frustration building. "What would you do... if you were in my position?"

She sighs, her expression softening. "I don't know. I guess I'd keep going through the games."

"And leave Ro, Juliette, and Dade behind, knowing what you know about this place?"

Her eyes flicker with something like sympathy. "The choice is never going to be easy, but you've only known

Dade, Juliette, and Ro for a few months. You've been Jenny's sister her whole life. She's the reason you chose to come into Hell in the first place."

Even when she lays it out like that, it still feels wrong, like every decision is a betrayal. But what else can I realistically do? She's right. I came here for Jenny.

I thank her and say goodbye, hoping that talking to Twila would give me some kind of clarity, maybe even comfort. But as I walk away, the hopelessness tightens its grip. Instead of finding a way forward, I just feel more lost than ever.

14

HOW MANY TIMES CAN ONE PERSON BREAK BEFORE THEY SHATTER?

JULIETTE

When my eyes flutter open, the world is a blur of white and sterile smells. My head throbs with a dull ache, and for a moment, I can't remember where I am or why I'm here. The beeping of machines and the sterile scent of antiseptics slowly bring me back to reality. I'm in a hospital. Hell's hospital, no doubt. I shift slightly, my body protesting with every movement.

That's when I see him. Tomas is slumped in an uncomfortable-looking chair beside my bed, his head resting on his chest. He looks exhausted, dark circles under his eyes, his usually neat hair disheveled. He's here. He stayed.

I can't remember the last time I saw him look so vulnerable. My heart clenches with a confusing mix of emotions—anger, hurt, relief, and something dangerously close to affection. Damn him for once again making me care.

I try to speak, but my throat is dry and only a raspy whisper escapes. "Tomas…"

His eyes snap open, and for a moment, he looks disoriented. Then his gaze locks onto mine, and relief floods his features. He's on his feet in an instant, moving to my side, his hand reaching out to gently brush a strand of hair from my face.

"Juliette," he breathes, his voice thick with emotion. "Thank God, you're awake. I was so scared..."

I want to be angry, to push him away and demand why he cares now after everything we've been through. But the words die in my throat when I see the genuine concern in his eyes.

"You... you stayed?" I manage to croak out. He nods and gives me a small smile.

The exhaustion tugs at me, but I fight to stay awake a little longer. "Tomas," I whisper, my voice weak. "What happened? How did I end up here?"

He takes a deep breath, his face growing somber. "You were poisoned during the second trial. The doctors weren't sure if you'd make it. You've been in a coma for two days."

Poisoned. The memory hits me like a freight train. The Earthery, the food, the trial... everything comes rushing back in a chaotic whirl. "The others... are they okay?"

"Rowena's still unconscious," Tomas says softly, his brow furrowing with worry. "But Dade and the others are holding on. It's been rough on everyone."

A pang of pain twists in my chest as I look down the row of beds and see Ro on the very end, her eyes closed. I'm not sure if I'm hallucinating, but Felix appears to be holding her hand.

"Tomas. Is Felix really over there by Ro, or am I imagining it?"

Tomas twists his head to look behind him, scanning the room. "He's not left her bedside since you all came in."

Tears spring to my eyes, surprising me. I try to blink them away, but they spill over, trailing down my cheeks. I never fucking cry. What is it with this place that's turned me into a fucking faucet? Probably lack of food. It's enough to turn anyone into a pathetic crybaby.

"Why are you crying? Are you in pain?" Tomas's voice is filled with concern as he reaches out, brushing a tear away with his thumb. It's a sweet gesture that stirs my soul and brings me more comfort than I want to admit to myself.

"No." My eyes turn to the end bed again. Felix is the biggest asshole I know and yet right now, I can see the pain in his eyes. He really does care. It's sobering, and strangely saddening too, though I don't know why?

I close my eyes and try to parse my thoughts together. I'm sad because it's clear that Felix really does care about Ro. Anthura must have absolutely balled him out, threatened him, no doubt, too, but he stayed anyway. He put all of his prejudices aside and changed. Like really changed. He's not the same man that came into Hell and that's all because of Ro.

But none of that changes the fact he was sleeping with underage girls, causing Quinn's sister to kill herself. He was a monster in life. Is sitting by the bedside of a woman that he's obviously fallen in love with an excuse to forgive him his previous sins? Sins that were so awful, so insurmountable, that I don't know if I'll ever be able to forgive him.

"I need to talk to him," I whisper, trying to pull myself out of bed.

Tomas stops me, his hands firm on my shoulders. "Not

right now, you don't. You've only just woken up from a coma. You need to see a doctor."

I want to argue that the demon hell doctors don't give a shit, but I'm so exhausted with my failed attempt to get out of bed that I let him leave to find one. As I lie back, I turn my gaze back to Felix and Ro. The sight of him by her side stirs something deep within me, a mix of anger and sorrow.

It suddenly hits me why I feel sadness on a different level than just having my best friend in a coma. Maybe Felix is a changed man. Maybe Ro's love has made him a different person than he used to be. And as he was the lowest of the low, that's a massive turnaround.

Tomas, on the other hand, was always attentive. If I'd have been in hospital back when we were both alive, he'd have been at my bedside, holding my hand. Except he'd have been texting one of his other women the whole time. Every part of my relationship with Tomas was a lie, and I've been pulled back into the lies one time too many.

Maybe Felix is capable of change, but Tomas most definitely isn't. And the sad thing is, if he is capable of change, he's told way too many lies for me to believe him ever again.

The weight of my realizations bears down on me, making it hard to breathe. Sure enough, I see Tomas discretely slipping his Hell Cell back into his pocket as he returns with a doctor.

"She's awake so she'll probably survive," The doctor says nonchalantly while barely bothering to look at me.

"Did you hear that Jules?" Tomas says, excitedly. "You're gonna be alright."

I nod and close my eyes. I'm tired but the truth is, I don't want to look at him right now. Knowing that his concern is probably just an act and he'll be out the door and fucking Tate the second I close my eyes again has me wishing him gone.

"Rest now," he murmurs, pressing a gentle kiss to my forehead. "You need your strength."

As sleep begins to pull me under, I cling to the warmth of his embrace, to the steady rhythm of his heartbeat. For the first time in what feels like forever, a flicker of peace settles inside me. And I really fricking hate that I feel it.

My eyes flutter open, a fragile hope swelling in my chest that maybe—just maybe—he's changed. I watch him as he walks away through the hospital ward door. But my heart clenches painfully when I catch a glimpse of silvery blonde hair. I blink, and just like that, it's gone. Was Tate waiting for him outside, or am I just losing my mind?

The problem is, I'll never know for sure, and I can't expect Tomas to tell me the truth.

Sleep takes me away for hours, and when I wake up, it's not Tomas by my bedside, but Quinn. I wave off the disappointment and give her a weak smile. "It's good to see you," I murmur. My throat is dry, but I know there's no point asking for water. Just like everything else, I'll have to suck it up.

"You have no idea how good it is to see you too." Tears make Quinn's eyes glisten, but she's smiling.

I hazard a glance toward the bed at the far end of the room. Rowena is still there. So is Felix. Quinn follows my gaze, her expression tightening.

"He hasn't left her side once."

"Maybe he's changed?" I suggest.

"Or maybe he's just watching over his assets," she snaps, her voice laced with bitterness.

I raise an eyebrow, waiting for her to elaborate.

"That's his baby she's carrying. Let's not pretend he gives a shit about Rowena," Quinn says, folding her arms. "His heir is more important."

"He's holding her hand," I point out softly.

"Yeah," she scoffs. "Like a leash." Quinn sighs and shakes her head. "Maybe he's trying to convince himself that he's capable of caring. But people like him don't change, Juliette. They just pretend to."

I look back at Felix and Ro, my heart heavy. I was telling myself the very same thing just a few hours ago about Tomas.

As I lay back, exhaustion pulling at me again, I can't help but wonder if there's any hope for redemption in this hellish place. For Felix. For Tomas. For any of us.

"Are any of us really capable of change, Quinn? These games were always about redemption, but we've played by the rules and nothing has changed. It's just getting harder and harder."

Quinn looks down. "I don't know if Tomas told you, but everyone who ate the food is out of the games."

I feel a lump form in my throat. "Out of the games? What does that mean?"

"I'm sorry." Her voice trembles with frustration and sorrow. "It means you're stuck here in Gluttony forever."

My entire world shatters. I shake my head vehemently and try to sit up before a bolt of nausea hits me causing me to lie back down. "No! I can't stay here. This can't be happening."

Quinn reaches out for me but I pull my arm from her reach. It's not her fault and I know I'm shooting the messenger, but I can't deal with this. Quinn is fine. She didn't eat the food. Felix is fine. The slimy bastard wormed his way through again. Maybe his waiting at Ro's bedside is guilt and nothing to do with love. I close my eyes. Tomas is going to go through... without me. I open my eyes and stare at Quinn. "Did Tate get through?"

She raises an eyebrow. "Does it matter?"

"Yes it fucking matters!" I snap.

"The people that got through the second trial don't automatically go through to the next circle. There's still the third trial," she reminds me. Sounds like I already know the answer. Fuck!

I feel my nails digging into my palms. "She'll get through and so will Tomas. I know they will." And they'll be fucking like bunnies, laughing at sad, pathetic old Juliette. Double fucking fuckity fuck.

Quinn gives me the saddest sort of look which does nothing to make me feel better. I don't want sympathy. "I'll say it again. Does it really matter?"

"No!" I reply, way too quickly. "The pair of them can both go to Hell."

And for the very first time, I understand what that really means. Hell has never really felt like the obscure fiery pit that I learned about growing up. It wasn't even that bad before now. Sure we've all had trials and it's not been plain sailing, but I've had my friends beside me, good food and hot men to entertain me. Now, in the worst possible circle, it's all been pulled out from under me. No food, my friends are leaving, and the only man I ever loved is going to go on to the next circle with the latest in his very long line of morally bankrupt whores. It matters. It matters more than anything has ever mattered because, despite all our history, I thought Tomas might have changed. I really fucking hate myself for even contemplating it because I've spent most of my existence hoping he might change, and I've let myself in for disappointment every single time.

I lie back, feeling the crushing weight of my own foolishness. How many times can a person be shattered before there's nothing left to break? The exhaustion tugs at me, but the turmoil inside keeps sleep at bay.

"I can't do this," I admit. "I'm not strong enough. I can't stay here... without you, without Tomas... without everyone I know."

Quinn has tears in her eyes as she grips my hand. "Ro is still here."

I look over to the bed at the end where Ro is still asleep. Felix's head is resting on the bed, his hand draped over her legs. His eyes are closed and I think he's asleep. He looks so peaceful. So innocent.

Quinn catches my eye line.

"Why is it," I start, my voice tight with frustration, "that men can do whatever they want? Lie, cheat, hurt the people they claim to love, destroy lives—and still come out looking like saints?" I nod towards Felix, sprawled out in peaceful sleep. "Look at him. He looks like butter wouldn't melt in his mouth. Part of me almost wants to get out of bed and comfort him."

Quinn draws in a deep breath, her gaze flicking to Felix. "I get the feeling he's in his own kind of hell."

"If he is, it's of his own making," I snap, bitterness creeping into my voice. "I always wondered about him. After everything he did to your sister, why is he here? Why did he end up in Purgatory? He should've ended up in a much lower circle."

Quinn's jaw tightens, her eyes darkening with unresolved pain. "I've wondered that since the moment I got here. Jenny's dead because of him. It's something I'll never forgive him for, but... the circles don't lie. We all end up where we're supposed to be."

My stomach twists at her words, my anger flaring again. "Tomas and his bitch entered the games from a circle they weren't even supposed to be in. I wouldn't put too much stock in these 'rules' about where we're meant to be."

Quinn stays quiet for a moment, her gaze drifting back to Felix, still asleep beside Ro. "Maybe he told the truth about Jenny," she murmurs. "Maybe he really didn't know her at all, and Jenny made it up."

I scoff, unable to believe it. "You had a photo of them together. Don't let the fact he looks like a sleeping angel make you doubt yourself."

She bites her lip, her voice shaking as she replies, "I don't want to change my mind. But if Jenny lied about Felix, the only reason left for why she killed herself is... because of me."

The weight of her confession presses down on me, my chest tight with empathy. "You should have gone to heaven," I remind her quietly. "If your sister killed herself because of something you did, you would have automatically come into hell, not begged to be let in."

Tears gather in her eyes as she whispers, "I didn't have time for her. I was working all the time, trying to keep us afloat, but I didn't bring in much money. We lived in shit-holes. Her whole life was nothing but loss after our parents died. I failed her."

I shake my head, my heart breaking for her. "You lived for her. You died for her. And now, in these twisted games, you're risking everything for her. If you ever did anything wrong in life, which I doubt, you've more than made up for it in death."

Quinn wipes at her eyes, her voice barely audible. "And if I don't get to her, then it's all been for nothing."

"No." I shake my head firmly. "It's never for nothing if you try. You're still in the games, Quinn. Go and do what the rest of us can't—get out of this place."

She lets out a shaky laugh, her eyes filled with a mix of hope and despair. "I only wish it was that easy."

15

I'VE FINALLY FOUND SOMETHING THAT JULIETTE PEREZ HASN'T FUCKED

ROWENA

I slowly drift back to consciousness, the darkness of my coma lifting like a heavy fog. My body feels heavy, but there's a strange warmth beside me. I blink my eyes open, and the dim, flickering light of a hospital room comes into focus.

Turning my head slightly, I see Felix. He's slumped in a chair, his head resting on the edge of my bed, his hand clutching mine. His usually stern face is softened in sleep, dark circles under his eyes hinting at the long hours he must have spent here. Holy crapola!

"Felix?" I whisper, my voice barely audible, throat dry and scratchy.

He stirs slightly but doesn't wake. I have no idea what to do. I'm not sure if I even want him to wake up right now, but his arm is resting over my legs and feels like it's been there for some time. It hurts. I squeeze his hand weakly, feeling a strange mix of emotions. This man, who I've fought with and raged against, is here, holding my hand like it's the most natural thing in the world.

I try to remember what happened, but the last thing I

remember is eating at the second trial. The memory of it comes back. The beautiful cabin, the amazing view. My dream for as long as I can remember... and Felix. If he wasn't holding my hand I'd have thought it was him that put me in here in the first place, but not even Felix would be stupid enough to put me in hospital, then stay by my bedside. Would he? I take a quick look around and spot a number of the other contestants. So I'm not the only one in here. Maybe Felix didn't try to off me after all. A few beds down, I catch Juliette grinning at me. Her eyes are red as though she's been crying recently, but the smirk on her face and her raised eyebrow gives me hope. Then she nods down at Felix and raises another eyebrow. Maybe she's grinning because I'm awake, but most of that smile on her face is because Felix is holding my hand. Embarrassment floods through me. Total complete and utter embarrassment, then anger, then, because my brain is on a mission to get me, a sense of happiness. Urgh.

"Felix," I try again, a bit louder this time, ripping my hand from his.

His eyes flutter open, and for a moment, he looks disoriented. Then his gaze meets mine, and a flicker of relief crosses his face. "Rowena," he breathes, sitting up straighter. "You're awake."

I nod slowly, still trying to process everything and trying not to notice that half the hospital wing is looking my way. "How long have I been out?"

"Two days," he says softly, his voice thick with exhaustion. "The baby is okay. I made sure to keep the doctors monitoring you both."

The baby. Our baby. I'd not even thought of it until I woke up. I was too caught up in why Felix was holding my hand. What kind of monster does that make me? I run my hand down to my stomach and feel the gentle curve of my belly.

"Two days..." I echo, my mind racing. "What happened?"

His face scrunches into an angry grimace. "It was a fucking joke. A ploy. The whole fucking thing."

"Spit it out, Felix," I say abruptly, thinking of at least three jokes about spitting it out but deciding now isn't the time. When did I get so boring around Felix? Probably around the time we slept together. I close my eyes and try to concentrate on what Felix is saying.

"You were poisoned. Half the contestants were. All those that ate the food ended up in here. You're the last to wake up."

I stare at him, my mind struggling to process what he's telling me. Slowly, it starts to sink in.

"I ate the food," I whisper, barely audible. "And now I'm here."

Felix's expression darkens. "You're out of the Games, Ro. I'm... sorry."

The weight of his words hits me like a sledgehammer, but somehow, I stay calm. My heart is racing, but I can feel the numbness spreading.

"You're still in?" I ask quietly.

He nods. "I'm sorry," he repeats.

"You're sorry," I echo, my voice hardening. I stare at him, and the pieces begin to fall into place. "You gave me the food. Insisted, even. And now, I'm poisoned and out of the Games, while you are still in?"

Felix's eyes widen, and he raises his hands in a defensive gesture as my voice rises. When he speaks, his voice is a low growl. "I didn't fucking know."

"But you didn't eat the food," I spit, sitting up

straighter, feeling the betrayal boil inside me. Anger surges through my veins. I'm such an idiot for the make believe running through my head that Felix Barclay might have suddenly changed.

"You must have known about the food being poisoned. Why else would you give it to me? You and Anthura planned all this."

"Ro..."

"My name is Rowena," I shout out, wondering why I'm making a big deal about him shortening my name when I kinda liked it before. "You and Anthura planned to get me out." I'm patently aware that we have the audience of the whole hospital wing now. Even the demon doctors have stopped what they are doing to watch my outburst.

Felix grabs my arm and pulls me close, his grip firm but not painful. He leans in, his breath hot against my ear as he growls low, his voice barely audible. "I didn't know."

I have to strain to hear him, his words vibrating against my skin. Despite everything—my anger, the betrayal—there's an unwanted spark in my chest. The heat of his breath sends a shiver down my spine, awakening something I desperately wish would stay buried. My body betrays me, desire flaring even as my mind screams at me to stay furious.

Damn him.

I'm about to retort when Juliette steps in. "Let her go, Barclay."

Felix stares up at her, anger flashing in his eyes.

"I'm talking to Rowena," Felix growls.

"And now you're done," Juliette snaps, her tone leaving no room for argument.

Felix's face darkens, but Juliette holds her own as he stands up to her.

He turns to me. "Rowena?"

"If I throw a stick, will you leave?" I snap, my voice laced with a nastiness that feels oddly satisfying, like slipping into a familiar old habit.

Felix's expression tightens for a moment, but he decides against responding. Instead, he turns on his heel and walks away. I watch him go, not shifting my gaze to Juliette until the door closes behind him with a soft click.

Juliette steps closer, her face full of concern. "I'm sorry, babes, but I couldn't sit there watching him argue with you when you've just woken up from a coma. The docs need to check you and the baby out." She waves one over.

I place my hand on my belly, feeling a wave of relief wash over me. Now that I don't have the suffocating feeling of Felix next to me, I can finally concentrate on the most important thing. The baby is fine. I can't feel it moving yet, but deep down, I know it's still there, still alive. I keep my mouth shut as one of the demon doctors gives me a perfunctory once-over. He barely looks at me before declaring, "You'll probably make it." Such comfort.

"We're out, but I guess you already know that," I say to Juliette once the demon has left.

She nods. "Dade is out too. Only Quinn got through."

"Felix got through," I point out, a bitter edge to my voice.

"Of course he got through," Juliette says, rolling her eyes. "Me and Quinn were talking about him earlier. You know, it never occurred to me that him and Anthura had planned all this."

I raise an eyebrow, incredulous. "Seriously? It's the first thing I thought about when he told me. First, he got me on his side in the first round, softening me up so I'd trust him, and then he and Anthura concocted this plan where I'd take the stupid food. She probably told George to put us together. I should have figured it out sooner. Since when has Felix ever chosen to do something for anyone but himself?"

Juliette looks thoughtful, her brow furrowed. "He's not left your side in two days, Ro. He punched George when he found out what happened to you."

"He punched George?" I echo, suddenly feeling sick.

"Yeah, right in the face. Apparently, he knocked him right over. Quinn told me. I was still out of it when it happened."

I stare at her, trying to process this new information. "Why would he do that?"

Juliette shrugs. "The guy is a grade A asshole, but maybe he really does care about you. Maybe there's more to him than we thought?"

Pain twists in my stomach that has nothing to do with the baby. He wouldn't have punched George if he wasn't really angry. Anthura I can believe was in on all this, but not George. There'd be no reason for him to stage it. If Juliette is right, Felix has more than likely given himself a one-way ticket out of the games... for me.

"Well, shit!"

Juliette smirks. "I wouldn't have thought he had it in him either, but there you go."

I close my eyes and let out a long, shaky breath. "I'm going to have to go apologize to him, aren't I?" I open my eyes again and look for Juliette's reaction. She screws up her face into a look of disgust.

"Eew. I wouldn't. If he fucked his chances up in the games, then that's on him. You had nothing to do with it. The way I see it is this. Either he did deliberately poison you with Anthura's help and he deserves everything that's coming to him, or he was looking out for you and took it too far. Either way, it's not your problem. Your problem is getting stronger, so we can both get out of this hospital wing and plead our case.

"You still want to be in the games... after everything that's happened to us?"

"Rowena, my darling. I'd rather fuck an angry porcupine than stay in this circle without food."

I laugh. "You mean you haven't already? I'd write it in my diary that I've finally found something that Juliette Perez hasn't fucked, but I can't seem to find a pen."

Juliette grins and suddenly the crippling worry and stress recede a little.

"You get yourself fighting fit, because I'm not doing this alone. You're coming with me."

"Dare I ask where? Not a porcupine sanctuary, I hope 'cause I already have a headache."

"In a few days when you are up and on your feet, we're going to find Hades and persuade him to let us back in the games," Juliette says with a determined look.

"Oh, and how do you propose we do that?" I ask, raising an eyebrow skeptically.

"I don't know yet," she admits, "but I'll think of something. Rest up for now, because we're getting out of this shithole and on to better things."

16

I'M OUT

FELIX

"I'm out!" I storm into the canteen, catching Hades' attention. Even seated, his presence is imposing, his dark eyes flicking up at me with mild surprise.

"You're out?" His deep voice carries an undertone of curiosity.

"Of the games. Out. I cheated." I steal a quick glance at Twila, who arches her eyebrows in surprise at my blunt admission. "I want Rowena to take my place, like when Quinn took Twila's in Purgatory."

Hades leans back, eyes narrowing as he studies me. I can practically see him weighing his options. What could he say? He can't bend the rules for one person just because he wants to spend eternity with her and not do the same for me.

"You cheated? You understand that admitting to that will have... very grave consequences."

I meet his gaze without hesitation. "And I'll take them all. Just put Rowena back in the games."

"You've treated Ro like shit since the moment you met her. Why the sudden turnaround?" Twila pipes up.

I turn toward her, the weight of her words stinging more than I'd care to admit. "Because..." My throat tightens, the reasons jumbling together in my mind. It's hard to put it all into words, to admit that the person I've been dismissing might actually mean something.

"I've been a coward," I admit quietly, forcing myself to meet Twila's eyes. "But that doesn't mean Ro deserves to be out of the games. She's better than me. She deserves a chance."

Hades' eyes narrow further, his expression inscrutable as he watches the exchange. After a long, tense moment, he rises to his full height, towering over us. "Very well. If you insist on taking Rowena's place, then so be it. But know this - the consequences of cheating in my games are not to be taken lightly."

A shiver runs down my spine at the ominous warning, but I refuse to back down. I nod, holding his gaze steadily. "I understand. I'm ready to face whatever comes."

"There you are," Anthura purrs, suddenly appearing from nowhere and linking her arm with mine. She flashes me a warning stare and digs her sharp talons into my arm, before smiling at Hades. "I thought I'd lost you. I know how upset you've been about the baby."

"He says he cheated and wants out of the games, Anthura," Hades says.

"Nonsense." Anthura digs her nails in deeper and smiles more widely at Hades. "He accidentally got some of Rowena's meds. There was a mixup in the hospital. Sedatives or something. Don't listen to a word he said. He's probably hallucinating."

"Anthura," I caution, but her nails are digging in to my flesh so hard, I can feel blood trickling down my wrist.

"Don't say another word. We need to get you back to

your room." She shakes her head dismissively. "He didn't cheat. He's just confused, aren't you?"

"I'm not..." I can't say another word as a flash of heat runs up my arm, scorching it. "See?" Anthura trills. "He's still in the games. Now come with me before you fall over, Felix."

She's shorter than me, but her strength surpasses mine as she drags me away from a confused looking Hades and Twila. It's not helping that my arm feels like it's on fire.

Anthura doesn't say a word all the way up on the platform but the second her apartment door closes, she lets rip.

"What the actual fuck are you thinking? Have you gone completely insane?"

"Me?" I rage at her, pulling my sleeve up to find my right arm red and blistered, with four puncture marks just above the wrist. "You burned me, you heinous bitch."

"Having you simpering after that freak is one thing, but putting me in danger?" Anthura's voice drips with venom. "That's something you're going to come to regret, Felix Barclay. What did you tell Hades?"

"I didn't even mention you," I shout back.

Anthura laughs bitterly, a sound that sends chills down my spine. "You're not that fucking bright to be able to cheat by yourself. Of course, they'll know I helped you. And for what? So you can go crawling back to that freak?"

I feel my fists clenching. "Damn it, Anthura. Stop calling her a freak."

Anthura narrows her eyes, a dangerous glint flashing in them. "What? It's not true? He's a freak, Felix. Always has been, always will be. But you? You're a fool for getting tangled up with him again. And now you've made a fool of me."

"Goodbye, Anthura." I turn to leave, but she grabs my arm and spins me back around to face her.

"Don't tell me you're going back to him."

I push my face into hers. "Her. Stop calling her a him. It's fucking gross, even by your standards."

"You called him a him plenty of times so don't come over all morally superior to me, you little shit." Her eyes widen and her mouth cranks into a malicious grin. "You've fallen in love with him. Fucking Hell, Felix, I knew you were dim, but I never thought you'd lower yourself."

My nerves are taught. "Let me go, Anthura," I warn her.

"You tell Hades you cheated again and he'll have you thrown in a pit with a hellbeast. And after that, I'll throw the love of your life right in there after you."

I hold her stare, anger filling my veins.

"You have to stay in the games. It's the only way to save your precious freak, because I'll be going through to the next circle with you." She shrugs. "I can't harm her if we're not in the same circle, can I?"

I'd damn her all the way to Hell if we weren't already here. "Fine. I'll stay in the games, but get this through your fucking ugly skull. I don't want anything to do with you ever again. I don't want to see you or hear you and if I hear that you've harmed one hair on Rowena's head, I'll drag you down to the hell beast's pit myself and gladly let him rip you limb from limb, even if it means sacrificing myself to do it."

I turn and this time she doesn't bother to stop me.

"Well, well, you do have it bad, don't you?"

I hear her cackling all the way down to my floor.

I slam my bedroom door shut and once again, push the dresser in front of it before punching the wall, leaving a fist sized hole.

I never lost my shit when I was alive. I was well known for keeping my composure, but there's something about this place... No, there's something about Anthura that riles me up. Probably the fact that I hate she's got something on me.

I sit on the bed, still hearing her last words to me. You do have it bad.

Now she thinks I'm in love with Rowena. How the fuck did I let that happen?

I pace around the room, my mind racing with thoughts of Rowena and the mess I've gotten myself into. I can't deny she's a fucking great lay, but love? That's a foreign concept to me, especially in this godforsaken place.

I've done what I can to protect Rowena from Anthura even if it means that she'll stay in this circle. That's enough. Then I can move on to the next circle and pretend she never existed.

A knock on the door startles me out of my spiraling thoughts. I freeze, hands gripping the edge of the dresser I've just shoved against the door. Anthura's smug grin flashes through my mind. Of course, she'd come after me now. I cautiously move the dresser and crack the door open, bracing myself.

But it's not Anthura. It's Rowena.

Well, shit.

"What do you want?" I huff, annoyed at both the situation and myself.

She glances at the dresser still blocking half the doorway, arching a brow. "Planning on an earthquake?"

"Fuck." I drag the dresser out of the way and when I look back, she's already in my room.

"You're supposed to stand in doorways during an earthquake," I say, trying to sound casual. "Blocking them won't help much."

"Right," she mutters. "Blocking doors for Active shooters and hiding under tables for earthquakes."

I roll my eyes, not in the mood for sarcasm. "Is there any particular reason you're here, or did you just want to critique my disaster preparedness?" My voice comes out sharper than I intended, but I can't help it. I'm on edge, and her presence only stirs things up further.

"Actually," she says, her tone shifting to something softer, something I'm not used to from her. "I came to apologize."

I drag my hands through my hair. "You don't need to."

She wanders around the room, almost like she's inspecting it before she comes to a stop and sits on the bed, her flowery dress sprayed out beneath her, her legs crossed at the ankles

She's not crying, but the weight of her sadness seems to fill the space between us. It lingers in the air, thick and unspoken, and for the first time since she walked in, I feel... unsettled. More than anything, though, I notice how beautiful she looks, her face framed by soft waves of dark blonde hair. It's almost disarming.

"Look," I mutter, trying to distract myself from whatever this is. "You don't have to—"

"I do," she cuts in.

I sigh and sit down beside her, the mattress dipping under our combined weight. The silence stretches between us.

"You stayed with me in hospital the whole time. Juliette told me."

"I had to make sure the baby was alright," I say dismissively, keeping my tone as flat as I can manage. No fucking point turning this into something it's not. I'm not in love with Rowena, no matter what Anthura might think. Our one night together was one fucking huge mistake. Just one that ended with consequences.

"Just the baby?" she presses, and I feel her eyes on me, like she's waiting for something more.

I tear my gaze away, staring at the wall as if it holds the answers. When I don't answer, she continues, "You didn't know about the food being poisoned, did you?"

"I already told you that." My voice is edged with frustration. She needs to get out of here before…

"Barclay, will you effing look at me?"

I turn to face her, my eyes meeting hers reluctantly. The intensity in her gaze catches me off guard, and I feel my resolve wavering. "What do you want me to say?" I ask, my voice rough with emotion I can't quite contain.

She reaches out, her hand gently cupping my cheek. "I want the truth."

I grab her wrist, pulling it away from my face. Funny how her touch burns worse than Anthura's, just not in quite the same way.

"You want the truth?" I reply, barely keeping the anger from my voice. "The truth is that I knocked you up, and that's it."

"Bullcrap."

I inhale a deep breath, frustration and anger pouring out of me. "Okay then. Here's the truth. I hate how you say bullcrap instead of bullshit and effing instead of fuck. I hate that you think you can just come in here like you own the place. I hate your fuck-awful dress and most of all I hate that..." I stop myself before I say the one thing I shouldn't.

She's not even shocked at my outburst. I hate that about her, too.

"You hate that you knocked me up?" she says, her voice not even wavering. "That's what you were going to say, wasn't it?"

"No," I grit back, blood raging through me. "I was going to say that despite all the things I hate about you, which, believe me, are plenty, I hate that I want to tear that fucking hideous dress off you and fuck you until you beg me to stop."

The world comes to a standstill, and for the first time, I see it—some flicker of emotion breaking through her usually guarded exterior. Rowena's eyes widen, her mouth parts in shock, and it hits me like a punch to the gut. I've never wanted to take back words more than I do right now.

Except I don't. I meant every damn word. I'm leaving, and she's staying. I'll never see her again.

Ten minutes ago, I was certain all I needed was space. Freedom. But now? Now, all I want is her.

She's staring at me like I've lost my mind, confusion and disbelief etched across her face. I can almost see the battle raging inside her, like she's wrestling with her own demons. The silence between us feels suffocating.

She moves closer to me slightly, leaning in. I swear I see something in her eyes—desire, maybe. For a moment, I think she's going to kiss me.

But then she stops. Shakes her head, barely moving. "I can't do this, Felix."

Before I can respond, she turns and slips out the door, shutting it softly behind her.

The moment the door clicks shut, the air feels like it's been sucked out of the room. I'm left standing there, frozen in place, my heart still pounding as if it hasn't caught up to the reality of what just happened.

I thought I saw something—something real, something more—but it slipped through my fingers just as quickly. What the hell was I thinking?

I sink down onto the bed, my hands clenching into fists. I don't know whether to be angry at her for leaving or at myself for letting her go. Probably both. Either which way, getting away from her to the next circle will be the best fucking thing for all of us.

17

EARTH TO JULIETTE

QUINN

"He's fine. He can go back to his room now," the doctor says, her voice curt and dismissive.

I glance down at Dade, who looks paler than ever, though at least he's conscious. I don't know if he ate more of the poisoned food than everyone else or if they gave him a stronger dose, but he's the only one left in the hospital wing. Rowena and Juliette were both released earlier, one by one, and I had to watch as the others left. Now, it's just Dade and me.

"Can't he stay the night?" I ask, trying to keep the worry out of my voice.

"It's fine, Valentine. You heard the doctor," Dade mutters, his voice hoarse but laced with that familiar stubbornness.

I want to argue, but I know how this goes. Last time, when a demon practically twisted his leg off, he shrugged it off and acted like it was nothing. Always hiding the pain, always pretending he's invincible.

"You're a stubborn ass," I say, exasperation leaking into my tone as he drags himself out of bed.

He smirks faintly, but his eyes still carry the weight of exhaustion. It doesn't escape my notice that he's putting enough of his weight on me that he can't stand up fully by himself.

I half walk, half drag him back up to his room, where he collapses onto the bed, the mattress dipping under his weight. Dade settles in with a barely concealed wince, his face pale as death, the dark circles under his eyes making him look like he hasn't slept in weeks. He looks awful, and the sight of him sends a pang of guilt through me.

"You could've died... again!" I snap, the fear and frustration boiling over. "And again, you did it to save my life."

Dade gives a weak chuckle, his voice raspy. "And I'd do it again, Valentine." He pauses, his expression softening before he continues. "But you're forgetting something." His eyes meet mine. "I didn't know eating all that food would save your life. I only ate because you demanded I eat up."

"Semantics. You'd have eaten the food anyway."

"I would, but so would you had you known it was poisoned."

I slip onto the bed next to him and he rests his head on my chest. He's not wrong. We'd both do anything for each other but that wouldn't change the fact that after the final trial, we won't see each other again.

"Don't even think about it, Quinn," he murmurs, even though his eyes are closed.

"Think about what?"

"Going down into the lower levels to kill that beast."

I sigh and stroke his long dark hair from his face. "I did think about it, but Twila says that it's impossible to pass. Only an Angel can pass it. Apparently Satan himself is the only person that can tame it because he used to be a fallen angel."

A small snore erupts from his throat as my Hell Cell beeps. Extracting my arm from under him, I read the message.

BABE, COME HANG OUT WITH US IN THE CANTEEN

I'd planned to spend the night with Dade, but he needs to sleep and I need to figure a way to get us both out of this. After spending most of the day at the hospital I'm desperate for some time with friends.

I type back a reply to Juliette that I'll be there in a minute and leave Dade to sleep.

Juliette barely glances at me as I take a seat opposite her in the canteen. She's glaring at someone or something over my shoulder. Probably Tomas. I turn and find my suspicions confirmed. He's sat with Tate and they both seem deep in conversation.

I wave my hand in front of Juliette's eyes to catch her attention.

"Earth to Juliette!"

She blinks, her eyes sliding over to meet mine. "Sorry," she mutters distractedly. "Why is he talking to her? Why?"

I glance over at the scene she's obsessing over. I've never seen Juliette like this—so fixated on someone. Normally, she's detached, cool with the people she's sleeping with. In the last circle, she didn't even bother to mention who she was hooking up with. I shrug my shoulders. "I don't know. Maybe they're friends?"

Juliette's face twists into a frown, clearly not the answer she wanted. "Look at her, with her perfect boobs and perfect hair. Friends, my ass. I'm going over there."

Before she can stand, Rowena slips into the seat beside

her, effectively blocking her escape. Her face is flushed, and her usually frizzy hair is a mess. She looks like she just ran a marathon—or got out of bed.

"Did you just get out of bed?" I ask, partly to shift Juliette's focus away from her jealous rage.

Ro's cheeks deepen into an even brighter shade of pink as she mumbles, "I needed a nap. Pregnancy is exhausting."

"Can you please get it through to Juliette that obsessing over her ex—the one she's called a rat multiple times—is pointless?" I ask, glancing at Ro.

"I'm not obsessing," Juliette mutters, crossing her arms defensively. But even as she says it, her eyes flicker back to the table behind us, watching Tomas and Tate.

Ro sighs. "You don't want him. He's single, remember? And don't you always say the best way to get over a man is to get under another one?"

"I am over him," Juliette protests. "Besides, you two already have the hottest guys here. You've got Dade, and you've got Felix," she says, pointing at each of us.

Ro looks like she's been slapped. "I can assure you, I do not have Felix."

"Well, whatever. I don't want your sloppy seconds, anyway. And who else is there? Everyone here looks like a walking skeleton, except George, and I wouldn't fuck him with someone else's pussy." She mimes gagging for extra effect.

"May I remind you I'm pregnant and, despite not eating since the poisoning, I still have the ability to throw up," Ro warns.

"Sorry," Juliette says, sounding more annoyed than apologetic. "You're right. I need to stop thinking about Tomas and his brazen ho..." She flashes a look at Ro. "And don't start lecturing me about slut-shaming. I don't give a shit. Look at her with her perfect legs out in that skimpy dress. She is a slut."

Ro rolls her eyes but wisely holds her tongue, turning to me instead. "How's Dade? Has he been discharged yet?"

"Yep. He's in his room. I'll go check on him after we're done here. Actually, I wanted to ask you both something."

Juliette's still zoning out, her gaze locked on Tomas, so I direct my question to Ro. "I need to figure out how to get past a hell beast. Any ideas? We can't kill it, fight it, subdue it, or talk to it."

Ro raises an eyebrow. "Do I even want to know what a hell beast is?"

"Think of the scariest monster and you'll be close. You two are out of the games. So is Dade. I can't stand the thought of going down to the next circle without any of you, so we need to figure out how to get past this hell beast in the lower level and find the elevator to the lower circles."

"Have you tried fucking it?" Juliette says, finally entering the conversation. "I find a good fuck calms the most savage beast."

I notice Ro rubbing her temples as I shake my head. I don't know why I'm even surprised by Juliette. At least I've taken her mind off Tomas.

"Funnily enough, when it was lunging at me with its razor-sharp teeth, I didn't think to throw my clothes off and try to seduce it. I was too preoccupied with getting out of there in one piece," I say. "Twila told me that the only way past it is if there's an angel there with us."

Juliette snorts. "You won't find many of those in here."

"There must be some other way to get past it," I insist.

"There has to be or all of you will be stuck here and I'll be going down to the next circle on my own."

Rowena sighs. "I'm pregnant. I don't want to stay here, but I can't run through the underbelly of the underworld with hellbeasts and demons chasing me. I have to stay here whether I like it or not."

"No. I'm not going without you. Juliette. You'll come and help me get past this hellbeast right?"

She looks at Ro, who won't match her gaze. "I would fight a million hellbeasts if it meant getting out of this fleapit, but I can't leave Ro on her own. I was thinking of speaking to Hades to demand he let us back in the games."

I sigh in exasperation. "Hades won't capitulate to demands. And no one is being left alone. We're all getting out of here, or none of us are."

Ro raises an eyebrow. "You considering dropping out of the games and staying with us?"

I rub my forehead. "I can't drop out of the games. I have to get to Jenny."

"Then we're at an impasse," Juliette says, crossing her arms. "Because we're not leaving Rowena, and you're not staying. So unless you can magically conjure up an angel or tame that hellbeast, and if you're right about Hades, then I don't see a way forward."

There has to be a solution. I can't abandon my friends here, but I also can't give up on reaching Jenny. She needs me. We all need to get out of this infernal place.

Suddenly, an idea strikes me. It's crazy, probably suicidal, but it's the only option I can think of.

"What if we create a diversion?" I say slowly. "One of us lures the beast away while the others make a run for the elevator."

Rowena shakes her head vehemently. "And who is going to volunteer to be eaten by a hellbeast to save our sorry asses?"

"I think I've found someone." Juliette sits up straight and pastes on a smug grin as Tate appears next to us, her genuine smile brightening the dimness of our surroundings. "Hey, ladies. I was wondering if I could join you. It's a little lonely down here."

Juliette scowls, crossing her arms defiantly. "You didn't look lonely when you were snuggling up to Tomas just then."

Tate furrows her eyebrows, her expression turning defensive. It's reasonable, considering that when I glanced over earlier, she and Tomas were sitting at opposite sides of a table, hardly what I'd call snuggling.

"I've already told you I'm not interested in Tomas. He's the only person that talks to me," she explains, her voice steady but tinged with frustration.

Juliette snorts, a hint of sarcasm lacing her words. "I bet he is."

"Anyway, is it okay to join you?" Tate gestures to the empty seat next to Juliette, her eyes hopeful.

"Of cour—" Rowena starts to respond, but Juliette shoots her a glare, cutting her off. "This seat is taken."

Tate raises an eyebrow at the obvious lie, glancing between Juliette and the empty chair. "Seriously? By who?"

"By her!" Juliette points across the canteen where Hades and Twila are chatting. "Twila!" She shouts across the canteen, then waves Twila over.

Tate's face falls, and she quickly walks away, clearly upset by Juliette's outburst.

"Why do you have to be such a bitch, Jules? She said

she was lonely," Ro says, giving Juliette a disappointed look.

Juliette shrugs unapologetically. "Do you really want her hearing us talk about how to get past a hellbeast? We don't even know if she's in with the leadership. How else did she get in the Games from Lust if she's not cozying up to one of them?"

"I thought we were done with that conversation," Ro mutters. "You were going to fuck it to give the rest of us a diversion, if I remember rightly."

Juliette gives her an annoyed smirk.

"It's not over yet," I interject, just as Twila takes the seat next to Juliette.

Twila looks between us with raised eyebrows. "What did I just walk into?" she asks, her voice teasing but her eyes sharp.

Ro glances at me, then back to Twila. "Quinn here is asking for hellbeast advice."

"Again?" Twila looks at me, unimpressed. "I thought I told you it was impossible, and now you're dragging Rowena and Juliette into this?"

Her words sting, and I feel like a scolded child. "There must be some way to get us all through this."

"I told you there wasn't," she snaps. "And you promised you'd stay in the games and forget about getting past the hellbeast."

"I didn't promise," I protest. "I said I'd think about it. You said Satan can control it. Is there any way to get him up here to talk to us?"

Twila gives me a withering look. "Don't you remember what I told you back in Purgatory? The only way to get to Satan is through the Inferno Games. That's why I joined them. That's why we all joined. I wanted to hook up with him, which I'm sure wasn't everyone else's objective, but no one can see him unless you make it to the ninth circle."

Frustration bubbles through me. I don't like being told no and I especially don't like being told something is impossible. I was told it was impossible to find a way out of Hell, but then I was introduced to the Inferno Games. There's always a way past things, even if they do seem impossible.

"What about getting Juliette, Rowena and Dade back in the games, then? Is that possible?"

She shrugs. "Possible but unlikely. Felix already tried that. I thought Hades was even considering it until Anthura pulled him away."

Ro's eyes open wide. "Felix tried to get back in the games? He was never out of them in the first place."

Twila's eyes wrinkle and she tilts her head to the side. "Didn't he tell you this? I thought you two were hooking up now?"

"We are not hooking up!" Ro says a little too loudly. Through gritted teeth, she carries on. "and no, he didn't tell me. Tell me what?"

"He came and pleaded with Hades to let you back in the games. He said that he'd cheated somehow and would step down if you could go back in."

Ro looks like she's about to faint. "Felix gave up his place in the games for me?"

"No. Anthura ran over and said he was crazy and drugged up and that he hadn't cheated and that was that. As far as I'm aware, he's still in the games and you're still out. Sorry."

"Can you all excuse me?' Rowena gets up, looking even paler than she did before."I think I need a nap."

"Didn't you just come down from a nap?" I ask, but she's already scurried away.

18

I'VE NOT FINISHED WITH YOU YET

ROWENA

My rational side is telling me that what I'm doing is insane as I knock on Felix's door and he opens it. My feminist side is shouting at me to run for the hills, but I've never seen such a look of angry desire on anyone's face directed as it is at me before now and it's intoxicating. I can't move and words seem to be stuck somewhere between my brain and my throat. The memory of the night we spent in his room and how effing amazing it felt comes crashing back to me.

"You said you wanted to fuck me," I whisper, barely getting in enough air to string a coherent sentence together. The tension between us is palpable. Heat pools low in my stomach, and my breath quickens, becoming shallow and uneven. Every inch of my skin feels hypersensitive, like the air itself is charged and brushing against me. My pulse is racing, thudding in my chest, in my throat, and lower, in places I can't ignore. I can feel my face growing warm, and a subtle, trembling ache spreads through me, making it impossible to stand still. And with all that happening inside me, I still don't know what I'm doing.

"I did. I do."

"Then why don't you?" I challenge, my voice barely above a rasp.

Felix's eyes darken, his gaze intensifying as he steps closer, closing the distance between us. His hand reaches out, fingers grazing my cheek before sliding into my hair, his grip gentle but firm. His presence is overwhelming, the heat of his body seeping into mine. I can feel the heat radiating off his body, the scent of him enveloping me - a heady mix of sandalwood and something uniquely Felix. My heart is hammering in my chest as he leans in, his lips just a breath away from mine.

Something flashes in his eyes, a mixture of hunger and disbelief. His hand comes up to cup my cheek, his thumb brushing over my bottom lip. I part my lips instinctively, and his breath catches. "You're playing with fire," he warns.

"Maybe I like the burn," I whisper, my heart hammering in my chest.

A growl rumbles in his throat, and then his mouth is on mine. His kiss is searing, demanding, his lips moving against mine with a fierce intensity that steals my breath. I melt into him, my hands grasping at his shoulders, his back, anything to pull him closer. He deepens the kiss, his tongue delving into my mouth to tangle with mine. It's a duel for dominance, a clash of wills, and I surrender willingly, eager to be consumed by the inferno of his passion.

Somehow I'm either pulled into his room or I'm pushing him into it, but either way, I slam his door shut with my foot before we tumble to the bed.

Felix's hands roam over my body, leaving trails of fire

in their wake. He grips my hips, hauling me against him, and I can feel the evidence of his desire pressing insistently against my stomach. A moan escapes me, swallowed by his greedy mouth. I arch into him, craving more, needing to be closer, to feel his skin against mine. He tears his mouth away, trailing hot, open-mouthed kisses along my collarbone. I move to pull the dress over my head, but he stops me with a hand. "Don't. I like the fucking dress."

"You told me earlier that you hated it," I cry out breathlessly as he ducks under the hem of it.

"I lied," he mumbles, finally tearing down my panties and flinging them across the room.

I thought I remembered what this felt like. I've played the moment Felix went down on me last time over and over in my mind like a broken record stuck on a loop, but as his tongue touches my clit, all those memories are blown out of the water.

I let out a gasp as Felix pushes me back onto the bed, the sudden movement sending a shockwave through my body. My head hits the soft comforter, and before I can catch my breath, he's already lifting the skirt of my dress, throwing it up and over my head, leaving me exposed. My skin prickles, the cool air hitting my thighs, a stark contrast to the heat radiating off me.

His touch is firm, unyielding, and every nerve in my body is on fire. I grip the sheets beneath me, trying to anchor myself to something, anything, as my pulse races, and a soft moan escapes my lips.

My hips buck as I break apart round him and yet he doesn't stop.

"Stop," I pant out, almost squeaking out the words.

He doesn't listen, but then when does Felix ever listen to anything I say?

"Stop," I say again, this time louder. "Please!"

This time he does, pulling my dress from my face and giving me a look that only a man that knows he's gotten exactly what he wants can have. He said he wanted me to beg him to stop and he got it, but I don't want him to stop. I want more.

"Fuck me, Felix Barclay."

His face goes hard. "I don't want to hurt the baby."

"You won't," I assure him, desperation in my voice.

"Then I'll eff you all you want."

Was that a joke? I open my mouth to ask, but the chance is stolen when he grabs my neck from underneath and roughly pulls me to him.

His lips crash against mine, demanding and insistent. I melt into his kiss, parting my lips to grant his probing tongue access. Felix's hand slides from my neck down my body, his fingers grazing the side of my breast before settling on my hip. He grips me tightly, pressing his arousal against my aching core.

I whimper into his mouth, my hands sliding under his shirt to trace the hard planes of his muscular back. Felix breaks the kiss and trails his lips along my jaw, nipping and sucking at the sensitive skin. "You drive me wild," he growls, his hot breath fanning my ear. "I need to be inside you."

Coherent thoughts flee my mind as a fresh wave of desire crashes over me. I can only nod, frantic with need. Felix makes quick work of freeing himself from the confines of his pants.

Felix's piercing gaze never leaves mine as he positions himself between my thighs. With deliberate slowness, he runs the tip of his length along my slick folds, teasing me mercilessly. I arch my back, silently pleading for more.

With a primal growl, he thrusts into me, filling me completely in one powerful stroke. I cry out, my walls stretching to accommodate his impressive size. Felix sets a relentless pace, each deep plunge stoking the fire within me higher and higher.

I cling to his shoulders, my nails digging into his flesh as he drives me closer to the edge. Felix's hand snakes between our joined bodies, his skilled fingers finding my most sensitive spot. Felix's fingers circle my sensitive nub in time with his deep thrusts, the dual sensations sending shockwaves of pleasure throughout my body. I can feel the coil within me winding tighter and tighter, threatening to snap at any moment.

Felix pants, his rhythm growing more erratic. "Let go for me."

His words are my undoing. With a keening cry, I shatter around him, wave after wave of ecstasy crashing over me. Felix follows me over the edge with a hoarse shout, spilling himself deep inside me.

We cling to each other as we slowly float down from our highs, our ragged breaths mingling in the charged air between us.

Well, I've done it again and this time I can't blame alcohol or having a concussion. I can't even blame the drugs the docs at the hospital wing gave me for pain because they are safely tucked away in my bag. I had sex with Felix Barclay for the simple reason that I wanted to... or insanity. If any of my friends ask, I'll go with that excuse.

My friends. I close my eyes. I can't tell them about this. Juliette already thinks I'm crazy for sleeping with him the first time, a theory I'm not sure I can dispel, and Quinn still thinks Felix is the reason she's in Hell in the first place.

My eyes flutter open when Felix brushes a tender kiss against my temple. The sex felt inevitable. It was highly charged and in the moment, but the soft kiss on my head reminds me that things have changed between us. And I'm not sure how I feel about it. In an ideal world, having a man kiss me tenderly after wild and amazing sex is the dream, but with Felix doing it, it makes me fearful. He's the father of my baby and yet, all I've ever known from him is months of hate and vitriol followed by two sex sessions and now a kiss on the head.

I turn to him and prop myself up on an elbow. His hair is messed up, making him appear almost human and not the put together, in control businessman I'm used to. He's, dare I say it, cute. He looks happy. It's not an emotion I've come to expect from Felix. "I almost miss the days where you hated me," I admit. "It was kinda fun coming up with put downs."

"I can call you a bitch if it makes you feel better."

"Well, I still think you're an asshole so go right ahead."

He laughs and lays back, facing the ceiling, cradling his head in his hands.

Why does this feel so normal? There's nothing normal about it. And yet it does. Still I can't get the feeling out of my head that this is still some kind of joke or a game. And I'm not used to playing.

"Felix?"

"Mmm?"

"You lied to me about my dress."

"Maybe a bit," he offers, turning back to me again. He fingers the flowery sleeve between his fingers "They aren't the type of thing I usually see on the women I used to hang out with, but your crazy dresses are growing on me. They remind me of you and I like that."

It's quite the admission coming from Felix. I'll be the first to admit that the dresses I make are never going to be shown in any fashion magazines.

The dress lie was one thing, but now another weighs on my mind—one secret I can't ignore any longer. I shouldn't have come here, knowing this, but now that I am here, I need answers.

"What happened between you and Sylvia Rothwell?" I force the question out, every syllable laced with a dread that gnaws at me.

Felix freezes, and the color drains from his face as if he's been struck. "How do you know about her?"

"You didn't hide it as well as you thought. Did you force her to abort her child?" My voice wavers, but I keep my gaze locked on him, bracing myself. His expression is answer enough, and my stomach knots.

He sighs, rubbing his chin, looking older and more worn than I've ever seen him. "Sylvia Rothwell was my girlfriend. Well... one of many."

"Of course," I snap, bile rising as the anger coils around my heart.

"Do you want the truth or not?" His tone sharpens defensively. "You know I wasn't exactly faithful when I was alive."

I cross my arms, my expression unwavering. "Keep going."

He inhales deeply, running a hand through his hair. "I'd been out of the country for months on business. She was doing modeling assignments, couldn't join me. When I got back, she told me she was pregnant. But it wasn't mine."

I blink, my throat tightening. "It wasn't your baby? Is that why you made her abort it?"

HIS SHOULDERS SAG, eyes flashing with hurt. "Is that what you think?" His voice drops to a whisper, raw. "No wonder you hate me. No, Ro. I didn't make her abort it. She'd been with someone else—a well-known, very married Hollywood actor. The baby was his. He was the one who pressured her to end the pregnancy. Not me."

I want to believe him, but something keeps me from falling completely into his words. "So what happened?"

"I offered to take care of her, of the baby. I even told her we'd say it was mine. But she wouldn't do it. The timelines didn't add up—I'd been gone, and people would have figured it out." He sighs, a touch of bitterness in his voice. "So I gave her a massive sum of money, to help her and the baby. Her career was coming to an end, and she hated modeling anyway. She left, moved to Montana. Last I heard, she married a cowboy, had the baby, had more kids."

"She had the baby?" My voice falters, doubt creeping in. "That's not what she said in the interview."

"What interview?" His face contorts with confusion, then softens with a weary smile. "Doesn't matter. She probably made it up to protect herself or to get back at that actor. She was the top supermodel in the world before she disappeared; people wanted reasons. Maybe she spun that story because it was easier."

"But I'd figured out it was you... she called him some rich egotistical asshole who got her pregnant."

Felix chuckles softly, and it's a strange, sad sound. "That's why you thought it was me?" He lets out a wry laugh, shaking his head. "I deserve that, I guess. But no, Ro. Sylvia and I were friends in the end, nothing more. No abortion. I've done plenty wrong—I admit I avoided fatherhood, kept people at arm's length. But with you..." His gaze softens, and he reaches a tentative hand toward my belly. "You were the first person I slept with without protection. I thought... I thought you couldn't get pregnant."

"But I did," I whisper, emotion heavy in my chest.

His hand brushes my belly, gentle and reverent. "And I'm glad. I'm glad I'm the father, and I'm glad it's you. It took someone like you to show me what really matters."

His words strike me with fear so much worse than what I thought he'd done. He wants me. He wants the baby. Its unnerving and scary and downright terrifying. I don't know if I can do this. I wasn't expecting such raw honesty from Felix. I slip out of bed and retrieve my panties from the floor, feeling nervous now the flush of sex has cleared my head a bit. "I should probably go," I explain as I put them on.

"I was hoping you might stay a while."

Another admission. None of this feels real. Maybe I've slipped into an alternate reality.

Crazy sex fuelled by either desire or insanity is one thing. Hanging around for cuddles is something else entirely. It's frightening and everything I've ever wanted all wrapped up together. I look up at him, scared what I might see in his expression.

Felix licks his lips as I dither by the bed, full of fear and uncertainty.

"Get your ass back in this bed Ro, and take those panties back off. I've not finished with you yet.

19

LIKE OLD TIMES

JULIETTE

"How is it that slutty Tate got through and my ex got through, but not your friends?" I snap, sounding more pissed off than I should. It's not Twila's fault, I know that. But she's had it easy, waltzing through these circles without having to do anything more dangerous than sucking Hades' cock—a job I used to want, once upon a time.

"The trial was the trial," Twila says, holding her hands up in surrender. "You know I don't get any say in it. And don't ask about the next one either. I have no idea what it is."

"I'm not even in the next trial," I grumble, crossing my arms and slumping in my seat.

It's not like me to give up, but without fucking Hades myself, I don't know how to sneak my way back into the games, and I doubt Twila will take too kindly to me trying it on with her partner. Besides, however much I hate to admit it, Hades has never even looked my way once Twila was on the scene. I'd try fucking Anthura, but look how that turned out for Felix. The guy has done nothing but argue with the woman since we got to this circle and he looks completely miserable. Besides, the thought makes me feel almost as nauseous as fucking Orlin. Then the thought changes. "Fuck me, I've got it!"

Quinn raises her eyebrows. "Herpes?"

I give her a deadpan stare. "Very funny. I've figured a way to get us all back in the games. Me, Rowena and Dade."

"Do I want to hear this?" Twila asks.

I look at her and weigh up her question. On one hand, she's my friend and I trust her, but on the other she is still sleeping with Hades and I'm not sure I want this to get back to him.

"Probably not. Sorry."

Twila gives me a grin. "Thank fuck. I was worried I was going to have to sit here with my fingers in my ears singing la la la, or worse still, have to listen to another harebrained scheme. I think Hades is probably ready for bed now, anyway." She stands up from the table.

"Bed?" Quinn looks at her Hell Cell. "It's half-past six."

Twila winks. "I never said he would be sleeping."

"I love that girl," I say as she wanders back across to Hades on the other side of the canteen. Sure enough, they both leave together, his hand on her ass the whole way to the elevators.

"So?" Quinn leans across the table, her expression one of excitement. "How do we get past the hellbeast? Don't tell me you were actually thinking of fucking it. I thought that was a joke."

"It was," I reply, keeping my voice low, so no one else can hear. "It wasn't the hellbeast I was thinking of, although I could be persuaded to change my mind. What does it look like, anyway?"

"Like a big hairy monster."

I raise an eyebrow.

"It had teeth longer than my forearm and claws like scythes." She brings up a photo of it on her Hell Cell.

I scrunch up my nose. It was worth a thought and probably sexier than the alternative, which I put to Quinn.

"So Twila is hooking up with Hades and basically has a free passport through the circles. Felix has been hooking up with Anthura and by some unknown miracle has managed to get through unscathed," I say sarcastically.

"What are you saying? You're going to seduce George?"

I shrug my shoulders nonchalantly, as though the thought doesn't make me feel sick to my stomach. "I honestly thought I was going to have to fuck Orlin throughout the last circle."

"Which you didn't?"

"No! I fucked those two gorgeous bodyguards of Noémi's, which also turned out to be revolting imps, but there's my point. I know I can seduce even the grossest of creatures and not lose my lunch if it gets me what I want."

Quinn's face is a screwed up picture of disgust. "Are you serious?"

"Have you figured out a way to get past the hellbeast yet?"

"No."

I cross my arms. "Then I'm serious. I'll charm my way into George's bed and when I have him wrapped round my little finger, I'll put it to him that I want me, Ro and Dade to be back in the games. Call it taking one for the team."

"Well, I can't say you're not a devoted friend, but

George? I think I would rather fuck Orlin, and that's saying something."

"I'd rather fuck anyone than George. Hell, I'd even rather fuck Tate, but needs must. I'm not staying in this circle, doomed to an eternity without a bacon sandwich. I know how to seduce men, Quinn. It's probably all I am good for."

Quinn reaches out and places her hand on my arm. "That's bullshit and you know it."

I shake my head, determined to finally do something to help my friends, no matter how awful. "Where do you think he'll be?"

Quinn shakes her head as though I've lost it and I probably have. What I'm considering is horrific. Trying to push the image of a naked George to the back of my head, I stand before I change my mind.

"I'm going to check on Dade," Quinn says on a sigh, "But do me a favor. If George tries to eat you, send me a message on the Hell Cell and I'll come and save you."

Being eaten by George. I hadn't thought of that. My stomach lurches, but as I've not got any food in it and I haven't developed Ro's weird ability to puke nothing, I put my best foot forward and head to the elevator. I don't have a marble key to get to the demon level like Dade has, so I press the button to the lowest level I can get to. The level with the Earthery.

Once down there, I don't know which way to turn. It's a long shot he'll be down here anyway, but half of me is hoping I don't find him so I can't put this ridiculous plan into action. Infernos' red lights shine brightly, illuminating the cobbled courtyard. If only they served something other than imaginary alcohol, I'd go in there and get drunk. As they don't, I head right and walk down the long row of classrooms. I've only ever seen the classrooms full of Inferno Games competitors, but now as I open the doors to peek into each one, I find the skeletal inhabitants of Gluttony taking night school classes. I almost stop in the one where they are learning to decorate cakes until I see they are using cardboard cakes and shaving foam as the buttercream. I try a few more, coming to a stop in the painting class. Scanning the room, I hope to see Rowena, who I know signed up for this class, but she's not here. I guess she's sick or tired. She did leave rather swiftly earlier. I remember my own pregnancies and how tired I felt all the time. Closing the door, I head into the last classroom. My breath catches when I see Tate. The class seems to be dressmaking as the room is filled with a variety of tailor's dummies, all of which are wider than the painfully thin people who are busy with pins and scissors and material. Tate is making some kind of flowing white dress. Surprising really, as everything I've seen her wear so far has been uber slutty with less material than a hand-kerchief. I mentally say sorry to Rowena for thinking of the word slut, but then take it back as I watch the way Tate runs her hand over the white material, bending over, revealing her tits at the front and ass at the back much to the delight of the skinny tutor. She's probably making a wedding gown to marry Tomas in. I close the door before she sees me and head back along the corridor. With no idea where to go next, I wander down the other way, past the shops. In the previous circles, this area was always bustling with people and featured shops I'd actually want to visit, like bakeries and cafes. Now, the shops are deserted except for the bored-looking demon shopkeepers, their eyes glazed with disinterest.

Even the clothes shops that I loved hold no interest for

me. The clothes in the windows are not even size zero owing to the fact that no one here has an ounce of flesh on them. Maybe I should have signed up to the dressmaking class too, but then I remember Tate is in it.

George isn't here. I honestly didn't think he would be, but my plan is the only way I can think to get us all out of this shit hole. I know I told Quinn I'd stay with Rowena, and I will if I have to, but going an eternity without ever tasting food again will drive me crazy within weeks.

At the end of the corridor, just as I turn to head back, something slams me into the wall, knocking the wind out of me. My first instinct is to fight back, thinking it's one of the demons lurking around. I knee it hard between the legs, but it pulls back quickly, and I catch a glimpse of the person in the dim light.

"What the fuck is wrong with you, Juliette?" she snaps, stepping closer again. "I've never been anything but nice to you, and you treat me like an annoying bitch."

"If the shoe fits," I mutter, straightening up as she finally steps back, giving me space to breathe.

She crosses her arms, her expression full of frustration. "Why? Why am I a bitch, Juliette? I know you have some seriously fucked-up unresolved issues with Tomas, but I've told you time and time again—I'm not fucking him. I get that men lie, but I don't have any reason to. I like him, yes, but not in that way."

"Every time I see him, you're there, simpering with those damn puppy-dog eyes. It's pathetic," I spit back, refusing to let up.

Her jaw tightens, and for a moment, she looks like she's about to walk away. But then she squares her shoulders and leans in so closely that I can feel her breath on my cheek. "You want to know why I sit with Tomas? Because he's my only friend in this place. And all he ever talks about is you, Juliette. Every single conversation is about you and how to get through your thick skull, how much he still loves you."

Her words hang heavy in the air, and for a second, I don't know how to respond.

"Tomas has always loved me," I say, my gaze narrowing as I take in her silvery blonde hair and full lips, "but never enough to stop him from cheating on me with every blonde that catches his eye."

Tate puts her arm to the wall behind me, effectively hemming me in. Frustration is visible in every line of her body that's almost pressing me to the wall. "Maybe he's changed. As far as I know, he's not with anyone else, and for the millionth time, he's definitely not with me. I don't know how to make it any clearer."

I scoff, but before I can say anything, she cuts me off. "You need to figure this out, Juliette. Either go find Tomas and get back with him, or tell him it's over for good. But whatever you do, leave me out of it. This is none of my business, and I'm sick of you glaring at me every time I come down to the canteen and stalking me when I'm in my classes."

Indignation comes over me. As if I'd stalk anybody let alone her, but she's already walking away.

Thoughts of fucking George have flown out the window as I ponder Tate's words. She's right about one thing—I need to figure out what I want, and I can't do that wandering aimlessly around the lower level of Gluttony. My heart pounds as I take the elevator back up to the main floor and head to the platform that leads to Tomas's room. The image of her face and the way she glared at me, inches from my own face, don't leave me as the platform ascends. I'm still not sure what I want when I knock on his door, but I know I have to face him, one way or another.

The door swings open, and the surprise on his face is unmistakable. "Jules. What a nice surprise. Come in."

His tone is casual, but his eyes search mine as he steps aside to let me in. My gaze sweeps over the room, immediately scanning for signs of another woman. His bed is roughly made, yesterday's clothes scattered on the floor, but there's no evidence that anyone else has been here recently. I can't smell perfume or anything suspicious— just the ever-present scent of bacon that permeates Gluttony, mixed with the faint sulfur smell that's everywhere in Hell.

"Sorry about the mess," Tomas says, picking up his clothes and tossing them into the walk-in wardrobe. "I'd have cleaned up if I knew you were coming. Everything alright?"

"I'm fine," I say, though the tightness in my chest betrays me, my heart still racing. My mind struggles to catch up with the whirlwind of emotions I'm drowning in. I sit down on the edge of the bed, feeling the weight of the question I've been avoiding for far too long pressing against my lips. "Tomas," I begin, my voice barely above a whisper, "do you love me?"

He stiffens, his eyes widening in disbelief. "Jules," he breathes, hurt flickering across his face. "How can you ask that? You know I love you. I've loved you since the moment we met in school."

His words hang in the air, familiar yet distant. I want to believe him, but a part of me can't shake the doubt that's been growing inside, slowly, like a thorn digging deeper with each lie, each betrayal. I search his face for something—anything—that will make it all make sense, but all I feel is the same old ache. I know he thinks he means it, but maybe our versions of love are different. Mine don't include having multiple partners behind his back.

He sits on the bed next to me and pulls my chin up so I'm looking into his eyes. Brown, with a twinkle that would make my heart race once upon a time. "You are the love of my life, the mother of my kids, the sun to my moon."

I shake my head sadly. I remember the first time he said that to me. I'd thought it was so romantic. Now it sounds like a cheesy cliché. "Are you sleeping with Tate?"

He doesn't look surprised by my question. I've insinuated it enough in the last few weeks. He shakes his head. "No. Never."

"She was with you at the hospital. I saw her."

Finally I see surprise in his eyes. Of course he didn't think I'd have noticed. The look in his eyes confirm I wasn't imagining it.

"She came down to see how you were."

"Bullshit!" I shake my head and close my eyes.

"Fine. She might have come down to see how I was holding up, but that's all. I didn't sleep with her."

I open my eyes and look at him. This time I believe him. My bullshit detector has grown over the years, but this time he might actually be telling the truth. "What about anyone else?"

"Since the moment I saw that you were down here, I haven't looked at another woman. I don't want anyone else. It's only you. It's only ever been you."

His words churn my stomach, but when he leans in to

kiss me and the familiar taste of him hits me, I find myself yearning for a time when we were younger and things were easy. And then I find myself falling into his kiss.

20

TWO WEEKS ISN'T ENOUGH

FELIX

I've never let a woman spend the night in my bed before—not unless I intended to kick her out before dawn. I like my space, my freedom to spread out without the inconvenience of someone else in the way. But with Ro... I couldn't bring myself to throw her out after last night. I wanted her there, her warmth pressed against me, her breathing slow and steady as she slept. Waking up with her curled at my side felt strange, but hell, it felt good. Now, I find myself studying her sleeping form like an idiot, like I don't already know every inch of her by heart. Her hair's a wild mess across the pillow, frizzy blonde strands splayed out, and her lips are parted just slightly, letting out a soft sigh every now and then. It hits me hard, this realization that her body feels like it was made to fit mine. The way her head rests on my chest, her hand draped across me—it's so damn natural. It's right. Carefully, almost against my own instincts, I brush a stray lock of hair from her face. Her skin's warm, soft, like she's never had a bad day in her life, and my chest tightens with something I can't explain. It's both exhilarating and terrifying, a strange twist of emotions I don't usually allow myself to feel. I let out a low growl, frustrated at myself for keeping this at bay for so long just because of my own bullshit fears. Me, terrified—that's a hell of a thing to admit. And yet, here I am, holding onto her like I've found something I didn't even know I was looking for, and realizing that maybe, just maybe, I never want to let go. Ro stirs, her eyelids fluttering open, revealing those captivating brown eyes. She blinks up at me, a sleepy smile tugging at her lips. I never thought anything could scare me, but Ro blew all that out of the water. At first it was because I didn't understand her. Then it was because I began to feel something for her. Now I'm terrified she'll realize this has all been some huge mistake and leave.

But then it hits me—I'm the one leaving, and she's the one staying. I swallow hard, pushing down whatever the hell it is that's tightening in my chest.

"I have something to tell you," I admit, my voice gruffer than I intended.

"Don't tell me. You used to be a woman?"

I stare at her until her beautiful lips curl up into a grin. Fuck me. This is why she's under my skin. She's the only person that's ever been able to tease me and get away with it. And I like it. All the atrocious banter between us... okay bullying on my part, was foreplay leading up to this.

"Not quite. I spoke to Hades yesterday and asked him if I could swap places with you in the games."

She doesn't look surprised. She already knows.

"Twila told me," she confirms.

A sudden realization hits me. "That's why you came to me last night."

She brushes her frizzy blonde hair back, avoiding my gaze. "That might have been part of it," she admits. "I also wanted to see if there was more to us than just a one-time drunken fumble."

"And is there?"

She hesitates, then sniffs the air with a dry smile. "I guess now it's a two-time fumble, and since I don't smell any alcohol on you... maybe it is more. I don't know. I think I want it to be more, but..."

Her voice trails off, leaving the unspoken doubt hanging between us. I know what she's thinking. She doesn't trust me—not that I've given her any real reason to. Part of me still resents her, hates her even. But those darker parts of myself, the ones that once craved perfection and power, are slowly being won over by her. It's strange, this unfamiliar feeling of wanting something deeper. Not something I'm used to—nor something I'll have the chance to get used to.

Ro and I were over the moment she was out of the games. In a week or so, we'll be in different circles of Hell. I wait for that sense of relief, the comfort of knowing I'll be free of this... complication. But instead, what rises is a suffocating urge to keep her with me, no matter what.

"Fuck!" I whisper harshly, running my hands through my hair. I get up out of the bed, feeling powerless. It's not a feeling I'm used to. Ro sits up and pulls the covers up to her neck. Fear now etches her features. Fear that I've caused. In all the times I've been nasty to her and threatened her, not once did she look at me with anything but an expression of defiance.

"Anthura wouldn't let me. She told me if I stay here and you move on, she'll torture you and the baby." The bile rises in my throat, bitter and acidic, at the thought of what Anthura is capable of.

Ro gives a sad, mirthless snort. "I kinda figured that part out for myself, Barclay."

Once again, I'm left staring at her. She knew the whole time and yet she still came to me.

"I can't save you," I reiterate. "Whatever I do, my hands are tied by Anthura."

"I'm sure it's not the first time she's tied you up. Maybe the first time, metaphorically speaking."

Fuck. I can't do this. With every ounce of energy I posses, I push my dresser back in front of the door, almost slamming it against the door frame.

"You can't keep her out forever," Ro says as I get back into bed with her.

"No, but I can keep her out long enough for the games to move onto the next circle. Anthura doesn't give a flying fuck about me, but she does want to get through the games. She wants it more than anything. Once she finds that I'm not leaving, she'll go through by herself.

"You're not leaving?"

I run my hand over her belly, feeling the gentle swell and curve of it.

Ro pulls back, almost stumbling out of bed. "You can't do that. You can't leave the games for me."

It wasn't the reaction I expected.

"Why the fuck not? Last night was fucking amazing. You are fucking amazing and you're carrying my child. Why wouldn't I stay?"

She gapes at me as though I've said something stupid. Until I met Ro, I was always cocksure about everything I said, but now I fumble over everything I say.

"Two weeks ago, you couldn't stand the sight of me. Two weeks ago, you called me a bitch. Two weeks ago, you'd gladly have seen me dead and would probably have danced on my grave, Barclay."

Her words cut through me like a knife. Her voice isn't even raised, but I can see a hint of panic as though she's trying to hide her emotions as she pulls her dress over her head. The worst thing is, every word she's saying is true. Two weeks ago, I would have pushed her under a bus if it meant securing my place in the games.

"This isn't two weeks ago. This is now, and I'm willing to stay here in Gluttony for you and for our child."

She shakes her head sadly, no longer hiding her emotions. "Two weeks might be enough to forget everything you said and did to me, but it's not enough for me. The sex I had with you made me feel things I didn't think possible and I'm sure you think you've changed, but it's not enough. It's nowhere close to being enough. Go and do the third trial and get through to the next circle."

Without a glance back, she walks across the room to the other door, not the one barricaded by the dresser. She opens it and steps through, her back still to me.

"Goodbye, Barclay."

And just like that, she's gone, taking my heart and my sanity with her.

21

THE THIRD TRIAL

ROWENA

I'm not crying. I refuse to shed tears for a man who bullied me, just like everyone else who has torn me down over the years. And I definitely won't cry over something that had the potential to be real.

Having a man stand up for me—that's never been my reality. The idea of someone sacrificing anything for me is so foreign; I don't even know how to process it. For a fleeting moment, I saw forever in his eyes. I glimpsed a future I've only ever dared to dream of. But dreams like that don't belong to me. They're not for people like me.

If Felix stays here, trapped with me in this place of emptiness—no food, no distractions, nothing of value— he'll start to resent me. It's inevitable, and it will happen sooner rather than later. I know he thinks he wants this, thinks he's made some grand decision overnight, but I've spent a lifetime imagining my perfect future. And none of those dreams ever involved being stuck in a one-bedroom corner of Hell with a man who, just two weeks ago, admitted he hated me.

The man slept with Quinn's under age sister, making

her kill herself. What other dark secrets lie in his past that I don't know about? Getting involved with Felix Barclay was a stupid mistake and though he might have changed, the things he has hidden in his past are unforgivable. I mentally berate myself for going back to him It was a moment of weakness that won't be repeated. Next week, he'll have moved on, and I'll pretend he never existed, like a fleeting shadow I can erase. I'm halfway down the third set of stairs when something stops me cold. A flutter. I freeze, my hand instinctively going to my stomach. Did I imagine it? I stand still, waiting for it to happen again. This pregnancy has been speeding by, faster than anything I ever imagined, so is it really too far-fetched to think I might have felt a kick already? Then there it is again. Stronger this time. Definite. A spark of life. Joy floods through me, drowning the misery and the uncertainty. I might never see Felix again after the final trial, but I'll always have this—a part of him that no one can take from me. The temptation to hide away in my room, nursing the heartbreak, is strong, but this moment—the small but undeniable kicks inside me—is something I can't keep to myself. It's a reminder that there's something bigger than the trials and the pain. Something real. I spot Quinn, Twila, and Juliette sitting at our usual booth. Juliette's head rests on her hands, not even looking up as I approach. I slide into the booth next to her. "What's happened now?"

Quinn answers. "Juliette had this grand plan to seduce George, but she somehow ended up in bed with Tomas instead."

I raise an eyebrow, glad of the distraction. I've known Juliette to hook up with some weird people and even the odd demon, but George? "That's a lot to unpick. Dare I ask why you were trying to seduce George?"

Juliette just groans from under her hair, so Quinn answers for her again.

"She planned to seduce George as a ploy to get everyone back in the games. She's not quite mentioned how she ended up with Tomas instead, but I think I can hazard a guess that it didn't go well." She looks down at Jules, who just snorts in response.

"You won't get back in the games by seducing George." Twila says, ignoring the very long sigh that seems to be emanating from somewhere under Jules's hair. "I would have told you that if I'd have known."

"But you only tell us what we can't do, not what we can do," argues Quinn.

"Will you two shut up arguing?" Juliette says, pushing her hair out of her face and sitting up. "Twila. You are right. Seducing George was a terrible idea, not least because the thought makes me want to hurl. I went to see Tomas to have it out with him and then he kissed me and it was like old times. It was perfect and wonderful and awful at the same time."

"I get that," I reply before realizing what I've just said. Quinn gives me an odd look before turning back to Juliette. "I don't get it. Was it good or was it awful?"

Juliette shrugs, looking defeated. "Sex with Tomas was always good. Maybe that's why I stayed through whore after whore. It was familiar. It was nice. It was home."

"But?"

"But all I could think of was those other women. It turns out that thinking of a line of women standing out the door ready to give him a blow job the second I left kinda put a dampener on it."

"That would do it," Quinn quips.

"I don't know," Twila chimes in. "Might be fun if those women join you?"

Juliette snorts. "I'm not into women, thanks."

"So, do you still think Tate is with him?" I ask, mostly to keep the conversation away from me.

Juliette shrugs again. "Actually, I saw her last night. I think maybe I was wrong about her. Maybe she isn't sleeping with him after all. He probably wants to, though. She's beautiful and blonde."

"So... Do you think you'll sleep with him again?" I ask.

"No." Juliette answers quickly. "Last night was a fond farewell. It felt like a goodbye." She sighs. "I guess it was a goodbye. He'll be leaving this place anyway soon. Once the third trial is over, I'll never see him again." I never thought Juliette and my life would share the same path, but here we are. It's both ironic and sad.

Quinn slams her fist down on the table, making all of us jump. "We are going to get out of here. I'm not letting them win."

"If by they, you mean Hades and George and Anthura, they've already won. You can't beat them." Twila looks over in my direction. "Look at Felix. He tried and Anthura dragged him off."

I try to remain impassive as the talk turns to Felix. When Quinn turns to look at me, I swear she knows, or at least she suspects something. "Do you know what that was all about? Have you seen Felix recently?"

It's like she can see right through me, but I can't tell her the truth. She's made it perfectly clear what she thinks of Felix. I can't tell her that I slept with him again. It would destroy our friendship. For the first time ever, I lie to a friend. "No. I don't know. It doesn't matter, anyway. Just like Tomas, he'll be gone next week, too."

Quinn grimaces. "Why is everybody being so complacent? We have to find a way to get back in the games, or get past the hellbeast." She looks at Twila pleadingly.

Twila shakes her head, her eyes filled with resignation. "Quinn, you don't understand. There's no way past that hellbeast. It's not just a guard dog - it's a creature straight out of nightmares. Even if you could somehow get by it, Hades and the others would hunt you down. They have eyes everywhere."

Quinn's jaw tightens with determination. "Then we find another way. There has to be something we haven't thought of yet. A secret passage, a hidden exit, anything."

Twila sighs. "I know you've been down there a lot. If there was a secret passage, you'd have found it by now." Quinn goes quiet for a moment, her face lost in thought. Then, suddenly, her eyes light up, and she pulls out her Hell Cell. We all watch as she types something quickly, a triumphant smile creeping across her lips before she punches the air.

"Are you going to tell us what you've just done?" I ask, raising an eyebrow.

"Nope." Quinn grins at me. "But don't feel defeated yet. I'm going to get us all out of this."

She stands and is halfway out of her seat when all of our Hell Cells buzz. I pull mine out and read the message:

GEORGE: NOW THAT EVERYONE IS FIGHTING FIT AFTER THE LAST CHALLENGE, THE THIRD TRIAL WILL START NOW. MEET IN THE ATRIUM IN FIFTEEN MINUTES.

. . .

A HEAVY SENSE of dread settles in my chest. "Well, whatever plan you had, you'd better act fast. The trial starts in fifteen minutes."

The color drains from Quinn's face. "No, no, no. There isn't enough time."

It's only then that I realize Quinn is the only one of us still in the games. The one person I believed might find a way to get us through, even if it was a long shot... and now, that last glimmer of hope is slipping away.

Quinn looks around at each of us, a storm of emotions brewing in her eyes. "I guess that's it, then. If I get through, tomorrow I'll be gone."

My heart clenches painfully at the look on her face. She was our hope, and now it feels like everything is slipping away faster than we can grasp it. "Twila, do something!" I plead.

Twila looks distraught. "I'll go speak to Hades. I'll do what I can." She runs off toward the atrium quickly, but I think we all know she won't be successful in persuading Hades to let us all back in. She's told us enough times.

"I'm sorry, Quinn," I say, standing up and pulling her into a hug. Hear head rests on my shoulder as her body racks with silent sobs. Suddenly, there's another pair of arms around us. "I never thought we'd be parted," Juliette whispers as we pull together in a three-way hug.

Eventually, we have to part. George, Hades and Anthura are already waiting by the sofas.

"We were quite the team," Quinn says, tears streaking her face. "I'll miss you. Take care of that baby of yours."

I hold her hand to my stomach. "I felt it kick this morning. I forgot to mention it."

Her face breaks out into a sad smile. "So soon?"

"I guess time has no meaning in here. Come on. We'll walk with you."

Juliette takes one of Quinn's hands as I take the other.

We make our way slowly to the sofas, savoring our last moments together. The enormity of what's about to happen weighs heavily on all of us. Quinn's hand trembles in mine as we approach the others. Hades regards us solemnly, his dark eyes filled with an emotion I can't quite place. Is it pity? Regret? It's hard to tell with him. Beside him, Twila gives us all a slight shake of her head. It was a long shot. Anthura stands beside them, her expression a smug grin. "That's everyone. Quinn, take a seat on the sofa. The rest of you have no place here, but don't worry—you can watch everything on the big screen." She narrows her eyes, locking onto mine. "Wouldn't want you to miss out on watching your friends suffer now, would we?" A wave of hatred crashes over me, seething through my veins like poison. She knows how much it will hurt me to see Quinn in pain... but then I realize she's not talking about Quinn at all. My gaze shifts to where Felix sits on the sofa, staring at me as though he wants to say something. But the time for words has passed. Tomorrow he'll be gone. I shouldn't have left things the way I did.

"Now, now, Anthura, there's no need for such words," Hades interjects, though I don't catch the rest of his sentence as Juliette pulls me away.

Juliette and I sit back in our booth, a heavy silence enveloping us as we watch the remaining contestants in the games receive their grim assignments. Each face is etched with fear, and as they stand to head toward the elevator doors, a wave of desperation washes over me. I want to leap up, to run after them, but my body is frozen in place, paralyzed by the weight of what's happening.

"I slept with Felix again last night," I finally admit, my voice barely above a whisper once they've all disappeared from sight. The confession feels like a boulder dropped into a deep, dark well; my heart sinks, heavy as stone. There's no point in hiding it anymore. Quinn would have hated me for this. J Juliette will probably just roll her eyes and think I'm an idiot—which, deep down, I know I am.

Juliette turns to me, her grip tightening around my hand. "I guess I wasn't the only one saying goodbye," she says softly, her eyes filled with empathy. In that moment, I see the reflection of my own pain in her gaze, and it makes everything feel even more real. The weight of regret and longing crashes down on me.

"We should have tried," I murmur, my voice cracking under the weight of what-ifs. "Quinn never gave up, and we just... did nothing."

Juliette's lips twitch into a sad, knowing smile. "Quinn was always stronger than us."

I shake my head, the knot of regret tightening in my chest. "Do you think she would have gotten us all through?"

Juliette shrugs. "I don't know. She certainly looked like she had a good idea, but then we got the text. I guess we'll never know."

Suddenly the lights flicker and the image on the giant screen that surrounds the canteen changes from floating cakes to Anthura smiling straight at the camera. I want to throw something at the screen but I have nothing to hand.

"Welcome to the third trial of the Inferno Games."

Her voice booms out throughout the whole building and grates through me.

"As usual, the trial will take place in the Earthery. Just like the last two trials, the images you see are what the contestants will see. Only to them, everything they encounter will look, smell, and feel very real. Now George, can you tell us a little about this trial? What can the remaining contestants expect?"

It's funny. I've never seen the games from this side before. I knew we were being watched, but it never really hit home what everyone was seeing before now. I glance to the side to see the canteen filling up with people. In the last circle, we were celebrities. Down here, the emaciated population never seemed to care about the Inferno Games, but now I see I was wrong in that assumption. They just weren't as forthcoming as the residents of Purgatory and Lust. Now they are coming in droves to watch the final Trial.

The camera pans to George who's almost shuddering in excitement. His belly wobbles as he talks. "The idea for this trial was actually inspired by Hades."

The screen quickly cuts to a shot of Hades, his expression stoic.

"It's a labyrinth of sorts," George announces, his voice bubbling with excitement when the scene returns to him.

"So what makes your labyrinth different from Hades' famous labyrinth?" Anthura inquires, her tone laced with excitement.

"In Gluttony, we feel hunger, but we cannot perish from it," George explains, a strange gleam lighting up his eyes.

"I doubt the bastard has ever felt hunger a day in his existence," Juliette hisses beside me, her contempt palpable.

"We can wither to bones and skin," George continues,

"but it cannot truly kill us unless..." He presses his fingers together and giggles, his jowly chin wobbling comically. "Unless they are in the Labyrinth."

"Are you saying that people can starve to death in there?"

"They can and they will. Within the walls of the labyrinth, there is food. Some will be easy to find; others will be much more elusive. But here's the catch: there's only enough for about two or three of the contestants to survive more than a few days. As the days drag on, people will begin to wither and eventually die of starvation."

"Days?" Anthura presses.

"Yes. This trial will only end when there are five people left alive. Those five will advance to the next circle."

"Wow," Anthura exclaims directly to the camera, her delight unmistakable. "So it's either get through or die."

"That's about it," George affirms, a grin spreading across his face, though it sends a chill through me.

"I'm excited, and I know those of you watching this on the big screen and on your portals are excited too. But before we go live into the Earthery, let's have a recap of our contestants."

A photo of Tate flashes up on the screen. She really was quite extraordinarily beautiful. I barely knew her thanks to Juliette's unreasonable hatred of her, but I think we'd have been friends in another life. We both suffered similar fates that brought us here in the first place. I wait for words of derision from Juliette as Anthura reads out a short bio about Tate, but it never comes. I glance over at her. She just looks sad.

The next picture to flash up is Tomas. I grip Juliette's hand as her ex husband stares down at her unknowingly from the big screen. Her grip on me tightens as Tomas is replaced with Felix. I'll never get over how I ended things with him. I had good reason, but I could have been better.

His bio is the longest one yet, but I learn nothing new from it. His list of earthly accomplishments never interested me.

When Quinn's face flashes up, there's an almighty bellow from behind us. Juliette and I crane our heads back to see a flash of black wings rushing through the crowd now filling the atrium.

Juliette gives me a panicked look. "Shit! I forgot about Dade."

She's up and out of her seat before I can say anything. I stand and watch as she pushes her way through the crowd. Dade is an impressive character, especially with his wings outstretched as they are now, but he doesn't look like he's going to get past the two demons with pitchforks guarding the elevator doors. Juliette rushes up to him, and though I can't hear what they are saying from so far away, I get the impression she's trying to calm him down. His wings falter as she points over to where I'm sitting. I give a half hearted wave. At least Juliette and I were able to say goodbye. Dade wasn't offered that chance.

Dade's wings fold behind his back as he follows Juliette through the crowd. His face is a mask of barely contained grief and anger.

"I'm so sorry, Dade," I say softly when they reach me. "It all happened so fast."

He nods curtly, not trusting himself to speak. Juliette puts a comforting hand on his arm.

"Let's sit," she suggests gently, guiding him into a chair. "The next trial will begin soon."

"I was asleep'" he explains. "The damned poison is still affecting me. Why didn't she come to me?"

"There was no time. She had an idea to get us all into the trial, or at least out of here, but then she had to go. I'm sorry."

His face blazes with anger and grief that echoes in my own soul. I've never spent much time with Dade, but being this close to him I can practically feel the dark emotion roll off him. I'm glad I'm on his side, that's all I can say. I wouldn't like to be opposing him, and I get the feeling that if Juliette hadn't guided him away from the demons, he would have put himself in jeopardy. The three of us can only watch as the final picture – Orlin's – fades and finally we see the inside of the labyrinth.

Memories of Hades' Labyrinth come back to me with its poisonous bushes creating the walls, but this is very different. The walls are all made of stone.

The ten contestants are all standing huddled at the very start.

My eyes seek out Felix, but it's Quinn they come to rest on. She looks so determined. I guess she has something that the other contestants don't. She has Jenny spurring her on.

George's voice once again comes over the tannoy, but this time it's clear the contestants in the Earthery hear it too.

"Welcome to my labyrinth. The objective of the labyrinth is to find the centre. When you do, you'll find a button to press. If you are in the first five people to press the button, you are through to the next circle – Avarice. The rest of you will head back to Gluttony."

I look at Juliette who appears as confused as I feel.

That's not what was said earlier. The image cuts back to Anthura, stranding smugly outside the Earthery.

"Of course, only we know that there is no centre of the labyrinth." She winks at the camera. "And no one is getting out of there alive if they don't find enough food."

My blood boils at the duplicity of it all.

"That's not fair!" Juliette screams out, but her voice is deafened by the rest of the crowd cheering. It's then that it dawns on me that this is what I'll have to look forward to, losing my soul as I spend centuries here with only the thrill of watching people being tortured by the Inferno Games, every time it passes through.

22

BACK IN THE LABYRINTH
QUINN

A claxon blares through the air, its sharp, jarring sound igniting a surge of adrenaline within me. Instinct kicks in, and I spring into motion, my heart pounding as I survey the labyrinth unfolding before me—a tangled web of stone walls that seem to tighten with each frantic breath.

Panic surges within me as I realize the urgency of the moment. The shouts and hurried footsteps of others reverberate around me, a cacophony of desperation as they dash in various directions, their choices echoing against the cold stone. I can almost taste the tension in the air, thick and suffocating. My heart hurts knowing I'll never see Dade again and I never got to say goodbye to him. He'll probably be watching all this upstairs. I take in a deep breath. I will not put him through the agony of watching me die. I will survive this. I have to.

Which way to go? The long path ahead offers no comfort; its darkness feels alive, ready to swallow any flicker of hope I cling to. The left seems too constricted, an uncertain alley that might offer safety or ensnare me in its grasp. The right, with its beckoning light, calls out, yet I can't shake the feeling that it could lead to even greater peril.

Every instinct screams at me to act, to make a choice, but the weight of indecision bears down on me. I can't afford to hesitate. My heart races as I make a split-second decision and dart toward the right, praying that the flicker of light signals hope rather than another cruel twist in this treacherous maze. The walls seem to shift around me, closing in as I plunge into the darkness, forcing me to confront the dread lurking in every shadow.

The light at the end of the pathway grows brighter as I race forward, my footsteps echoing against the stone walls. The vines seem to reach out, grasping at my ankles, trying to slow my progress. I push onward, my lungs burning with each labored breath, the claxon's blare fading behind me.

Suddenly, the passage opens into a vast chamber; the light revealing a scene that stops me dead in my tracks. In the center of the room stands a towering stone altar. Surrounding the altar are dozens of hooded figures, their faces obscured by shadows, their chanting rising in a haunting crescendo.

I freeze, realizing too late that I've stumbled into something far more sinister than a mere maze. The figures turn towards me, their chanting ceasing abruptly. As they start moving toward me, I see what it was they were guarding. A massive cake stands in the centre of the altar.

All this for cake?

I stand paralyzed at the bizarre scene for only half a second before the hooded figures slowly pull back their hoods. My heart lurches. Their faces are grotesque—like melted wax, distorted and oozing, with long, jagged teeth that gleam under the dim light. A wave of revulsion sweeps over me, every instinct screaming run. I don't wait to find out the whys or wherefores. In an instant, I spin on my heel and bolt back the way I came, my pulse thundering in my ears. Footsteps echo around me, but to my relief, they don't follow. As the Earthery can conjure up just about anything, I guess I can count on rooms like this throughout, with varying degrees of horrifying things. I remember the massive wolf like creatures in Hades Labyrinth and how I was able to beat one. I can do this! But as I turn yet another corner, I realize that I'm alone. Even though in reality the other contestants are somewhere in the warehouse sized Earthery, I can no longer hear them. I'm completely alone.

The eerie silence is punctuated only by my ragged breaths and the thud of my footsteps reverberating off the stone walls. Doubts begin to creep in as I wonder if I'll ever escape this twisted maze, or if I'm doomed to wander these nightmarish passages for eternity. At least in the original Labyrinth, I could see the light of the exits. Here, every passageway blends into the next, indistinguishable and oppressive.

I glance up at the towering walls that stretch into the darkness above. They're not real, I remind myself; there's no point in trying to climb them. Hours slip by in silence, and just as despair threatens to engulf me, I round a corner and nearly collide with Orlin. Relief washes over me at the sight of a familiar face, even one as emotionless as his. "Thank god," I gasp. "Are you ok? What have you seen so far?"

He shrugs, his indifference palpable. "Not much." He doesn't even stop, and I hastily run after him.

"That way is a room with these weird hooded people

guarding a cake," I say, pointing back the way I came. "I got out of there quickly, but I thought you should know."

"Okay," he replies, barely acknowledging my words.

Once again, I'm left to ponder if he truly understands the gravity of our situation. When he turns back down the passage I just mentioned, frustration bubbles within me. Spending time alone feels preferable to choosing Orlin as an ally, so I take the opposite passage and head in the opposite direction, hoping to bump into someone else. Anyone. I should have thought of forming a team of allies before we came in here, but there wasn't time. I didn't even get chance to say goodbye to Dade. Pain fills my chest, almost suffocating me. I have to push it down if I want to get through this. There will be time for grief later. Instead of thinking about Dade, I pull a picture of Jenny laughing from the depths of my mind and concentrate on it. Jenny is why I'm here. Jenny is the reason I have to survive this.

Ten minutes later, my energy begins to wane, and I flop down against one of the cold, unyielding walls. Hours have passed, and apart from that bizarre cake room, all I've seen are walls. Surely, something should have happened by now? The Inferno Games have always been about entertaining the demons of each circle, never truly about us humans. I realized that long ago, so why does this trial feel so dreadfully monotonous? The hooded figures didn't even put up a fight.

As I ponder this, half-hoping a giant monster will leap out to break the tedium, my stomach grumbles, cutting through the silence. I'm accustomed to hunger after spending the last two weeks in Gluttony, but this time it feels different—more insistent.

My stomach grumbles again, louder this time, and I

clutch at it with both hands. The hunger gnaws at my insides, twisting and churning like a living thing. I try to ignore it, but the more I resist, the more intense it becomes.

Suddenly, a mouth-watering aroma fills the air, and I freeze. Cake. My head snaps up, and my stomach twists in hunger, the scent wrapping around me like a cruel temptation. My mouth waters, and the ache in my empty belly grows sharper. I feel like I've spent the entire day walking away from the room with the cake and the hooded figures. Yet, as I turn the corner, I find myself standing right back where I started, at the entrance to the labyrinth. The Earthery has pulled me back, like a rubber band snapping me into place.

I shouldn't be surprised. Everything in this place is a construct of the minds trapped inside it, twisting and shifting to amuse the audience above. I knew from the start that this was never a fair race. The labyrinth changes constantly, adapting to the will of whoever—or whatever —is controlling it. And me? The most thrilling thing I've done today is whine about my blisters, so clearly, the Earthery is pushing me back toward the one thing I avoided: the cake room.

Maybe I was supposed to fight the hooded figures. Maybe that was the point all along.

I sigh heavily, shoulders sagging as I turn toward the scent of chocolate, the promise of cake pulling me in like a magnet. I don't have a weapon, nothing to defend myself with, but what if I somehow manage to take them down? Would I finally be rewarded with that mountain of cake? God, I could use it right now.. My stomach rumbles in agreement.

I pause at the threshold, eyeing the towering cake

warily. The hooded figures are gone, but something about this feels wrong, as though it's a trap. Taking a tentative step forward, I suddenly notice something I hadn't seen before. Behind the cake, the floor is stained with the unmistakable crimson of blood. My first thought goes to Orlin and the horrible thought that it was me that sent him here, albeit whilst trying to warn him about it. As I walk around the display, a gasp escapes my lips when I find the body of one of the other contestants sprawled on the ground. Just like in the underwater area in Purgatory, someone has decapitated him, the head missing. I'm momentarily pacified by the fact it isn't Orlin. I look closely at the bloody shirt of the headless man. It's one of the contestants. I didn't know him well, but he seemed nice enough. David something or other. Bile rises in my throat, and I quickly clamp my hand over my mouth to suppress it. We never did find out who killed Michael and Lucia. I thought that after nothing happened that wasn't explained in Lust, the murderer must have been out of the games, but evidently not.

My thoughts spiral to the contestants still trapped in this labyrinth with me. A few names flicker through my mind, but one stands out: Felix Barclay. I don't want to believe it, especially after how he's been these past few weeks, but the thought gnaws at me. He always had a nasty streak, and I can't shake the fear that this is precisely what the games are about—surviving at any cost.

Fighting the urge to panic, I quickly grab a handful of cake, the rich frosting sticking to my fingers, and race away from the gruesome scene. My heart pounds in my chest as I navigate the labyrinth once more, adrenaline coursing through me.

When I can run no more, I find a corner and sit,

looking at the sticky chocolate frosting coating my hands. I have no idea what will happen to me if I eat this. It could be filled with poison, like in the second trail. It might render me confused. I sit looking at it for an inordinate amount of time as my stomach's grumbling gets louder. In the end, I eat it all, licking my sticky fingers until there is nothing left. Then, because I'm too exhausted to carry on, I tuck my legs up to my chest and fall asleep.

23

WATCHING FROM ABOVE
ROWENA

P regnancy sickness forced me back into my room, but nothing can keep me away from watching everything going on in the Earthery below. We've all been offered snacks of popcorn, which is the first food any of us have had that hasn't had anything to do with the games. I brought mine back to my room where I've hunkered down with my Hell Cell, watching the trial play out on that rather than the big screen surrounded by people that view it as entertainment rather than the nightmare it is. The screen hops between the contestants so my view of the people I care about is fragmented, but my heart lurches every time it shows Quinn or Felix.

Nausea churns in my stomach and the popcorn isn't helping. It's late and most of the contestants have fallen asleep. Two are already dead, and not from starvation like George had warned. My heart had been in my throat when Quinn stumbled upon David's body, though the Hell Cell conveniently skipped the part where he was actually killed. They never show the whole truth.

I focus on Felix, one of the few still wandering the dark

labyrinth, his movements calculated and steady. He found water and food early on, and somehow has yet to face any of the creatures or traps the others have encountered. Luck? Or is Anthura still pulling strings for him behind the scenes? I don't know, and that's what unsettles me the most. My pulse quickens as I watch, unsure if any of this is real. It's frighteningly easy for them to warp what I'm seeing, to bend the truth into something darker. How much of this is real, and how much is just another layer of their twisted game?

I'm so exhausted that my eyes keep fluttering shut, but it's only when Felix finally stops and lays down on a patch of earth and closes his eyes that I finally sleep.

It's late into the night, or maybe early in the morning, when a knocking on my door wakes me from a fitful sleep. My eyes dart to my Hell Cell that's still playing out the events in the Earthery, but it seems to be all quiet there at the moment, or at least, they are only showing the quiet parts.

Fear grips me tightly, despite the relative safety of my room. No monsters can reach me here, but a messenger could, bearing the news I dread most—news that Quinn or Felix is dead.

"Who is it?" I call, my voice shaky.

"Babes, let me in." Juliette. I open the door to find her standing there, eyes rimmed with dark circles, her face drawn and exhausted.

"Can I sleep with you tonight?" she asks softly.

I nod, too weary to question her. As I rummage for a pair of pajamas, she shuffles toward the bathroom, and I call out, "I fell asleep a couple of hours ago. Anything else happen?"

The bathroom door creaks open just enough for her

voice to slip through. "David's dead. One of the girls too. Anita something. He was murdered. I don't know about her... they didn't show it."

I wince at her words, even though I already knew. Two more names etched into the growing list of the lost. A twinge of guilt flickers in my chest—relief, selfish and cold, that it wasn't Quinn or Felix. They're still safe. For now, at least.

I shuffle over to make space as Juliette slips into bed beside me. She sighs heavily, her voice low. "I just left Dade. I had to stay with him or I'd have come to bed earlier. He's mad. I've never seen him so crazy. I thought he was going to do something stupid."

I shrug, pulling the blanket higher around us. "What isn't stupid here? He's fought demons before and survived. Maybe you should have let him."

Juliette gives a small, tired laugh, but it's strained. "I know that. But I couldn't bear the thought of Quinn going through all that while her boyfriend ends up being eaten by a demon or something." She pauses, rubbing her eyes. "Besides, we all have enough going on without adding more stress. I waited until he looked too exhausted to do anything, then walked him to his room. Do you want these?"

I glance over and catch Juliette eyeing the leftover popcorn in the box.

"Go ahead, have it," I offer. "If I eat it, I'll just throw it all up tomorrow, anyway."

Juliette doesn't need to be told twice. She grabs the box and tips it, letting the popcorn spill straight into her mouth, sending stray kernels scattering all over the bed. Out of nowhere, she says, "I shouldn't have left things with Tomas the way I did. In my mind, we had forever. How stupid is that?"

I brush the kernels off the bed and snuggle up beside her, trying to give her some comfort. "We've been manipulated since the second we entered Hell. Tomas wasn't even supposed to be here, but he came anyway. Quinn got letters. I got letters..."

"And I got Tomas," she sighs deeply.

"I think maybe you were the luckiest of us all," I say softly. "The letters sent to Quinn and me were meant to break us. Maybe Tomas being here was meant to break you, but you found the closure in death that you never found in life."

Juliette leans against me, her voice quieter now. "I'm so glad I found you here. I don't think I would've made it through all this without you."

I hold her a little tighter. "Get some sleep. We don't want to miss whatever hellish thing they have planned for tomorrow."

She's silent for a while, and I think she's fallen asleep, but then her voice breaks the stillness again.

"If Tomas was sent here to break me, why was Tate brought here? She shouldn't have been able to enter the games either. As far as I know, she doesn't know anyone here besides Tomas."

I think for a moment, then say, "Maybe she did exactly what the leadership team wanted her to do."

Juliette frowns. "What do you mean?"

"She made you jealous. And for a long time, it worked. It wasn't Tomas who was your horrible letter. It was Tate, all along. And I bet she has no idea that she's just a pawn."

THE TWIN BEEPING of Juliette's and my Hell Cells fills the air, sending a spike of adrenaline through my veins. My heart races as I grab my Hell Cell from beneath my pillow.

A text message flashes across the screen, one sent to all of us.

IG LEADERS: DAY TWO: 8 CONTESTANTS LEFT.

I rub my eyes, stifling a yawn. I already knew that, of course, but I guess the ear-piercing shriek of the Hell Cells was the game's way of ensuring no one missed the update—whether we wanted to hear it or not.

"God, I hope we get more popcorn today," Juliette mutters, shaking the empty box as if it might miraculously refill itself.

"They're awake," I say, pointing the Hell Cell screen toward her. "How long do you think this will go on for?"

Juliette taps something into her own Hell Cell, her brows furrowing in concentration. Then suddenly, her eyes widen. "Holy shit!"

"What?"

"People can live up to three weeks without food."

I close my eyes, feeling the weight of that statement settle over me like a suffocating blanket. Three weeks. I can't go through this for three weeks.

"But they can only survive a few days without water," she adds quickly, as if offering some kind of twisted reassurance.

"There's water in there. Felix found a stream pretty early on, and I saw Tomas drinking from a pail. The only food I saw was that cake, though. I don't think they're going to let them die quickly. Water isn't the issue."

"Urgh," Juliette groans, flopping back against the pillows. "This sucks."

I nod grimly. "But someone in there is killing them off, so it probably won't last as long as we think."

Juliette's face darkens. "It's just like back in Purgatory. We never found out who it was then. We never figured out who sent those letters, either."

"No." Quinn said it was Anthura, but then Hades corrected her. I almost snigger at the thought of Anthura being framed, like she'd even care.

"I'm going downstairs to see if they are giving us more food. Do you want to come?"

I shake my head. I can't bear watching the Earthery on the big screen.

When Juliette leaves, I turn my attention back to the Hell Cell. Anthura's smug face fills the screen, speaking directly into the camera outside the Earthery. Despite my instinct to mute her grating voice, I turn the volume up.

"...the throes of day two. Only eight contestants are left. Yesterday they had cake; what will they find inside the labyrinth today?"

The scene cuts to one of the contestants I don't know well, sprinting through the labyrinth as if speed alone will save him. I almost want to shout at the screen—*there's nothing chasing you, and running will only waste precious calories!*—but there's no point. He can't hear me.

Next, the feed shifts to Tate, kneeling by the stream Felix found yesterday, filling a pot with water.

"Good girl," I think, mentally cheering her on, though I know Juliette wouldn't share the sentiment. It's not that I want anyone to die. Quite the opposite—I want them all to win, to make it out alive. No one in the Earthery deserves an agonizing death. I just want Felix and Quinn to survive more than the others.

They're my priority, but my heart twists with guilt,

knowing that rooting for them means hoping someone else falls.

The camera cuts away from Tate and focuses on a group of three contestants huddled together, whispering furtively. I lean forward, straining to hear their conversation, but the audio is too muffled. Their shifty eyes and tense body language suggest they're plotting something, perhaps an alliance or a trap for the others.

Suddenly, a piercing scream rips through the labyrinth, causing them to scatter like startled rabbits. The feed switches to another camera, revealing a young woman writhing on the ground, clutching her stomach. Blood seeps through her fingers, staining her tattered clothing a dark crimson.

My heart races as I watch helplessly, silently praying for her suffering to end swiftly. The camera lingers on her contorted face, capturing every excruciating moment. Finally, her body goes still, her eyes glazing over, and then the Hell Cell goes dark. Panic surges through me. I shake the device, then check the other apps; everything works fine except for the live feed from the Earthery. With my heart pounding in my chest, I leap out of bed, hastily pulling on the first dress I find. I sprint out the back door and call the platform, watching it rise slowly before me. Impatience ignites my urgency, and as soon as I step on, I'm slamming the button with my foot, willing it to move faster.

The atrium and canteen are packed tightly with emaciated demons, and it takes me a few minutes to push through the crowd to reach the canteen. For the first time since entering Gluttony, I catch a scent that isn't just donuts and sulfur; there's the unmistakable smell of bacon and eggs wafting through the air. As I spot Juliette in our usual booth, I notice a plate of breakfast in front of her. It's a mark of her fear that she's not cramming bacon into her mouth, her eyes glued to the dark screen above us.

"What's happening?" I ask, sliding into the seat next to her.

"I don't know, but I don't like it. No one has told us anything," she replies, her voice tense.

Before I can respond, a gruff voice growls from behind me. "These murders weren't part of the plan." I turn to see Dade slipping into our booth opposite us. He looks dreadful—dark circles under his eyes betray a sleepless night, and his pallor is alarming.

He beckons us closer, and I lean so far forward that my nose is almost buried in the mountain of bacon on the table between us. Dade shifts his glance to the sides, ensuring we're not being overheard. The other people in this level seem oblivious, too engrossed in the sheer joy of food for the first time in what feels like ages, cramming it into their mouths like a wild food orgy.

"I spent the night sneaking around, listening to the demons," he starts, but he's cut off by Juliette.

"I took you to your room so you would sleep," she admonishes.

"I can't sleep knowing Quinn is in danger. I won't sleep until I know she's safe."

"It can take three weeks to starve to death," I interject. "Juliette looked it up. May I remind you that you may look like a demon, but you're still human. You won't help Quinn by killing yourself." I push the plate of bacon toward him. "At least have some breakfast."

He manages a sad smile, the tension in his shoulders easing slightly. "Have you eaten yet?"

"We all should eat, and then tell us what you found out," I insist, nudging the plate closer to him.

Dade hesitates, glancing from the food to our worried faces, then finally picks up a piece of bacon and takes a tentative bite. "Alright, alright. You win," he mumbles, chewing slowly. "You eat too. I'm not stealing a pregnant woman's food."

I don't want to eat. The little food I've managed to keep down since being here has ended up in the bottom of a toilet bowl thanks to morning sickness. Yet, as I take a bite of the bacon, my stomach settles just a bit. Juliette hands us both a knife and fork, and between us, we share the massive plate of breakfast food.

"What did you hear?" I finally ask, keeping my voice low enough to avoid attracting attention.

Dade's pale face darkens, and his eyes flash with intensity. I can see Quinn's appeal in him, though he's too dark for my taste. I almost shiver when he speaks. "The Games leaders are in a state of panic. They don't actually want the contestants being killed off so quickly. The point was to watch them slowly starve to death. Apparently, that's more fun for the people here, though I can't think why. George planned this to last a couple of weeks at least, but now they are dropping like flies. That's probably why the screens are off."

Almost as soon as he finishes speaking, the screen goes back on. A cheer erupts among the people, but as Quinn's face looks back at us in terror, I can't find anything to cheer about.

"I can't watch this here. I'm going back up to the room." I look to Juliette as she stands up to follow me. Then my eyes turn to Dade. He looks dangerous. Manic.

There's something dark come over him like a mask. "You want to come up to my room too?" I ask tentatively.

He shakes his head, his face turned down into a grimace, and though I care about him on some level, I'm almost relieved when he says no.

This is hard enough without watching Dade give in to his demons.

24

AN UNEXPECTED ALLIANCE
QUINN

I never expected to see any of the game leaders in the labyrinth, especially not Anthura, but it's she who wakes me from an unsettled sleep. When I open my eyes, the walls of the labyrinth have gone, to be replaced by darkness. The little light there is shows Anthura looming over me, her arms crossed and an expression of fury on her face.

"Show me your hands!" she demands, her voice sharp and commanding.

I pull myself up and hold my hands out to her, which she grabs, turning them over roughly in hers. The last time she touched me, a burning sensation ran up my wrists, but this time they remain fine.

"Why do you want to see my hands?" I ask, my heart racing as I wonder if this is somehow related to the chocolate cake I consumed yesterday.

"Someone is murdering the contestants, and unfortunately, it isn't us. I was checking for blood. What's this under your nails?" She grabs my wrist and holds it up in front of my face.

"Chocolate frosting. Mud, maybe." I feel a mix of relief and irritation. "So you're saying that David's death had nothing to do with you?" I suspected as much, but to hear it confirmed by Anthura is another thing. Seeing her mad about it is yet another thing. I thought she would find glee in watching us suffer, but I guess we're messing up her plans—boo fucking hoo.

"Is this the same person that killed Michael and Lucia in Purgatory?"

She keeps hold of my wrist, and this time I feel heat start to build. I wrench it from her grip before she can blister my skin like she has done so many times before. "That's what I'm trying to find out. There aren't many of you left from my tower in Purgatory, but you are on my list."

"I had no reason to kill Michael and Lucia," I bite back. "Just like I had no reason to kill David."

Her eyes narrow, full of venom. "Of course you'd say that, but here you are, in the games, trying to survive. I don't trust you."

"Then it's a mutual feeling," I almost laugh, rubbing my wrist, trying to dispel the lingering heat from her grasp.

She pushes her face so close to mine that I almost choke on her sulfurous perfume. "David isn't the only one murdered. Anita was killed last night; Marybeth from the other tower was killed this morning. If I find you had anything to do with fucking up these games, so help me, I will hunt you down myself and make you wish you'd never lived and then never died."

The menace in her voice sends a shiver down my spine. "You think I'm the one who's messing things up? I'm just trying to stay alive, just like everyone else."

"Survival doesn't absolve you of suspicion," she hisses, her eyes narrowing. "You're too clever for your own good, and that makes you dangerous. Remember, the only way out of here is through the games, and the games don't care who you are or where you come from. They only care about the bloodshed."

"Then maybe you should be more concerned about who's actually behind the murders rather than wasting time accusing me," I snap back, trying to hold my ground.

Anthura steps back, her expression shifting slightly, as if I've struck a nerve. "Don't forget who has the power here," she warns, her tone chillingly calm. "You might want to keep your head down and your mouth shut if you don't want to become the next target."

I watch her walk away into the darkness and then the safety of the outside of the Earthery.

Then, just like that, I'm back in the labyrinth. Only now I have to contend with a murderer picking off contestants.

It doesn't take long for the thought of murderers to be overtaken by crippling thirst. I didn't drink yesterday and went to bed with a sore throat. Now the sore throat is back with a vengeance, and added to it is a monster of a headache. I need water. Just like the gnawing hunger yesterday, this feels urgent. I've not had any liquid for weeks, but in here, I know I need it.

So, murderers aside, my first job is to find a source of water. If I'm right, and judging by my thick head, I am dehydrated, then there must be water in here unless they want us to die of thirst.

I listen out for the sound of running water. I hear the sound of someone or something running. It sounds close, but distance is so relative here. I could be standing right next to someone in real life and not know it. I follow the sound anyway. The sound grows louder as I approach, my heart pounding in my chest. I can't tell if it's from fear or anticipation. Maybe both. The darkness seems to close in around me, suffocating and endless. Suddenly, my foot catches on something and I stumble, barely catching myself before I face-plant into the hard ground. I reach down, my fingers brushing against what feels like a small metal pipe. I follow it, hand over hand, until I reach a spigot. I twist the handle and water gushes out, splashing over my hands and face. I cup my palms, drinking greedily. It tastes metallic and stale, but in that moment, it's the sweetest thing I've ever had.

As I drink, I hear the sound of running footsteps again, closer this time. I freeze, water dripping down my chin. It's getting nearer, and panic grips me. I can't decide whether the person coming around the corner will be a friend, a murderer, or one of the many creatures I expect to find down here. It's only when it's too late that I remember I have no friends down here—only the distant voices of my allies upstairs, watching this nightmare unfold on the big screen.

I let out a sigh of relief when Tate rounds the corner. She isn't my friend, but she's no monster, and she can't be the murderer either; she wasn't with us in Purgatory. In a funny way, she's the only person I can really trust in here.

I hold back, waiting for her to say something. The games have pitted us against each other and being trapped in this nightmare changes people. When she sees me, she smiles—a genuine smile that momentarily eases my tension. It widens further when she spots the water gushing freely behind me.

"Oh, thank goodness." She takes a step closer, then notices my hesitance. "May I?" she points to the tap.

I hesitate, unsure if I can trust her. Juliette hates her, but to be honest, I've never had a problem with her. I step aside, moving from the tap so she can drink.

"Did you get a visit from Anthura this morning?" she asks after taking her fill.

"I did," I reply, my eyes narrowing.

"Do you know who it is?" she presses, wiping water from her mouth with the back of her hand.

I hesitate, weighing my options. "No, not yet. But the games leaders must be freaked out enough to send Anthura in. They'll have hidden cameras all over the place in here and if the murderer managed to kill three people without being shown on the cameras, then we're dealing with someone much cleverer than I."

Tate nods, her expression serious. "It's not just the deaths. The games are becoming more chaotic, and people are getting desperate. I heard whispers of alliances forming, but I don't trust anyone. Not anymore."

"Neither do I," I admit, glancing around to ensure we're still alone. "It's every contestant for themselves in here."

She looks down for a minute, then raises her eyes to mine. "Maybe we could form an alliance?"

It would be nice to have someone to watch my back and it would help to stick together if we came up against anyone who wanted us dead, but the truth is, I don't know her and even if I did trust her, she's wearing a skintight dress and high heels. She wouldn't outrun a murderous sloth.

I shake my head. "I can't. I'm sorry. The second the leadership team sees us forming a partnership, they'll put more danger in our way to split us up. It's probably safer staying apart. Besides, Anthura really is out to get me. She's hated me since the second I got to Hell."

"Any particular reason?"

I shake my head. "It's a long story and I really hope I can tell it to you some time, but you will be much safer staying away from me."

She nods her head sadly. "I understand. Thanks for the water, anyway." She begins to walk away, then turns. "I was always told to keep turning left in a maze, so that's what I'm doing. You can do the same if you want, but if you don't want to, if you go down the path I just came from, there's a kind of clearing with some food on a plinth. I ate some of it, but there was plenty when I left."

Regret nags at me long after Tate disappears down the path. Maybe I should have taken her offer to form an alliance. She didn't have to tell me about the food. Trust is hard to come by here, but her gesture feels genuine. Still, I shake off the second-guessing. Trusting too easily can be deadly in these games.

As I walk, my stomach growls louder, a hollow ache building with each step. I ate last night, but that chocolate cake barely touched my hunger, and now it's growing impossible to ignore. The more I walk, the more ravenous I feel, like a pit in my stomach widening with every breath. Something about it feels wrong. Too intense, too fast. My thoughts snap to the water. They must have put something in it to mess with my hunger. Cursing Hades for inventing these stupid games and George for no doubt coming up with the water trick, I follow Tate's directions. I walk in a straight line for about an hour when I come upon the clearing she talked about.

Just like she said, in the center is a plinth with food on it. I move closer and my stomach tightens.

A grilled cheese sandwich with chili sauce. Of course. These games love to toy with me. I've been craving that exact sandwich for weeks, ever since Jenny and I used to devour them back in the day. Driven by hunger, I step forward, only to stumble over something. After dusting myself off, I glance down and see a crossbow, already loaded. My first instinct is to ignore it, but with a murderer on the loose and me still unarmed, I grab it and inspect it closely.

Suddenly, a sound makes me freeze. From the other side of the clearing, Felix emerges, another crossbow in his hand. The second he sees me, he raises it, aiming directly at me.

"Snowflake," he says, voice cold.

"Felix," I reply cautiously, not lowering my own weapon.

His eyes flick toward the grilled cheese, and even from here, I can hear his stomach rumble.

The tension in the air thickens as we stand there, crossbows raised, staring at each other across the clearing. The absurdity of the moment isn't lost on me—two people armed to the teeth, ready to kill over a grilled cheese sandwich. Yet, I can't deny how the scent of it fills the clearing, teasing my already starved senses, making my mouth water in anticipation. My stomach churns angrily, but I can't afford to lose focus. Felix looks just as hungry, his eyes flicking from me to the sandwich with barely concealed desperation.

"Let's be smart about this," I say, trying to keep my voice steady. "It's a sandwich, Felix. There's no need to go down this path."

His eyes narrow, his grip tightening on the crossbow. "Maybe not, but it's survival now, Snowflake. And that sandwich is all that's between us and starvation."

"We don't have to kill each other over food." My heart hammers in my chest, but I keep my weapon raised. "We could share."

A bitter laugh escapes him. "Share? You think they'll let us do that? They're watching. We both know how this works."

He's right, of course. This is exactly what the games are designed for—pushing us to desperation, making us turn on each other. I glance at the grilled cheese, the temptation gnawing at me, but the idea of killing Felix for it is unthinkable. We've both come too far for that.

"I'm not going to shoot you," I finally say, lowering my crossbow with slow, deliberate movements. My fingers tremble as I release the weapon, laying it carefully on the ground between us. "If you want the sandwich, take it."

The ache in my stomach is relentless, a gnawing, primal hunger that feels like it's clawing at my insides. I want nothing more than to devour that sandwich, but it's not worth losing everything over. Pain is familiar to me— I've endured far worse in Hell.

I glance up at Felix, searching his eyes for any sign of humanity. Instead, I find something darker, something unhinged. There's a madness in his gaze, a wild glint that makes my blood run cold. Anthura's words echo in my head. Wasn't Felix the first person I suspected when she told me there was a murderer among us?

My heart sinks. I've made a terrible mistake.

I squeeze my eyes shut and hold my breath, bracing for the worst.

I hear the arrow's deadly whistle before I feel the impact.

25

THE END OF AN ERA
JULIETTE

I glance away for just a second, rummaging through my handbag to grab more of the bacon I'd stashed earlier. Before I can take a bite, Ro's piercing scream sends me tumbling off the bed and onto the floor.

"What the fuck, Ro! What happened?" I ask, scrambling back up in a panic.

"Shit, fuck, poop," she mutters, eyes wide, glued to the screen. Ro never swears unless it's serious, so I know something big just went down.

I whip my head toward the Hell Cell, and all I see is Quinn, standing frozen, her eyes shut tight. The camera pans, revealing an arrow lodged between the eyes of a statue of George, about five feet from where Quinn is standing. "What the shit fuck poop happened?"

"Felix looked like he was about to shoot Quinn over a grilled cheese sandwich, but then he moved the crossbow to the side and shot the statue instead."

"He was going to shoot Quinn over a sandwich?" I ask incredulously before remembering I'd have willfully murdered half of Hell for a bacon sandwich before they decided to grace us with breakfast this morning. I chew on the last slice thoughtfully. "actually, I kinda get it."

We both watch as Quinn cautiously opens one eye, then the other. A split second later, she's sprinting toward the sandwich like her life depends on it.

"So, where's Felix now?" I ask.

Ro sits up, her brow furrowed. "I don't know. He's starving. He needs food, but he gave up his last chance for Quinn." Frustrated, she shakes the Hell Cell in her hands. "Cut to Felix, dammit!"

I grab the device from her before she can do more damage. "Careful. You're going to shake the baby loose."

Her eyes widen, and she presses a hand protectively to her belly. "Is that possible?"

I shrug. "I don't know, but all this stress can't be good for it. I get that Felix was a good lay, but don't lose your head over the guy."

"But he did something selfless," she protests, almost defensively.

"You seem surprised," I say, raising an eyebrow.

She sighs, sinking back into the pillows. "I guess I am. He really looked like he was going to shoot Quinn and for a split second I actually thought he might."

"About time!" I exclaim as the screen finally cuts to Tomas. They've barely shown him at all. I get it, though— he looks about thirty years older and thirty pounds heavier than the other contestants. The cameras are too busy showing Tate mincing around in her heels and barely-there dress, or focusing on the Quinn and Felix drama, but at least that was exciting. The only person they've shown less than Tomas is Orlin, but again, I understand. Orlin probably hasn't moved an inch since the claxon went off yesterday.

I sigh, watching Tomas clutch his stomach, ambling along like a man lost in his own misery. Poor guy was never built for starving. If there was one thing Tomas loved more than his libido, it was his stomach. Sometimes I wondered if he stayed with me all those years just for my cooking.

"Maybe his size will help," Ro says, her voice casual. "I mean, he can stand to lose a few pounds."

"Don't fat shame!" I snap, sharper than I intended. I used to be a big woman. It's only since I died that I got back to my youthful figure, and I still remember what it felt like.

Ro flinches. "I don't fat shame. You know me better than that. I'm just trying to put your mind at ease. He'll probably fare better in there than the skinny ones."

We're turning on each other now, the tension getting to us. I sigh again, softer this time. "Sorry, Ro."

"This was never going to be easy. Look at us, sitting here worried about the fate of two men. Men that have treated us like crap in the past."

"Men that we'll never see again," I say, the truth of it sobering both of us. "I'm glad I slept with Tomas that last time. I needed to put the past behind me."

Rowena squeezes my hand, silent. What is there to say? It's clear she's falling for Felix in a big way. I don't get it, and maybe I never will. Then again, I never understood why I stayed with Tomas for so long, despite all his cheating. My head always knew better, but my heart never quite let go. It still hasn't.

We stay in bed all day, watching the games. We cheer when Felix finally finds food, holding our breath every time someone we care about appears on screen. The hours pass, but the hunger in my belly doesn't.

"I'm going downstairs to see if they've put out more food for us. I'll bring back whatever I can fit in my bag."

Ro barely looks up from the screen. She's too absorbed in watching Felix's every move.

Downstairs, the atrium is far busier than it was this morning. It feels like everyone in the tower is gathered around the big screen, eyes glued to the action. I can barely make out Tate on the screen over their heads. She's not looking good. Earlier, she was attacked by one of those huge beasts from Hades' labyrinth. The memory sends a shudder through me, and to my surprise, a pang of sadness for her.

I'm too emotionally drained after watching the games all day to muster up hate anymore. The sharp edges of my resentment toward Tate have worn down to almost nothing. I don't even think I'd feel bad if Tomas and Tate ended up helping each other in the Earthery. My old jealousy about the two of them possibly hooking up seems ridiculous now that they're both just trying to survive. I push past the crowds to the canteen, where there are indeed plates of food on the tables. I pick up a plate and empty the pile of sandwiches into a bag. I pick up another sandwich with the intention of eating it when an almighty cheer sounds out around me. I glance up at the screen and drop the sandwich back on the table. It's not just Tate that's in a bad way. Quinn is with her and she looks like she's bleeding out, too.

Fuck! I stare at the screen open mouthed with my heart in my throat. All around me, the cretinous assholes are still stuffing their faces and cheering on the action. I try to make sense of the image before me. It looks like Tate is trying to comfort Quinn. Quinn is whispering in

Tate's ear while Tate nods her head, tears streaming down her face.

The screen goes black then cuts to Anthura standing at the front of the Earthery, the same malignant grin on her face that she's been giving updates of contestant deaths with all day.

Despite the leader's best efforts to have these games go on for weeks, the contestants have been dropping like flies, partly due to the monsters they put in there and the one monster they can't find — the mysterious murderer.

"There's been another death!" Anthura trills into the camera. My heart stops. Not Quinn. Anyone but Quinn! Suddenly, a roar erupts from behind me, shaking me out of my stupor. I twist around just in time to see Dade, his massive black wings unfurling as he launches himself off one of the balconies. He's moving like a storm, straight toward the demons guarding the elevator. They barely have time to react before he takes them down, knocking them aside like they're nothing.

I shove through the crowd, trying to catch up, but by the time I reach the elevator, Dade's already gone. Panic rises as I look back at the screen, but I can only see the top of it through the crowd. Then I catch a glimpse of him— Dade, swooping in on Anthura and tossing her aside like a rag doll. The last thing I see before I bolt toward the platform to get back to Ro's room is Dade's black wings disappearing into the Earthery.

26

DADE TO THE RESCUE

ROWENA

I can't breathe. The moment Juliette steps into my room, her face says it all. She knows. She knows what's happened. I can see the pain etched into every line on her face, raw and agonizing.

"I'm so sorry, Jules!" The words barely escape my throat as I see her sit on the edge of the bed, her bag slipping from her hand and hitting the floor, spilling a pile of sandwiches everywhere.

"I can't believe she's dead!" Juliette sobs, collapsing into me. She rests her head on my shoulder, and it breaks my heart in ways I never imagined. Juliette doesn't cry—she never cries—but now she's drowning in her tears, her sobs shaking both of us as I hold her close.

"She?"

"Quinn. I saw her with Tate. There was blood everywhere. Dade went in there."

My heart clenches, tightening in a way that feels unbearable. "Jules, it's not Quinn who died. Didn't you see what happened after Dade went in?"

Juliette wipes her eyes with her hand, smearing the

tears across her face before wiping her nose. "No. I came up here as fast as I could. I couldn't stand all the cheering after Anthura announced the death. If it wasn't Quinn... who was it?"

My heart clenches in my chest as I struggle to find the words that will shatter her world all over again. How do I tell her that the person she loves is gone forever?

My grip tightens around her hand as I realize I have to say it before Anthura's face fills the screen again, before she repeats it like it's some twisted joke.

"It's Tomas," I say, my voice barely audible above Juliette's cries. "He's been murdered."

She's survived his death once, but now... now there's no coming back. Not for the already dead. There's no second afterlife.

Juliette's eyes widen, her breath catching as the words sink in. "Tomas? My Tomas?" Juliette's voice cracks. "No!!!!"

I let her wail, holding her close until my shoulder is wet with tears and she runs out of breath. I've never seen Juliette like this before and because she's usually so laid back, her sorrow is all the worse. It's palpable, heartbreaking. Painful.

Losing someone we care about has always been a probability in the Inferno Games. I guess neither of us thought it would really happen. Once again, they don't know who murdered him. It wasn't caught on camera. It's almost as if the murderer knows the labyrinth and where the cameras are, but how could he... or she? I don't know who it is, but the list of suspects is getting smaller and smaller.

I shake Juliette gently as Quinn appears on the screen. She still looks like crap, but she isn't dead yet. I'm holding onto hope that she'll make it despite how bad she looks.

We both watch, Jules holding my arm as though if she let go, she'd fly away.

Dade appears, swooping in to where Quinn and Tate are. I'm surprised the games makers haven't dragged him out, but I'm sure they'll punish him enough when he eventually does come back out. He's crazy to think otherwise.

It looks like he and Quinn are arguing, but both are whispering so quietly that I can't hear what they are saying despite the volume being way up on my Hell Cell.

I glance at the stats to the side of the screen. Tomas's death has brought the count down to six. Just one more, and it's over—they'll be through to the next circle. Do they even realize how close they are? Dade's impulsive move to go after Quinn might have been the biggest mistake of all. She's covered in blood, but she's still holding on, and Tate is right there with her. If he'd only waited, they could have made it. Now, I wouldn't be surprised if they all end up thrown out of the games.

Frustration bubbles inside me as I watch Quinn embrace Dade. His massive black wings unfurl, wrapping around them both, and then Tate too. The screen goes dark, swallowed by the vastness of those wings.

"What's he doing?" Jules asks, leaning in so close she's practically in my lap.

Whatever it is they are doing, it goes on for ages, until Dade's wings contract and then flap until he's in the air.

"He's flying Quinn out of the Earthery!" Jules says, her voice an octave higher than usual.

I stare at the screen incredulous. "That's not Quinn he's holding. He's flying Tate out!"

27

CAPTURED IN CHARCOAL

JULIETTE

"What the fuck is going on?" My voice shakes, but I don't care. Nothing makes sense, nothing feels real, and the weight of it is crushing me. I know Rowena doesn't have the answers any more than I do, but I can't seem to get a grip on anything.

Tomas might have been a leech, but he was always there. Even when he wasn't, I always thought he'd find a way back to me. I guess deep down I hoped he'd change someday, that we'd get our happily ever after. Hell, even when he died, I still believed that maybe, somehow, we'd be reunited in heaven. I snort at the absurdity of that thought now. Heaven? Yeah, right? Well, we did end up together in the end, didn't we? But it wasn't some fairy tale reunion—it was Hell, and in Hell, he actually changed. He really changed. But now he's gone. Truly gone for good this time.

No happily ever after. Just a bittersweet end to our messy, twisted love story, and then a brutal, final end to his life. His existence. My heart is a tangled, soggy mess, and I don't know what to do with it. This grief is different —messier, uglier than anything I've ever felt. I ended it with him for good the other night, and I was happy with that decision. I was ready to move on. And still... it stings.

I could've told him I loved him one last time. I could've said goodbye in a way that didn't involve sex. But no, everything with Tomas was always about sex. Ha. It was how we connected, how we fell apart, how we said good-bye. I sigh as Rowena drags herself out of bed.

"Where are you going?" I ask between hiccupping sobs.

"I'm going to get you a tissue before you soak my bed sheets through and then I'm going to find Dade."

That's what I need. A plan. A sense of purpose, so I don't have to think about Tomas. I follow her to the bath-room where she passes me a pulled off piece of toilet paper.

"Come on. We have to keep going," Rowena says soothingly as I blow noisily into the tissue.

The noise is deafening as we step onto the circular balcony, the chaos below swelling like a tidal wave crashing against the stone walls of the atrium. I grip the balustrade tightly, my knuckles white as I peer down at the mass of people. They're jumping up and down, screaming like this is some kind of celebration, as though my heart and soul hasn't just been beheaded by a fucking monster.

Hate ignites in my veins, burning for them, for Hell, for every damned thing in this place. I want to scream at them, make them see the raw gaping wound inside me, but all I can do is swallow it down.

"Why are we going down this way?" I ask, eyeing the rounded sets of stairs that spiral below us like some twisted carnival ride. "We should have used the platform at the back."

"Dade isn't going to use the platform. Look." Ro's voice is barely audible over the roar of the crowd, but she points downward, two floors beneath us, to the elevator doors.

Sure enough, they open, and Dade bursts through them in a flash, Tate in his arms, his wings spreading wide as he bowls over the guards yet again. They scramble to their feet, only to be knocked down like dominoes, barely able to catch their breath before he takes to the air. The crowd goes wild, swarming like insects, desperate to be near him, to touch him.

He's magnificent. A dark, beautiful demon in flight, wings cutting through the air like scythes. As he passes us, the wind from his wings stirs the air around us, brushing my face with the same icy sharpness of his presence. For a brief moment, I forget the rage tearing me apart—he's something otherworldly, a force beyond all of this madness. But then the reality crashes back in, heavier than before.

"Come on!" Ro grabs my hand, pulling me toward the stairs with urgency. We race up, my legs burning as we spiral around to the second set. By the time we reach Dade's floor, my chest heaves with each breath. I've never been in his room before, but I know exactly where it is— Quinn has described it enough times.

The door is open, as if he's waiting for us.

We burst in, the door swinging wide as we enter. Dade is hunched over Tate, who is barely conscious; her limp body sprawled on the bed. The sight of her sends a prickle of hatred through me, sharp and instinctive. My mind flashes to Tomas, to the unfairness of it all—why him and not her?

But the thought is fleeting, disappearing as quickly as it comes. She's done nothing wrong. She doesn't deserve my anger. I know that. Still, my reaction to her is visceral, something I can't explain. It knots in my gut, a twisted mix of jealousy and resentment I don't even fully understand. But it's not helping now. She needs help, not my bitterness.

I force myself to look at her as she really is—not as a symbol of everything I've lost, but as a person hanging on by a thread. Her face is pale, her breathing shallow. Dade is frantic, his hands trembling as he hovers over her, unsure of what to do next.

Seconds later, Ro is at my side, a glass of water in hand, procured from Dade's bathroom. She moves swiftly, her urgency palpable.

"Dade, help me get her into a sitting position," Rowena orders, her voice sharp with tension. The three of us work together, lifting Tate until she's sitting upright, but her head lolls to the side, her eyes barely open, flickering like a dying candle.

"Drink," Rowena urges, pressing the glass to Tate's lips. She manages a few tentative sips, but then her eyes close completely, her body sagging against me. I glance down at my shirt—it's already soaked through with blood, the crimson staining Tate's legs and Dade's bed sheets.

"She needs to go to the hospital wing," I say, my voice tight, barely concealing the panic clawing at my throat.

Dade finally looks up, his face drawn and grim. "And she will. The Games leaders will be here in seconds, but I needed to talk to you two first before they get here."

"Wanna start with telling us why you didn't get Quinn out of there? She looked to be in a worse state than Tate!"

The words spill out harsher than I intend, laced with bitterness and frustration.

Dade doesn't flinch. He's used to this, I realize. He's seen worse. Felt worse. We're all frayed at the edges, barely holding it together.

"Quinn was barely awake when I went in," Dade says, his voice low, rough with exhaustion. "But she was strong enough to be adamant that I bring Tate back. She wouldn't let me near her."

His face is as impassive as ever, but I can feel the despair radiating off him in waves. It's dark, oppressive, suffocating. This must be what Quinn feels when she's near him, that heavy sense of doom. I don't know how she stands it—being near him like this is unbearable.

"I think I know," Rowena says. "Quick. Help me block the doors!" She runs to the dresser and starts pushing it to the front door before Dade presses a hand to her. "You're pregnant. Sit. I'll do this."

He swiftly moves the dress to block the front doorway and then does the same to the back door, using the side table. It won't hold for long.

"If one more person dies in the labyrinth, Quinn will go through to the next circle," Ro says.

Dade and I stare at her. "We know."

"Don't you remember what Felix looked like at the end of the last circle? His head was so disfigured he had to wear a mask to Noémi's party, but the very next morning he looked normal." She sighs when we don't get it straight away. "We heal quickly in Hell anyway, but there's something about moving between circles that makes us back to normal overnight. Quinn knew if you brought her out, she'd spend a week or more in the hospital wing and lose her chance to get to Jenny. Dade. She's going to be okay. She's going to survive."

Dade's face tightens, his eyes shadowed with doubt. "If someone dies before she does," he mutters, his voice raw.

As though summoned by his words, all of our Hell Cells beep at once. My heart lurches in my chest as I pull mine out, dreading what I might see. The notification is stark and brutal—the announcement of the last death in the labyrinth. My breath catches, and for a moment, everything freezes. But then I see the name, and my heart squeezes with relief. It's Tate. She's not dead. I can plainly see her still breathing on the bed, but I guess they've chosen her as the last contestant out.

The feeling is bittersweet, a heavy mix of relief and sorrow. I'm about to say something when a violent banging erupts against the front door.

"Open this fucking door!" Anthura's voice screams through the wood, filled with fury. The lock clicks ominously, no doubt thanks to her Hell Cell, which can unlock any door. But the dresser buys us a little time—it'll take her at least a minute or two to push past it.

I rush to the door, throwing my weight against the dresser, my back pressed hard against the wood as I push with everything I have. On the other side, Anthura shoves against it, the force of her blows shaking the entire frame. My arms strain, the muscles burning as I hold the dresser in place.

"What now?" I whisper in anguish, the words barely escaping me.

"Let her in," Rowena says, her voice calm.

"Are you fucking kidding me? You just asked us to block the doors."

"Yes I did, but then I realized that Tate is the key to this and having her bleed out on the bed isn't going to help.

"Key to what? If Anthura gets in here, Dade will be captured and you know what Anthura is capable of. He's already on his last chance with her after everything that happened in the last circle." I shouldn't care about Dade as much as I do, but he's the love of Quinn's life and it would kill her to know we were just giving him up.

Rowena looks between me and Dade. I can almost see the cogs whirring in her mind. "Dade. You want to make a run for it? Fly out the back door?"

Dade shakes his head. "No. There is only one way out of this tower and I've yet to get to it. Flying away now will only prolong the time until they capture me. Move out of the way, Juliette."

I don't move. Anthura is spitting feathers behind me. She's out for blood after her stupid trial was ruined, first by a rogue murderer and then by Dade sweeping in and stealing one of the contestants away.

"No."

Dade steps up to me. His sheer presence is over-whelming. "Juliette. I am so very grateful that you are trying to protect me, but in doing so, you are putting your-self in danger. I cannot and will not ask you to do that for me. I will have to face Anthura at some point. It may as well be now, and as Rowena said, I can't be responsible for Tate dying. It was Quinn's lat request to me to get Tate to safety. I have to honor that."

Damn him and damn logic. Why can't we just all stay here in Dade's room forever? There's nothing for me on the outside of it. Not anymore. Still, I move to the side and watch as he shifts the giant dresser to the side.

Anthura slams the door open and glares at Dade, her face almost as red as her outfit.

"Dade Angelis!" she spits. "You are done for now."

Dade hands his wrists out to her as though he expects her to cuff them. "Do whatever you need to do with me, but take Tate to the hospital wing first. She's going to die."

Anthura's face twists into a grimace, but she glances over at Tate before turning back to Dade.

"Get out," she hisses. "I'll have someone come up to deal with her."

My heart doesn't stop hammering until a couple of skinny demons come up and take Tate out on a stretcher, leaving me and Rowena alone on Dade's blood stained bed. It's silent and suffocating. Ro and I are the only two left.

"Look at all this," Ro says softly, glancing around the room.

I follow her gaze, and my breath catches in my throat as I take in the drawings covering Dade's walls. Charcoal sketches stretch across nearly every inch of space, dark strokes mingling with soft shadows to create a haunting beauty that's just like him—dark, intense, and yet stunning. Most of the drawings are of Quinn, each one capturing a different side of her. But as I scan the walls, I realize he's drawn all of us. There's barely any blank wall left, each square filled with faces frozen in moments of stillness.

My eyes land on a drawing of myself, and I feel a bittersweet smile tug at my lips. He's made me look so much more beautiful than I really am. It's like he's taken something buried deep inside me, something I can't even see, and brought it to life through his art. I feel exposed, vulnerable, like Dade has seen straight into my soul and translated it onto paper.

I stand and gently take the pin holding the picture next to mine. It's a sketch of Tomas. His eyes glimmer with that familiar, hopeful spark, and his smile is captured perfectly, as though Dade had seen him in one of those rare, unguarded moments. I wonder what Tomas was doing when Dade caught him like this. Looking at me? Thinking about the past?

"I'm sure Dade won't mind if you take this," Ro says, stepping up beside me. Her voice is gentle, understanding.

I've cried so much in the last half hour that my tears have dried, leaving me hollow inside. I've been through every emotion I can name, from anger to despair to fleeting hope. But now, there's a sense of calm. I had the goodbye with Tomas that I spent the latter half of my life hoping for. And it was beautiful. I feel like he's finally set me free.

"I think we should go down to the hospital wing and see if Tate is going to be okay," I say, folding the picture of Tomas and slipping it into my pocket.

Rowena reaches out, her hand warm as she takes mine. "I think that's a good idea. I have a feeling Quinn wanted us to talk to her." She squeezes my hand gently before adding, "Before that, we need to find out what's going to happen to Dade. Quinn would never forgive us if we let Anthura hurt him."

Rowena's right, but Quinn will never know. Whatever happens now, Quinn is going to be in another circle and we're stuck forever in a place where our friends have gone and we can't eat. I glance down at the Hell Cell in my hand, its once flickering screen now black, as empty and hollow as I feel. The Games are over. There are no more cameras, no more challenges. It's all over—for us.

There's no moving on, no next circle. Just this never-ending hunger gnawing at our insides, reminding us that Hell isn't just a place of fire and brimstone. It's a place of emptiness, of things you can never have. Food. Freedom. The people you care about. They slip through your fingers like smoke, and no matter how hard you fight, you can never get them back.

I pocket the Hell Cell, swallowing the lump in my throat. "Let's go," I say softly, my voice barely holding together. We can't afford to break down now. We need to see Tate, and we need to protect Dade. For Quinn, even if she'll never know. Even if it won't change anything.

As we head toward the door, I cast one last glance at the walls, at the faces that will forever be etched in charcoal—captured, but gone. Just like us.

28

QUINN'S IDEA

TATE

My head spins, and my leg burns like holy hell as I come back from the darkness. It takes a moment for my brain to catch up to my eyes. Juliette is sitting in the seat next to my bed and Rowena is sitting on the end of the bed itself. It's then I realize I'm in hospital. I'm in the very bed Juliette was in after the poisoning.

"What happened... Quinn!"

"Quinn got through," Juliette reassures me. "She's fine. She's more than fine, probably. You're the one we have to worry about."

I give her a small smile and am shocked to see it reciprocated.

I close my eyes and try to picture how I got from the labyrinth to a hospital bed, but everything is fuzzy. I was bitten by a hell hound. Quinn tried to save me, but she was bitten too. I remember both of us laying on the ground waiting for death. I remember being glad that she was with me and that I wouldn't die alone. I don't remember anything else.

"How did I get here?" I ask, opening my eyes and looking at Juliette.

"Dade flew in and saved you. He brought you out."

I don't remember Dade being in the Labyrinth at all. "Why did he take me out? I thought he and Quinn were dating?"

Rowena sits forward, so my attention turns to her. "We hoped you'd be able to tell us. Dade said that Quinn made him take you out. I thought it might be because if she was pulled back here, she'd not be able to go through to the next circle, but I think it was something else too. Quinn was desperate to get to her sister in a lower circle, but she wouldn't have taken your chance to get through away from you unless she had good reason. What did she say to you?"

I look between hers and Juliette's faces. I'm glad they are here. I had no friends in Lust and I didn't think I had any here, but I can't help them "I can't remember much," I murmur, shaking my head. "I don't know. I'm sorry. She saved my life. She risked hers for me. Do you know if she was taken to the hospital in the lower circle?"

Rowena's expression softens, and she shakes her head. "I doubt it. She won't need to. The second they take her to the next circle, her body will reset. It'll be like she was never bitten at all. She'll be perfectly fine."

I should feel relief at that, but instead, a fresh wave of guilt crashes over me. "And Dade?" I ask quietly.

Rowena goes silent, her gaze falling to the floor, and Juliette's eyes drop to the bed. The answer is written in their hesitation.

"He's down on the demon level," Rowena says at last, her voice barely above a whisper. "With Anthura, George, and Hades. They wouldn't let us down there to find out what his punishment will be."

My stomach twists, and I struggle to understand. Why did Dade take me out? Why would Quinn let him face punishment for my sake? None of this makes sense. I swallow hard, the words heavy in my throat. "This is my fault. I'm to blame for all of this. I'm sorry."

Juliette reaches out, her hand brushing against mine. The contact sends a jolt of electricity up my arm, unexpected and sharp. It's the first time she's touched me, the first time she's shown me anything other than the derision I've come to expect. Her fingers tighten briefly around mine, and for a moment, the anger I've felt from her is gone, replaced by something I can't quite name.

"This isn't your fault. Quinn had her reasons for wanting you back here and no one can force Dade to do something he doesn't want to do. Quinn wanted you to be saved and Dade did that. Whether he did that for her sake or because he's a fucking good guy, I don't know, but don't waste the sentiment by getting sicker. You need to recover and Rowena and I need to find out what's happening to Dade."

She stands. When she lets go of my hand, the coldness seeps in. "Don't go!"

The second the words leave my mouth, I clamp my lips shut, embarrassment washing over me. Juliette isn't my friend. Neither is Rowena.

Juliette pauses, her back to me, and for a moment, I wonder if she'll turn around. But she doesn't. Rowena glances back, her face soft with understanding, though she says nothing about my outburst.

"We'll come back," Rowena assures me.

When the door finally clicks shut behind them, the

emptiness rushes back in, suffocating and cold. I take a deep breath, pushing the heavy covers off my leg, and brace myself for the sight beneath. The sharp intake of breath echoes in the sterile silence of the room as I take in the damage. Stitches crisscross my skin, ugly and jagged, leaving my leg looking like a grotesque patchwork— Frankenstein's monster reborn. The Hell Hound really did a number on me.

The pain is sharp, burning, but it almost feels like a relief. It's tangible, something I can focus on instead of the heavier weight pressing on my chest. I try to tell myself the pain is enough to drown out the guilt, but it isn't. Not really. Beneath the throbbing in my leg, the guilt gnaws at me, relentless.

Quinn wanted me back here for a reason. And it had nothing to do with her trying to get through to the next circle. I didn't know her well, but I remember her face, her determination as she threw herself into danger to save me. She put her life on the line for mine. Why?

If she didn't care, she would've let that Hell Beast tear me apart. She could've run, saved herself, and let me die. But she didn't. She risked everything for me.

There's something there—something that doesn't add up. I can feel it lurking in the fog of my mind, just out of reach, like a puzzle with too many missing pieces. I can't shake the feeling that whatever it is, it's important. Something more than just survival. Something Quinn knew that I don't. I just need to figure out how to access it. How to clear the fog and see what it was that she expected from me. The lights in the hospital wing dim, signaling it's time to sleep. I glance around, realizing I'm the only one here. Does that make me one of the unlucky ones, or the lucky ones? I survived. Many others didn't. The stillness of the room presses down on me, heavy and suffocating, but I don't feel relief.

I close my eyes, trying to force my mind back to the labyrinth, to the last thing I remember. It's a blur of fear, blood, and desperation. The memories swim just out of reach, tangled in the fog of pain and exhaustion. I need to piece it together, to make sense of it, but it's slipping through my fingers.

I've done this before. I know how to retreat. Back in the days when I sold my body to survive—when men took more than I was ever willing to give—I learned how to escape without leaving. My body would be there, but my mind? My mind could be somewhere else. Far away. It was my only way out when I couldn't physically leave. Meditation, they'd call it now, but back then it was survival. A way to endure the unbearable.

So I do it again, letting myself slip back into that familiar space, blocking out the pain in my leg, the questions swirling in my mind. I mentally pull myself away from the present, back to the labyrinth, trying to grab onto the last clear memory. I focus on my breathing, slowing it down, like I used to when I couldn't fight back. There's something buried there, something that Quinn knew and I need to uncover.

We were both injured. My leg had nearly been torn off. Quinn had injuries all over herself. It was hard to see any part of her clothes that weren't red with blood. Both hers and mine. She kept it together better than I did. Even then, my mind was dizzy, swirling. I remember her talking to me. Soothing me. She told me that I'd get out of here. Had she known then that Dade would come in to save us? No. I don't think so. It was just words of comfort. Then Dade came. I heard her arguing with him. Insisting that he take me and leave her. I open my eyes and force in a breath. Why did she do that? What am I missing? Her face comes to me. She looked so relieved, so happy to see Dade, but there was something else in her features. A grim determination. As Dade picked me up, she bit down on her bottom lip and gave me a nod. As though she was expecting me to do something. But what?

The images I conjured in my mind begin to fade as the darkness of sleep closes in around me. I've lost a lot of blood, and no matter how desperately I want to cling to the memory of Quinn, I let myself be pulled under, surrendering to the heaviness of slumber.

Hours later, I sit up straight in bed, my heart pounding, sweat soaking through my clothes, making them cling uncomfortably to my skin. Something stirred me. Something not just scary but... thrilling. I scan the hospital wing, my pulse racing. It's empty except for one of the demon doctors, sitting quietly at a desk at the far end. He hasn't looked up, so whatever woke me was either very quiet or—

A realization hits me like a bolt of lightning. It was Quinn who woke me up. No, not her physically, but the memory of her, transformed into a vivid dream. My unconscious mind did what my conscious mind couldn't; it recalled the brief, frantic moments between the Hell Hound's attack and Dade's arrival.

Quinn wanted me to do something. I can feel it, a flicker of urgency igniting in my chest. The fragments of the memory swirl in my mind like wisps of smoke. I strain to grasp them, to understand what she was trying to communicate. She wanted me to help Dade. But how? I lick my lips trying to pull the last remnants of information from my mind. She wanted me to dress him?

No... Yes! Suddenly it all falls into place as I remember the last conversation with Quinn. She wanted to save not just me and Dade, but Juliette and Rowena, too. And she knew how to do it. I drag my bed covers off and put a shaky leg to the floor. A jolt of pain shoots up my leg, but I grit my teeth and put my whole weight on it. This can't wait until I feel l better. I need to do this now, before they do whatever they have in store for Dade.

"Hey!" the demon doctor shouts over. His voice echoes through the empty room. "You shouldn't be out of bed."

Ignoring him, I hobble to the door of the hospital wing. It doesn't take long for him to catch up with me. He grips my shoulder and spins me around. "I said you need to stay in bed."

"Not today, Satan!" I mutter, then lift my fist and sock him right in the face. My knuckles scream in as much agony as my leg, but he tumbles to the ground, anyway. I allow myself a victorious grin, then hobble as fast as I can out of the Hospital wing.

The atrium is empty, though there are the remnants of what looks to have been a party. The huge screen at the far end of the canteen shows five faces. The winners of this Inferno Games. With relief, I see Quinn's face. She did make it. She's now down in the next circle. I wrack my brains to remember what the next circle is. I'd look it up on my portal, but they were taken from us when we entered the Earthery.

Avarice, I think. Not that it matters. Unless I can get Juliette and Rowena on board, and save Dade from the Demons that run this level, everything I do will be in vain. I make slow progress across the atrium and call for the platform. At Juliette's level, I step off and knock at her door. There's no answer, so I head up a few more levels to

Dade's room. The door has been left open. I didn't expect Dade to be here, but I hoped Juliette and Rowena might be.

"Juliette? Rowena?" I call quietly into the room. I can't run the risk of being seen by anyone. I might not be in trouble like Dade is, but I escaped the labyrinth. I can't see Anthura reacting well to that. I creep into the room, peering into the dark in the hope that I'm wrong and they are sleeping on the bed. They aren't, but something on the floor catches my eye. It's Dade's portal. It must have fallen off the nightstand when he moved it to block the back door. Picking it up, I type in Juliette's name and press call.

"Dade?" Her voice is muffled, groggy, like she's just woken up. Which she probably has.

"It's me, Tate. I went to find you in his room and stumbled onto his portal instead."

She doesn't respond immediately. Then I hear her speaking to someone—probably Rowena. "It's Tate. She's in Dade's room."

I swallow hard.

"We're in Ro's room. What's going on?" Juliette asks, her voice filled with unease.

"I know what Quinn wanted me to do, but I can't do it without you... and I can't do it without Dade."

There's a long pause, silence so thick I can hear my heart pounding. Then Juliette's voice comes back, heavy and low. "Well, you're fresh out of luck. Dade is dead."

THE WORDS HANG in the air, deafening, as my mind stumbles over them. Dade? Dead? That can't be right. My chest tightens as I try to make sense of it, but I can't.

Quinn had told me how to save them, but I need Dade to do it. I need him.

But he's gone.

I don't know how to respond; the phone slipping slightly in my hand. "Come down to Ro's room," Juliette sighs, as if trying to steady me. "Room Twenty-Four."

I hang up, my fingers trembling. A lump forms in my throat, growing thicker with every breath. I barely knew Dade, but he saved my life. And now, he's dead. Gone. Just like that. The last piece of hope Quinn had given me, the thing I was clinging to after he pulled me from the labyrinth, has shattered.

29

ANGEL IN DISGUISE

JULIETTE

I open the door and wait for Tate. When the platform descends to our floor with her on, I see that she's a mess. Dried blood coats her clothes and her leg is crisscrossed with stitches. She winces as she steps off the platform.

"Should you be out of the hospital?" I say, looking her up and down? Even her blonde silvery hair is tinged with red.

"Probably not, but I wanted to leave. I knocked a doctor out to get to you." She sighs. Her pale face looks even paler in the blue light of night. She stumbles forward and I catch her. I wrap my arm around her, holding up her weight as we step into Ro's room. She leans into me, resting her head on my shoulder.

"You can sleep here, but it's going to be a squeeze. You'll need a shower to wash all that blood off you, too."

She nods as I guide her into the bathroom and turn on the shower. "Are you going to be alright?"

She nods again, but I don't believe her. She looks half dead. I leave to grab her some pajamas of Ro's. When I get back, I find her sitting in the base of the shower, letting the water cascade over her. She's still fully clothed with the dress she was wearing in the labyrinth. It's clear that she doesn't have the strength to wash herself.

"Can I help you?" I sigh, placing both a towel and the pajamas on the vanity.

She barely raises her head, but I'll take that as a yes. She doesn't have the strength to stand, let alone clean herself. I help her out of her dress and underwear. And grab a sponge to wash the blood from her body. She clings to me limply as I run the sponge over her perfect skin. "Tomas would have loved watching this," I joke, to take away some of the tension I'm feeling. It's weird how that thought is comforting rather than painful. She doesn't even respond. I finish by washing her hair. By the time I pull her out of the shower, we're both soaked to the skin, but at least she's clean now. I towel dry her hair then work my way down her body, wiping away the rivulets of water. When I get to her mauled leg, I'm as gentle as I can be, but her breath still quickens. I stand to face her. Her expression is unreadable, but she looks exhausted. I hand her the pajamas then turn to leave. I'm going to have to find a fresh dry pair of pajamas for myself.

"Juliette?"

I turn to face her.

"Thank you." She closes the distance between us, wrapping her arms around my neck and burying her face against my shoulder. I hold her tight, feeling the warmth of her body against me. Just two days ago, this would have seemed unthinkable, but so much has changed in the last forty-eight hours. I try to push aside the fact that she's naked, focusing instead on offering her the comfort she needs right now. Her breath is warm against my neck as she clings to me, her body trembling slightly. I rub her back in slow, soothing circles, trying to calm her.

"It's going to be okay," I murmur, even though I have no idea if that's true. This feels so alien to me. I've seen so many naked people in my time, but generally they've been men's bodies.

She pulls back to look at me, her eyes shimmering with unshed tears. "Quinn wanted me to save you."

I don't know what to say to that. I just want to get into my own pajamas and fall into the void of oblivion. I have no emotional bandwidth left for anything else. I untangle myself from her and try not to look down at her naked body. "You're wet again. Dry up and come to bed. I'll get dry in Ro's closet.

She's still in the bathroom when I'm dry and redressed and I worry that she's fainted or something, but almost as soon as my head hits the pillow, I feel the weight of her getting into the bed next to me. Beside me on the other side, Rowena is snoring lightly. I shift over, allowing Tate some room, but as the bed is made for one, it's a tight squeeze. Tate's body presses up against mine and she gives a long sigh. I lay awake long after Tate drifts off, my mind racing with thoughts and emotions I can't seem to sort through.

In the moment between sleep and waking, I feel Tomas beside me, his arms around my waist, but my heart already knows what my sleepy brain cannot quite comprehend. I wake up and turn over to find Tate with her arm around me. Not Tomas. I move her arm and, because Rowena is still sleeping on the other side of me, have to shuffle down the bed to get out of the bottom of it.

Tomas is gone. Quinn is gone. All I have is Rowena... and, I guess, Tate. It's all so overwhelming. Hearing about

Tomas's death yesterday was compounded by the loss of Dade. And I had to hear it from Anthura. After leaving Tate in the hospital wing last night, Rowena and I had gone straight up to the very top floor of the tower. Anthura had the audacity to mock us when she told us that Dade had been killed because of his actions in the Labyrinth. At least I'll never have to see that bitch's face ever again. She'll have toddled off to the next circle at some point in the night. Now that everything is over, I have to find a way to get on with an eternity in this hell hole. I quietly change into one of Rowena's dresses, trying to keep the noise to a minimum as I rummage through her closet. After slipping out through the back door, I take a deep breath of the stale air. I need to be alone for a while. I need to grieve without Rowena offering platitudes or Tate... I'm not even sure how Tate will handle grief.

She was too sick to really deal with anything last night; she needs sleep to heal.

The atrium feels almost hollow now that the games are over, a stark contrast to the vibrant party atmosphere from the night before. I scan the canteen, my heart heavy, wondering if I can bear to sit there with the faces of the Inferno Games winners looming over me on the big screen. Those who died aren't shown. I suppose that would be too much of a downer. It's all fun and games watching the carnage unfold, but now that they are gone, there's nothing left to commemorate their existence.

"Hey, Juliette."

I turn to find Twila standing before me—well, more like face to stomach since she barely reaches five feet tall.

"I'm so sorry about what happened to Tomas." Her voice wavers. "We didn't intend for him to die like that."

"No, you just planned for him to starve to death or get

eaten by a hellhound," I shoot back, the bitterness spilling out before I can contain it.

Her eyes fill with sadness, her face etched in guilt, and that only makes me feel worse. I rub my forehead. "I'm really sorry. I know you don't have any control over these games."

"If I were you, I'd hate me too," she says,. "I have no clue what's going to happen next, but I get a free pass through the circles."

"I guess you'll be heading to Avarice now?"

She nods slowly, her expression somber. "Yep. Hades is waiting for me. I hoped..." She glances down, shame flickering in her eyes. "I hoped to say goodbye to you and Rowena before I left. I actually thought you were her in that dress until I saw your black hair."

I look down at the flowery dress, my chest tightening. "It belongs to Ro. She's still asleep. Should I go get her?"

Twila shakes her head, urgency in her voice. "There isn't really time. Hades is dealing with Dade right now, and we need to leave before the contestants wake up in Avarice."

My brow furrows in confusion. "Dealing with Dade? Anthura told us he was dead."

Her brow furrows. "Dead? No," she says, a glimmer of surprise breaking through the sorrow in her voice. "He's locked up on the demon level."

A wave of relief washes over me, momentarily pushing back the pain. "Take me to him."

She hesitates. "I can't. You know that." Her voice is firm, but her eyes hold a hint of compassion, as if she wishes she could help.

I want to tell her that Tate can get us out of here. All of us, but whether I like it or not, I can't trust her. Not while she's still hooking up with Hades. Until they split up, she's on their side.

"Quinn will never get over it if she knows Dade is being held hostage." I want to add that she'd never forgive Twila, but that might be overkill.

Twila screws her face up in frustration as her name is called out. We both turn to see Hades striding over to where we are.

Twila pulls me down to her height and gives me a hug. It feels hollow until I hear her whisper in my ear. "I'll see what I can do."

And then she's gone. Down into the elevator with Hades. Down to Avarice, where Quinn will be waking up, hopefully as good as new in a few minutes. I can't even follow them. The only person I know with an elevator marble key is Dade, and he's already down there.

I sit in the canteen, lost in my own thoughts and grief for almost an hour, before the elevator doors finally open and a man with giant black wings strides out. A spark of excitement and relief fills my chest with warmth. I rush to Dade and am in his arms with his wings wrapped round me before I know it.

"Quinn wasn't wrong when she said you give amazing hugs!" I mutter, suddenly feeling uncomfortable with the sudden public display of affection for a man I have barely talked to before. I don't even really know him.

"She said that?"

"No," I confess, cringing slightly. "She said you were an amazing lay, but I rephrased."

Dade's dark face brightens for a second, and then he laughs. It's a comforting sound, one I'm not used to coming from him.

"What happened?" I look up at him. "Anthura told us you were dead."

Dade looks thoughtful. "I guess I would have died, but Twila unlocked my chains before she left."

Anger fills me. Anthura would have left him there to die at the hands of the demons, and with no way for us to get down there, I guess she thought she was telling the truth.

"Tate came to Rowena's room in the middle of the night," I tell him. "She said that she remembered what Quinn wanted her to do, but she needed you. She said she could save us all."

Dade's expression turns thoughtful. "I don't know if redemption is on the table for any of us, but if she can get me to Quinn, then there's no time to waste."

I don't know what I was expecting, but it definitely wasn't for Dade to tighten his grip and launch us into the sky. My heart plummets as I cling to him, my arms instinctively wrapping tighter around his shoulders. A rush of wind whips past, and before I can catch my breath, we touch down on the second-floor balcony. The jolt of landing is still sinking in when the door swings open, Rowena already standing there, as if she heard us coming.

"Dade?" Rowena gapes at him, her eyes wide and mouth slightly open in shock.

"Anthura lied to us—big surprise there. I've got Dade. Where's Tate?"

Rowena blinks, still processing. "I just woke up and found both of you gone. I... I don't know where she is."

"Anthura, Hades and Twila have all gone down to Avarice, so it's doubtful they have her." I shrug my shoulders. "George might?"

"George is probably hiding out in the demon level

after his disaster of a games." Ro points out. "He's probably licking his wounds after a murderer took out half the contestants before he did."

A pang of sorrow hits me at her words, but none of us have time for grief now. If we get out of here, I can grieve then.

"Let's find her and get the fuck out of here." I grab Dade's hand so he doesn't get any more ideas about flying me anywhere, and drag him toward the stairs. Ro runs behind us.

"Shouldn't we split up?" she asks when she catches up.

"No. We're sticking together until we find her and then we're going to get Quinn, too."

Ro mumbles something that sounds suspiciously like 'Felix.' I've not put much thought into Felix. His face was up on the screen along with Quinn's, so he must have gotten through to Avarice too. He's the last of my concerns, despite Rowena being my best friend.

The atrium is mostly empty, save for a few stragglers. I pull Dade aside, lowering my voice. "We need to head down to the demon level and find George. I know Rowena doesn't think he's interested in Tate, but where else could she be? None of us know her room number, and she doesn't have her Hell Cell."

"Damn," Rowena mutters. "Dade's Hell Cell is still on my nightstand. I should've brought it."

Dade shakes his head. "Doesn't matter. We can't communicate between circles, anyway. The only one I want to talk to is Quinn. Besides, I'm not ready to tip my hand with George. He doesn't know I have the marble key to the demon level, and I intend to keep it that way. We need to exhaust all other options to find Tate first."

Dade makes sense, but I can't picture Tate heading

down to the Earthery level. Shopping or a trip to Infernos doesn't seem like her style—especially since the place doesn't even serve drinks. "Her leg was shredded. Wherever she went, it was deliberate. Unless... maybe she went back to her room?"

In the end, we pile into the elevator anyway and press down. I'm itching to go one more level down, but I respect Dade's wishes. We really need to find Tate.

The lower level is as miserable as usual in this circle, with sad looking shopkeepers and very few customers. A quick race down the shopping street tells us that Tate isn't here. I check in Infernos anyway. As I suspected, she isn't there either.

I'm just about to suggest we go looking for her room when Dade stills beside me. "She's in the Earthery."

I want to ask him how he could possibly know that, but then I look over and see her in the entrance talking to the demon that works behind the Earthery desk on days it's not being used for the games. She's carrying a huge bag on her shoulder. "I'd forgotten this place had other uses," I say as we walk inside.

Tate's face lights up when she sees us, and as her gaze shifts to Dade, she brightens even more. She turns back to the demon behind the desk. "Make that four."

The demon barely shrugs. "You've only got half an hour. I've got a booking after that. Don't make me come in there and drag you out."

Tate pulls us aside, out of earshot, though the demon seems far too disinterested to care. "I thought you were dead?" Tate says looking at Dade then throwing a questioning glace my way.

"Anthura lied," I say.

Tate grins. "I'm so glad," she whispers, leaning in to us.

"Quinn had a theory, but the only way to test it safely is in here." She glances up at Dade. "Once we're done, we'll need to head straight to the demon level. Quinn said you've got a key for the elevator?"

Dade gives a curt nod.

"I'm so glad you're here," she adds, relief flickering across her face. "This will be a lot easier with you than the alternative I had in mind."

"Time's ticking!" I cut in, nodding to the clock. The urgency in my voice matches the pace of my racing heart. "I don't know what you have planned, but I hope you can do it in thirty minutes." I hold my Hell Cell up to the pad next to the doors and they open.

"Let Dade think of the Demon Level," she whispers as we step into the darkness. "The rest of you let your minds go blank. The Earthery moulds itself to the minds of the people inside and we don't want distractions."

Seconds after the doors close behind us, a corridor begins to materialize. The walls are dull and gray, but lining them, stretching endlessly, is food. Cupcakes, candy, chips—everything I love.

Tate furrows her brow. "Is this what the demon level looks like?"

"There's no food there," Dade says flatly.

Everyone turns to me.

"Sorry." I shrug sheepishly. "I tried to think of nothing, but... I'm hungry."

Dade steps forward, glancing down the corridor. "It doesn't matter. The layout is the same. We're in the right place." He looks back at Tate. "What do we do now?"

"I need you to close your eyes and focus on where you got stuck last time," she instructs, then turns to me. "And you need to stop thinking about food. This has to be as real as possible."

"Like that's gonna happen," I mutter, but Rowena jabs me in the stomach. "Fine," I grumble, pouting. "I'll try."

Reluctantly, I close my eyes and force the thought of food to fade away.

A growl has me opening them.

"What the actual fuck is that?" I yelp, pressing myself against the wall as a massive, disgusting beast snarls and snaps in a crystal-lined room ahead of us.

"It's chained. It can't reach you," Dade says calmly. "But we can't get past it either."

Realization hits. "Oh, that's the beast Quinn mentioned. Yeah, I've changed my mind. Definitely don't want to fuck it. It's disgusting."

Tate and Dade give me matching looks of confusion, while Rowena just shakes her head.

"We're in the Earthery, though. This thing can't actually hurt us, right?" I say, peeling myself off the wall and stepping closer. The beast strains against its chains, baring yellowed teeth, its breath rancid enough to kill a cactus. I step back quickly, my heart pounding. It looks real enough

"Of course it can hurt us," Rowena says. "Did you forget everything that happened last night? That was in the Earthery, too, remember?"

"Well shit!"

"But in here we can all think of something safe and the room around us will change," Tate points out.

Dade steps in front of me, his eyes fixed on the beast. "This place has a mind of its own. Until we're sure, let's assume everything in here can hurt—and kill—us just as easily as in reality." He turns to Tate. "What did Quinn say to do next?"

"Quinn actually thought this would be safe, but I hear you about exercising caution." Tate drops the bag she's carrying to the floor. "She said that you couldn't fight it, get round it or..." she looks my way, "get past it by other means. She did say there was one way to get past it, though."

Rowena shakes her head, wrinkling her nose at the beast. "She said only Satan could get past that thing."

"No," Tate corrects, "she said Satan probably brought it here, but what Quinn actually said was that angels could get past it."

I cross my arms, staring at the hulking beast. "Unless you've got a spare angel stashed in that bag, I think we're wasting our time."

"Ye of little faith," Tate says with a grin. "Dade, step in front of it. Just don't get close enough for it to make you lunch."

Dade moves up cautiously, but the moment he's in front of the creature, it goes wild—snarling, snapping its teeth, and raking its massive claws into the ground, desperate to close the gap between them. The sight is terrifying, and this isn't even the real thing.

Tate pulls a massive wad of rolled-up white material from her bag and steps up behind Dade. "Extend your wings."

Dade glances over his shoulder, then complies, unfurling his magnificent wings.

No matter how many times I see it, the sight of Dade's wings never fails to take my breath away. The feathers shimmer in the dim light, radiating an ethereal glow.

"Wow!" I mouth, captivated.

The beast halts its frantic thrashing and seems to still slightly. I guess I'm not the only one mesmerized by Dade.

"I didn't have time to make a proper costume, but I'm hoping this is enough!" Tate exclaims, draping the white material over Dade's massive wings. He ducks slightly, allowing her to throw the fabric all the way to the tips.

"Help me!" she urges, nodding toward her bag.

Rowena and I dive in, pulling out the rest of the material along with the dress I saw her making the other day. Together, we wrap swathes of material around Dade, nearly turning him into a mummy. Finally, his black clothes are hidden beneath swathes of white, and his majestic wings appear almost angelic.

"Step back!" Tate whispers, taking my hand in hers. With my other hand. I take Rowena's and the three of us take a slow step back, leaving Dade to face the monster alone.

The beast seems confused for a second, but then, slowly, it lowers its head and drops to its front knees.

"Dade!" Tate whispers. "See if it lets you past."

Dade keeps his wings open as he takes a step around the beast. It watches him, but doesn't make a move, allowing Dade to get to the door. He pulls at the handle and the door opens. As it does, a light flashes a couple of times and then everything goes black.

30

FACING THE HELLBEAST

ROWENA

I instinctively clutch my growing stomach with one hand while Juliette's hand tightens around my other. It's only when the lights go back on that I realize that our time in the Earthery is over.

"Oy. I told you I had another booking!"

We must look a funny sight to the demon Earthery receptionist as we turn as a whole to face him. The three of us holding hands with Dade covered in white behind us. He doesn't seem in the slightest bit interested. I guess he sees it all down here.

"Sorry," mutters Tate, pulling the material from Dade and shoving it into her bag.

We leave the Earthery with a sense of determination I've not felt before. I told myself that Felix was gone and it was probably for the best, but the truth is, now that there's a chance of seeing him again, has my heart catching in my throat.

This time, as we enter the elevator, I'm going to one of the most dangerous places in all of Hell. On the floor below us, the demons don't have to pretend to like us.

They don't have to keep us safe. Down below us, we are no longer guests, we are prey. I swallow back a lump in my throat as Dade inserts the marble into the hole next to the elevator buttons. All the stories Quinn has told us about what she had gone through down there rush through my mind. The time when she saw Dade having his skin peeled back, the time they were chased by demons and let's not forget the time she was almost literally reduced to ash. Then she had Hades to save her, but we don't even have that. Hades isn't here in this circle anymore. He's even lower in the depths of Hell – a place we're actively trying to get to. As the doors to the elevator open, panic sets in. This is all too fast. I'm not ready. Can I put my unborn child into such a dangerous position? What kind of mother does that make me?

The others step out of the elevator, but I freeze. All I have to do is press the button, and I'll be taken back up to relative safety. Sure, I'll never taste food or drink again, but at least I won't be eaten by a demon.

"Ro?" Juliette's voice pulls me back, but I shake my head, unable to move.

"I can't do it. You go on without me," I whisper, my chest tight with fear.

The elevator doors begin to close, but Juliette jams her foot between them, holding them open. "I'm not going without you, Ro. You can do this!" She reaches out her hand toward me, her eyes pleading.

"I can't," I say, my voice trembling. "It's not just about me anymore."

Juliette's gaze drops to my stomach, then back to my eyes. "Don't let this baby grow up without her aunty Jules."

My body trembles uncontrollably, the weight of everything pressing down on me. I want to move, to take that step forward, but my legs won't listen. I stare at her hand, wanting to reach out, wanting to be strong, but the fear... the fear is suffocating. "Rowena Bagshott. You are the bravest person I've ever met. I know you can do this. Just step out of the elevator."

I stare at Juliette's outstretched hand, my heart pounding wildly in my chest. The fear is overwhelming, threatening to paralyze me completely. But then I think of my unborn child - the life growing inside me that depends on me to make the right choices. Can I really condemn her to an existence trapped in this hellish place, never knowing the taste of food or drink, always living in fear?

Everything I love is on the other side of those elevator doors. Juliette, Quinn... Felix?

Taking a deep, shaky breath, I reach out and grasp Juliette's hand tightly. Her fingers close around mine, warm and reassuring. With a determined nod, I step out of the elevator and onto the treacherous ground of the lower level.

The air down here is thick and oppressive, heavy with the stench of sulfur and decay.

Dade gives me a reassuring smile. "I'll do everything in my power to protect you. Come up here with me."

I release Juliette's hand and step closer to Dade's side. I won't lie; he used to scare me at one point. But now, as he wraps a wing around me, I feel an overwhelming sense of comfort. I silently apologize to Quinn for all the times I called her boyfriend an asshole. He takes my hand in his. "We're going to stick together. Thanks to Quinn's idea, we know what to do now. Okay?"

He makes it sound so simple. The difference is that the monster in the Earthery was just lurking there. Down here, we have to traverse miles of winding corridors to reach it. What are the odds we won't encounter a demon along the way?

I push the thought aside and let Dade lead me, with Juliette and Tate trailing behind. We've barely walked ten feet when a voice calls out from behind us.

"What are you doing down here?"

I don't need to turn around; I already recognize the voice—George.

"Lost?" Juliette tries to explain, but I can hear the tremor in her voice.

"There's no way to get down here unless you're with a demon. Who do you have helping you?" George demands.

"Anthura!" I lie, turning to face him. Cerby is panting next to him. "She let us down here before heading to Avarice."

George takes a step closer, his presence even more revolting in this dimly lit space. His teeth are stained yellow and brown, and his mottled skin looks worse than I remembered. He narrows his eyes at me, skepticism etched across his face. "Anthura left hours ago."

"We've been down here for hours," I manage, forcing the words out. "We were hoping to find some food."

George laughs, a harsh sound that echoes off the walls. "Any food you might find down here is definitely not meant for your stomachs."

"Okay then. Sorry! We'll head back upstairs!" I say, attempting to sidestep him, but he grips my wrist tightly. The sensation of his clammy skin against mine sends a jolt of revulsion through me, and I let out a yelp.

"Demons!" George shouts, his voice booming in the corridor. We wait with bated breath, but no one comes to his call.

"Very well. Everyone is upstairs, but they will relish this tasty meal when they get back."

He drags me down the dark corridor, his grip so tight it feels like he's trying to peel my skin off. The heat from his hand burns like acid, and I can almost smell my flesh sizzling.

Juliette lunges at him, but just like me, her fingers recoil from his touch. "You leave her alone!" she demands, anger lacing her voice.

"No. You will all come with me. If any of you try anything, I'll kill her in the most painful way possible."

Dade unfurls his wings again, a magnificent display meant to intimidate, but Tate jumps in front of him and reaches for me. Unfortunately, that gives George the chance to snatch her too, and almost immediately, I see her face contort in pain as her wrist begins to burn.

"You bastard!" Juliette seethes, but it's too late. We're already dragged into a dimly lit room.

"You two get yourselves into the manacles." He nods toward the heavy iron shackles bolted to the wall. "And don't try anything unless you want your friends burnt to a crisp. I missed out on a lot of deaths in the labyrinth, but I could have my fun with you four."

With a resigned sigh, Dade and Juliette comply as George clamps Tate and me into a pair of manacles each, the cold metal biting into my skin. When he's satisfied we're all chained to the wall, he claps his hands together, a sinister smile stretching across his face. "I don't know what will be more fun: torturing you alone or letting my demons feast on you for supper. I don't usually let them dine on the residents of Gluttony, but for you four, I think I can make an exception."

He strides over to Juliette, who glares at him with a

fierce intensity. "Ah, you're the one who demanded I serve you food on your first day here. I should have guessed you'd be trouble." He steeples his fingers, a look of mock contemplation crossing his face. "But I don't want to be too cruel. Here, have all the food you want."

With a flick of his wrist, the room transforms, bursting with every kind of food imaginable.

"I have to go attend to some business, but just in case any of you think about escaping, I'll leave Cerby here to keep you company." He smirks, glancing at the colossal creature lurking in the shadows. "Enjoy looking at all this food, because when I return with my demons, you'll be served up alongside it."

With that, George strides out of the room, the door slamming shut behind him.

"Oh my god, I'm so hungry!" Juliette whimpers, her eyes darting to the endless spread of food. "I really fucking hate this place. Anyone have any ideas on how we might get out of here? Oh, is that cheesecake?"

I shake my head, fighting the temptation myself.

"This is the demon lounge," Dade informs us, his voice steady yet laced with urgency. "This is where Quinn and I were nearly killed in the last circle."

Just effing great!

Tate leans closer, her voice dropping to a whisper. "I might have an idea. Cerby! Here, boy!"

Juliette shakes her head, disbelief evident. "You don't seriously expect that ugly beast to help us? It might have three heads, but it doesn't have opposable thumbs... or keys to use them, for that matter."

"There were keys on the wall over there last time." Dade nods to the far side of the room, where a massive keyring hangs from a hook.

"Already ahead of you," Tate says, determination glinting in her eyes. "Cerberus! Come here!"

"I thought it was called Cerby?" Juliette interjects.

"That's his nickname," Tate replies, undeterred. "Quinn said he prefers his full name."

"How in all Hell does she know that?" Juliette scoffs.

Tate shrugs. "I don't know. She told me about him in the Labyrinth."

"Is there anything she didn't tell you?" Juliette quips.

"She didn't mention how to get the keys from the wall, but Cerberus looks like a clever dog." Tate's eyes are fixed on the creature.

"I've seen dogs do more impressive things than just get keys from a wall. Do you really think it'll work?" I say.

Tate's resolve hardens. "Only one way to find out."

With that, she calls Cerberus's name again. This time, the creature pads over, all three heads swaying in unison, leaving a trail of drool that glistens on the floor.

"Hey baby. Can you get the keys?" She shakes her head toward the bunch of keys.

Cerberus sits, looking up at her, its tail wagging

"Keys. Can you fetch the keys? I'll get you a bone!"

Juliette lets out a groan.

"Keys Cerby. Can you fetch the keys?" Tate motions to the keyring again.

The three-headed dog cocks its heads, as if pondering the request. Then, with a sudden burst of energy, it bounds across the room, its massive paws thudding against the stone floor. It reaches the wall where the keys hang and rears up on its hind legs, its front paws scrabbling at the rough surface.

"Come on, Cerby! You can do it!" Tate cheers, her voice echoing in the cavernous space.

Juliette rolls her eyes. "This is ridiculous. There's no way that creature is going to-"

Her words are cut off by a triumphant bark as Cerberus manages to snag the keyring with one of its mouths. The keys jangle as the beast drops back down to all fours and trots back to Tate, its tail wagging furiously.

"Good boy!" Tate exclaims, easing the keyring from the dog's mouth with her foot. Deftly, she raises her leg and slips the keys into her fingers. We're all on tenterhooks as she tries key after key in the manacles, but eventually she gets the right one.

"Told you he could do it," Tate grins smugly as she unlocks Juliette's manacles.

"Fine," Juliette concedes, but it's still a mangy mutt."

"Don't listen to her, baby." Tate drops down and kisses all three heads of Cerberus.

While Tate unlocks Dade and I, Juliette stuffs her bra and face with cupcakes. I give her a scathing look.

"What? I've not eaten since yesterday, and who knows. We might have to throw cupcakes at that beast."

The thought sobers me instantly. We managed to get out of George's traps quickly enough, but we still have a long way to go.

"Come on."

Dade takes the lead, opening the door back to the corridor. He ushers us all outside. Cerberus follows wagging his tail.

"That thing is not coming!" Juliette warns, but Tate reaches down the front of Juliette's bra, pulls out three cup cakes and throws them to each of Cerberus's heads, rendering Juliette speechless for the first time in her life and death.

When she sees that her indignation is not going to be heeded, she follows us down the long corridor.

After about two hours of relentless walking or limping in Tate's case, Dade suddenly stops. "I'm going to have to take my shirt off."

I glance down at my swollen ankles, feeling the heat radiate off my skin. I'm exhausted and uncomfortable, but I don't have the luxury of being able to discard my shirt whenever I feel like it.

"Such a turn-on," Juliette jokes, a playful grin spreading across her face.

Dade shakes his head, amusement flickering in his eyes. With a swift motion, he pulls his shirt over his head. He shuffles it around, carefully guiding his wings through the fabric.

Despite my irritation, I can't help but draw in a breath when Dade turns his back to us. I'm not alone; beside me, Juliette and Tate gasp in unison.

"It's London," I say, gaping at the massive tattoo that sprawls across his back.

Juliette leans in closer to inspect it. "It's a map."

"A map of these corridors," Dade clarifies. "Quinn marked the beast's room with a red dot."

"Quinn did this?" I ask, stepping up beside Juliette, my curiosity piqued. "I never knew."

"I asked her to keep it a secret," Dade replies, reaching over his left shoulder to prod a specific area of the map. "I think we're around here somewhere. We just passed a fork and a T-junction."

I shake my head in awe as Juliette follows the path along Dade's back with her finger, tracing the intricate lines.

"It's right here!" Tate snaps, jabbing her finger down

just below Dade's left shoulder blade. "And the red dot is down by his right kidney. We need to take the next right, then a left, then another left."

Juliette raises her nose in the air, a hint of disdain evident on her face. When Dade, Tate, and Cerberus start moving, she pulls me back.

"Why is Tate even here?" she sniffs, crossing her arms.

"Uh, because she was the one who took us to the Earthery. She figured out how to get past the beast..."

"That was Quinn," Juliette reminds me, her tone sharp.

"Okay, fine. She was the one who got us all out of the manacles in the demon's lounge."

"Yeah. And now I'm three cupcakes lighter because of that slobbering mutt."

"You'd be a whole lot lighter than that if the demons had eaten you. Face it—we wouldn't even be here if it wasn't for Tate... or Cerberus. Now come on. We don't want to lose them."

It takes another four hours to reach the crystal room. Four hours of Juliette complaining about the dog and Tate.

I'd seen the beast before in the Earthery, but now, standing before the real thing, my fear creeps back in, settling like a heavy weight in my chest. Cerberus whines slightly, with one of its heads giving a timid bark. He slips behind Tate's legs and cowers. For a type of hellhound with three heads, he's an awful coward.

The hellbeast looks different—bigger, for starters. Its teeth gleam menacingly, longer and sharper than I remember.

It unleashes an almighty howl that reverberates off the walls, sending a chilling roar down the corridor. The force of it rustles our hair and sends shivers racing down my spine.

"Alright, Dade. You know the drill," Tate says, dropping her bag and pulling out the familiar white fabric we used before. She tosses the dress aside, quickly unraveling the material to drape over Dade's wings.

This was easier in the Earthery. There, the chance of being mauled to death was significantly lower. Now, the stakes feel terrifyingly real. The beast's breath reeks of sulfur, its jaws snapping with unnerving force. Yet, somehow, the three of us work together, dressing Dade in his angelic disguise.

When we're done, he looks like the most bedraggled angel ever—but he fooled the fake hellbeast. Maybe it'll work again.

I hold my breath as we step back, watching for any sign that the disguise will hold. If it doesn't, our only option is to retrace our steps all the way back to George and beg for mercy. Mercy that he has never shown.

The beast stares at Dade, its teeth bared. Dade is made of stronger stuff than I am. He's an inch from the snarling jaw of the beast—close enough for it to ruffle his hair and yet he holds steadfast. He's magnificent, his wings outstretched. The pressure he must be under, but he's like a rock, staring into the red eyes of the beast, willing it to submit.

Finally, the beast lowers its gaze, and I let out a slow, shaky breath. I make a move forward, but Tate's hand grips my arm, holding me back in warning.

Dade hangs there for a heartbeat, motionless, then steps toward the beast. It's as if a spell has been broken. The beast snaps out of its trance, lunging forward and striking at Dade. His quick reflexes save him, but not fast enough. The creature's jaws clamp down, tearing into his chest with a vicious bite.

I know I'm screaming. After hours of near silence, the sound of my voice echoes off the walls, sharp and piercing. Every instinct in me screams to help him, to pull him back, but I'm frozen, paralyzed. My mind fixates on the life growing inside me. Fear locks me in place.

Suddenly, a flash of white cuts through the chaos. In my frantic state, it takes a moment to register what I'm seeing. Tate. She's somehow managed to slip into the white dress we had discarded earlier, her body now between Dade and the beast. She's tall—standing on her tiptoes, she nearly reaches Dade's height.

The beast pauses, confused. I follow its gaze, trying to understand. Tate, with her flowing white-blonde hair, the ethereal dress, and Dade's white wings draped around them both, looks like something otherworldly—like an angel descending from the heavens.

And the beast seems to believe it.

It stops growling, its ferocity melting into submission as it lowers its massive head to the ground, like a work of art unfolding before my eyes.

"Wow," Juliette whispers, her voice filled with awe.

I snap back to reality, grabbing her hand and pulling her forward. But my heart pounds in dread as I glance at Dade—he's losing too much blood.

Between Juliette, Tate and I, we manage to hold Dade up, almost carrying him around the beast and finally bolting through the door at the opposite end of the room, slamming it behind us before the beast comes to its senses.

"Dade!" I whimper as he crashes to the ground.

He looks up at me and smiles. "Everything is healed

between circles remember," He huffs out. I'm momentarily confused until he nods to another set of doors. Elevator doors. The words 'Third Circle' are printed in gold above the double doors.

Tate rushes over to the elevator and slams her hand on the call button. We're here. We've done it!

We've managed something I never thought possible. Disbelief turns to excitement as the doors open. It takes us a couple of minutes to haul Dade to his feet and get him in the elevator, but between the three of us, we manage it. Cerby trots in behind us and I mentally add 'stealing a hell dog' to our list of crimes.

The exit to hell is in our reach and it takes everything I have not to press the button for the lowest circle. We only got out of here because of Quinn. We can't leave her in Hell on her own. Besides, getting to the inner circle of Hell puts us face to face with Lucifer himself and none of us have prepared for that.

There's a palpable charge in the air as the elevator descends, an electric tension that makes my heart race. The red velvet wallpaper and the strange painted walls depicting the nine circles are oppressive, but there's a feeling of joy too. When Dade shifts his shirt aside, revealing the once vicious gash from the Hellbeast miraculously healed, I can't contain myself. A burst of joy propels me forward, and I fling my arms around Tate, pulling her into a tight hug. The relief, the sheer victory of it all, washes over me.

I turn to Dade next, hugging him fiercely despite the sticky mess of blood still on his chest that smears across my dress. But I don't care. "I knew we'd get that baby of yours to safety," he whispers in my ear, and I smile up at him, warmth flooding my chest. Who would've thought the brooding, mysterious Dade had a heart underneath all that darkness?

I spin around, ready to embrace Juliette in my elation, only to freeze in place. My eyes widen as I take in the sight before me—Juliette's lips are locked with Tate's. Or maybe Tate's lips are on hers. I'm not even sure who initiated it.

My mouth hangs open in shock, the adrenaline in my veins now twisting into something completely unexpected. The soft ping of the elevator doors opening snaps me out of it, but Tate and Juliette remain entirely oblivious, lost in their moment.

"Ahem," I clear my throat, feeling the heat of embarrassment creeping up my neck.

Tate pulls away slowly, her face smug, like the cat that got the cream. Juliette, on the other hand, looks stunned, her eyes wide with shock.

"Maybe we should get out before the elevator decides to take us back up?" I suggest, trying to restore some sense of normalcy to the situation.

Tate struts out confidently, her long white dress trailing behind her, now smeared with Dade's blood across the front, looking like the goddess she is. Just like Dade, she has healed completely, the scars on her legs vanished.

"Are you coming?" I smirk at Juliette, who still seems too stunned to move.

"She kissed me," Juliette hisses as we trail behind Dade and Tate.

I glance up at the pair, striding ahead like royalty, their presence larger than life. They move with the kind of grace that feels otherworldly. Dade had shrugged off the white cloth he'd worn in the elevator, but Tate is still rocking the bloodstained white dress like some kind of warrior goddess.

"I hugged Dade. So what?" I shrug, still feeling the adrenaline. "Emotions were high. I probably would've kissed Tate too. I mean, she did save us."

Juliette suddenly stops, grabbing my arm and spinning me around to face her, her expression intense. "I didn't kiss Tate. She kissed me."

I try to keep my expression neutral, but amusement flickers in my eyes. "Maybe she was just happy we escaped."

"You're not getting this, Ro. She had her fricking tongue in my mouth!" Juliette's voice rises, flustered in a way I've never seen before.

A smirk pulls at my lips. I've never seen Juliette so rattled, and honestly, it's kind of hilarious.

"I wouldn't read much into it," I say calmly. I've noticed Tate's lingering looks at Juliette and the half smiles in the past day, but I didn't think much of it until now. Not that I'm going to tell Jules that. She stares at me as though I've gone crazy.

"Come on, or we'll lose them. We walked for hours to get from the tower and it's probably the same distance back to the Avarice tower."

I take a few steps, hurrying along to catch up with Dade and Tate, but I soon have to stop to see if Juliette is following.

"Do you want to lose them?" I ask, as she stands still, disbelief still covering her features. "May I remind you that our only map of this place is tattooed on Dade's back?"

"But she kissed me. What does it mean?"

I sigh. "Jules. You've fucked every man you've ever met.

Maybe this is the universe's way of telling you that you should try something new?"

"You just told me I shouldn't read anything into it and now you want me to fuck her? I'm not even a lesbian!"

I sigh, not in the mood for a lengthy conversation about Juliette's love life. "I don't want you to do anything other than get a move on. My feet are killing me. I've suddenly developed hunger that feels like my stomach is revolting against me and who knows what we'll come across down here. I doubt the hellbeast in Gluttony was the only one. Maybe stop thinking of Tate as someone who kissed you and start reminding yourself that she was the one who got us away from the hellbeast in the first place."

31

IN AVARICE

JULIETTE

I'm trapped in Hell. I've just fought a literal Hellbeast... well, kinda. My ex-husband has died—again, for the second time—and all I can think about is Tate's lips. Not exactly what I imagined would be occupying my thoughts right now, but here we are. It's almost enough to distract me from the hunger gnawing at my insides. Almost. Rowena's right, though—the hunger here hits differently. I thought Gluttony was bad, but this circle? If they don't feed us soon, I might actually die.

Watching Dade and Tate walk is like watching a movie preview with the two main characters walking away from a massive explosion. The juxtaposition between Dade with his long black hair and giant black wings, now folded up behind him standing next to Tate with her platinum blonde hair over the white dress is something else. The contrast between them is striking, almost surreal.

And here I am, stuck in Hell, hungry as ever, obsessing over a kiss I can't stop thinking about.

I must be going insane. Hunger has been known to do that to me. I try to look at Tate objectively. She's... pretty.

No, actually, she's not just pretty. Quinn, Ro, and Twila are all pretty in their own ways. Tate is striking—tall and almost fae-like in that white dress. There's something about her that demands attention. She's attractive, sure, but am I attracted to her? I can't be. I've never been into women.

I guess I fell for Tomas in school and spent the rest of my life—and death—revenge screwing my way through anyone who crossed my path because of all the hurt he caused me. Urgh, that sounds pathetic. Exactly the kind of thing Ro would raise an eyebrow at and have some wisecrack ready for. I make a mental note never to say this out loud in her presence. She's already offered me her ridiculous advice on the matter, and I don't need more of that nonsense.

I avert my eyes from Tate and focus on where we are, trying to make sense of the seemingly endless corridors. Maybe they're just like the other circles, but it's hard to tell. Everything smells of sulfur, way worse than it does upstairs, and the surroundings are dull—dull grey walls, dull grey ceiling, stretching out forever.

"Quinn better be down here," I mutter to Ro. "And she'd better have a bacon sandwich ready to hand over to her bestie." As if on cue, my stomach growls loudly, an obnoxious reminder of just how desperate I'm getting.

"Are we nearly there yet?" I shout out ahead of me.

Dade stops and moves his wings to show his entire back. "I think we're about a third of the way. You'll have to check on the map.

I stride forward, feeling self-conscious for the first time in my life. I can practically feel Tate's eyes on me, and it sends a shiver down my spine. I don't know where to look, so I focus on the one thing that feels safe—the map tattoo etched onto Dade's back.

"I think we're here," Tate says, her finger tracing a point on Dade's skin. "See, we passed a couple of T-junctions, which are here." Her touch is light, but it causes his muscles to ripple under her fingertips.

"Great," I manage to say. I glance at Tate and immediately regret it. That sly smile playing on her lips—like she's reading my thoughts, my embarrassing, ridiculous thoughts—makes my heart race in all the wrong ways.

Turning away quickly, I head back to Ro, who's standing a few feet away, observing the whole thing with a knowing grin. She even throws in a raised eyebrow for good measure. Seriously? Can everyone read me like an open book? Do my thoughts stand out as clearly as the map tattooed on Dade's back?

Urgh! "Come on, let's get going then," I say, trying to shake off the awkwardness. "Hopefully, we'll be there in time for breakfast."

It takes us hours to traipse the same path we've already done, but in reverse. It's only when we get near to the place where, in the upper circles, there is an elevator to the tower, that I begin to feel nervous. Thoughts of Tate and bacon drop away when Dade stills and holds a finger to his lips.

"We're really close to the elevator, which is good, but we're also close to the demon's lounge, which, obviously, is really bad. We need to get up to the tower without attracting any attention."

Tate shakes her head. "I say we go right to the Demon's lounge."

"What?" I stop dead, staring at Tate like she's lost her

mind. "You want to walk right into a demon's lounge? Are you crazy?"

Tate crosses her arms, that infuriating sly smile creeping back onto her face. "Yes. It's the fastest way, and if we keep sneaking around, we'll be spotted, eventually. We might as well go in boldly."

Dade shakes his head. "No. These demons will tear us apart if they catch us."

"They are going to catch us wherever we go. You think we'll be able to fit in with whatever the fuck's going on in the tower. You saw what the inhabitants of Gluttony looked like. We couldn't pass as human skeletons there and we won't be able to pass as whatever the hell they have going on in Avarice either."

Ro sighs dramatically, rubbing her temples like she's already exhausted by the idea of it. "At least there they might wait five seconds to listen to our side of the story before they rip the heads off our shoulders and eat them."

"That's two for holding out until we are upstairs. Juliette. You get the final vote."

"Tie goes to me," Tate says before I have time to answer.

"Fine!" Dade grits out.

Three pairs of eyes turn to me. I know Dade is right. Getting our asses upstairs sounds a lot more fun than heading into a pit of infernal murdering assholes, and let's be honest, there's probably bacon upstairs too, but when I open my mouth, I can barely believe the words that fall out. "I say we do what Tate says."

Tate licks her lips and slides her eyes over to Dade in a smug expression, before turning them to me and giving me a discrete wink that sends my tummy into a loop that has nothing to do with bacon.

Dade's features darken, but he turns and leads us down the corridor, more than likely to our agonizing deaths.

"You literally just called her crazy for wanting to go to the lounge," Ro whispers in my ear so that Tate and Dade can't hear.

"Sorry," I mumble back.

"Just remember, I'm pregnant and probably a very tasty snack right now."

"You're not the only tasty snack." My eyes flicker to Tate's retreating figure, and I immediately clamp a hand over my mouth, mortified.

Ro just shakes her head, chuckling. "Not interested, huh?"

I groan, utterly embarrassed. I need to get a grip.

"Last chance," Dade mutters as we approach the elevator to the tower.

No one says a word as we stride silently past our final means of escape. The tension hangs thick in the air.

"That's the door to the lounge," Dade says, stopping about twenty feet from it. He glances back at us. "Sure you don't want to change your minds?"

Tate stands firm. My stomach twists, but I'm not backing down now. I made my choice, and I'm going to stick to it, no matter how much my instincts are screaming to turn back.

Dade unfurls his wings, spreading them wide to shield us from the door. The dark feathers cast shadows over all of us, and I can't help but feel grateful for the protection. But Tate, calm and unflinching, steps forward and gently presses down on one of his wings. "Dade, I know you like to think of yourself as some kind of dark protector," she says softly, "but we're a team. We either go in together, or we don't go in at all."

Dade looks like he's about to argue—to insist that maybe we shouldn't go in at all—when the door to the demon's lounge swings open.

My heart plummets, and I brace myself for the inevitable, imagining that any second now, I'm going to be a demon's next meal. But then, to my shock, a figure steps out into the dim corridor.

A shocked voice echoes down the corridor. "Dade?"

I blink in disbelief at the sight of Twila.

"Twila!" Ro gasps, darting forward and nearly knocking her over as she throws her arms around her.

Twila stands there, looking utterly bewildered as she takes in the sight of us. I can't blame her—we must look like we've been through hell... which we literally have. Dade and Tate are both smeared with dried blood, and the rest of us are so worn down from walking for hours that I'm not sure I even have feeling in my feet anymore.

"What...what are you all doing here?" Twila asks, wide-eyed and visibly shaken. "Oh shit! You found a way past the Hellbeast?"

Ro nods, her weariness showing. "We made it, Twila."

"Fuck shit," Twila mutters under her breath, grabbing Ro's arm and pulling her back toward the group. "You can't be here."

I'm beyond exhausted and in no mood for this. "Well, we are."

Twila shakes her head, panic creeping across her face. It hits me that for all the time I spent obsessing over getting down to Avarice, I never stopped to think about what would happen once we arrived.

"They will cremate you," she hisses. "No one gets past

Satan's guards and walks away. Do you think this is a game?"

I let out a humorless laugh. "Yes, actually, I do. This whole shitshow has been a game since we stepped foot into Hell. It's literally called the Inferno Games, so yeah. I think it's a game."

"And we're crushing it," Tate adds, smirking. "So what if we broke a few rules? That last trial had a murderer chasing us down and decapitating people. Nobody in here follows the rules."

Twila's face hardens, her terror replaced with frustration. "This isn't just a broken rule," she snaps. "You've done the one thing no one should ever do. You've got one over on Satan."

"Fucking great!" I say, throwing my arms in the air. "Maybe we'll get a medal."

Twila narrows her eyes, clearly about to fire off a retort when the door to the demon's lounge opens again. In a split second, despite her petite frame, she manages to shove us all toward the elevator. She slams the call button with such force that I half expect it to break.

When the doors slide open, Twila ushers us inside. A tense silence hangs in the air, only broken when the elevator doors open again. "Where are we?" Ro asks, peering out.

"It's the Earthery floor," Twila says, her voice low and tense. "Stay close, act inconspicuously, and don't say a word until I tell you to."

Dade doesn't move, his eyes locked on her with a simmering intensity. "Take me to Quinn. Now!"

Twila spins around to face him, her patience thinning. "Not now. I'm taking you to get something to eat while we figure this mess out. I need some time to think."

His jaw clenches, unmoving. "I swore to protect her, and I couldn't. I'm not stepping out of this elevator until I know I can see Quinn."

Twila's expression softens just a fraction. "Quinn is fine. She's safely in bed. It's not Quinn you need to worry about right now. But if you try to fly up there, I can't stop whatever consequences might come your way. The safest thing for you to do is come with me."

Dade presses his hand against the elevator door, holding it open, his anger and despair almost palpable. I feel it too—the desperate need to see Quinn, to see Felix. But if we push too hard, we might lose everything. I lean in closer, my voice barely above a whisper. "Quinn will never forgive you if you get yourself killed. We've waited for days. We can wait another hour."

He growls low in his throat, but after a long, agonizing pause, he steps out of the elevator. The tension in the air shifts slightly, allowing me to follow him out. As I step onto the marble floor inlaid with gold, I hold my breath. Beside me, Ro whispers, "Wow," under her breath. It's clear this is the Earthery floor—the layout is the same as on the other levels—but here, it feels like stepping into the lobby of an exclusive hotel. A demon in a red uniform with gold braiding stands behind a sleek desk, looking oddly attentive for a change. Usually, the Earthery attendants seem bored.

We follow Twila as she walks quickly, and I can't help but be swept away by the grandeur around us. Towering columns rise on either side, and the arched ceilings are adorned with intricate gold detailing. We're moving past rows of shops and bars, but they're unlike anything I've seen in Hell before. Inferno's bar is in its usual spot, but a quick glance inside reveals rich mahogany paneling, gleaming gold accents, and the warm, inviting glow of a massive chandelier overhead. The scent of polished wood and expensive cologne fills the air—but then my nose catches something else. Food!

Many of the shops we pass feature the most delectable fashions, but we breeze past a patisserie, a boulangerie, and something that looks like an exclusive market. The sight of them makes my stomach churn with longing.

"I hope for Twila's sake there's food wherever she's taking us," I whisper as Ro drags me past a shop with a chocolate fountain in the window. "Otherwise, I might have to resort to eating her."

Tate turns her head and raises an eyebrow, clearly having heard me.

Luckily, Twila saves me from dealing with my runaway mouth by stopping at the Brimstone Bistro. It's like coming back to an old friend. It didn't even exist in Gluttony, because there was no need for restaurants in a place that doesn't have food.

We follow Twila inside. She holds her finger to her lips, signaling us to keep quiet. It's not my mouth making noise. My stomach is starting to sound like bongo drums to Ro's stomach percussion. The smell is enough to break a woman. It smells like nothing on Earth and yet I know whatever it is, I want it. I want lots of it.

"I need the VIP suite," Twila says to the concierge with a level of confidence that takes me by surprise. "Make sure no one bothers us. And have a waiter bring us four plates of the special of the day and a couple of bottles of wine."

I blink, trying to reconcile this commanding presence with the timid Twila I used to know. Where did she go? I guess fucking a literal Hell God has done wonders for her self-esteem.

The room at the back is so dark, I'm barely able to find a seat on the deep red velvet couch that runs along the length of a huge mahogany table. I don't know how they did it, but there's already place settings for four on the table. Even more amazingly, four plates of food, piping hot, at each place setting. "You may as well eat before they kill you all," Twila says, sliding into the head of the table —a chair that can only be described as a throne. I look around at the opulence, feeling like I've stumbled into the realm of royalty. So this is how the other half lives. Tate throws some of the meat from her plate to each of Cerby's heads. I grimace as they lap it up, drool dripping from each of them. I glance at Twila, who isn't bothering with a plate. I guess she's already eaten—or maybe she's just too preoccupied with our impending doom. Not that I care. My stomach's about to crawl out of my throat if I don't eat soon.

The moment the food touches my tongue, I let out a contented sigh. It's a thin slice of meat, though I wouldn't be able to tell you what animal it came from, even for a million dollars. Whatever it is, it's like an edible orgasm. As if on cue, Tate lets out a low grown which is nothing short of sexual, sending my stomach flipping again, but this time not because of the food.

I can't look at her. I don't want to. I have enough going on without adding my sexuality into the mix.

"I need to see Quinn," Dade says, his voice steady, though he doesn't touch the food in front of him. I'm impressed. After weeks of starving, I don't know how he can just sit there without devouring everything.

"I already told you. That's not possible right now," Twila replies, her distress clear. She keeps shaking her head as if she can't believe what's happening. "I can't believe you're here. Hades is going to be pissed."

Dade leans forward, his eyes focused on her. "What do you suggest we do?"

Twila grabs a bottle of wine and pours herself a generous glass. Without thinking, I grab the bottle next, pouring myself a drink before offering it to Ro. She glances at me and pats her stomach, reminding me she's pregnant.

"The baby's survived weeks without food. Surely it deserves a drink?" I joke lamely.

"I could use a drink," Tate says, reaching for the bottle. A jolt of electricity runs through me as she takes it from my grasp, her smile indulgent. I don't know how to feel about that, so I redirect my attention back to Twila. I'm sure Dade just asked her something important, but I've already forgotten what it was.

Twila shrugs. "I don't know. As far as I'm aware, no one has ever descended a circle via the main elevator without prior consent from his highness."

"His highness?" I echo, confusion creeping in.

"Satan," she whispers hurriedly, glancing around the dimly lit room as if we're being watched.

"Does it really matter? We made it here. I'm sure Satan will unleash even worse beasts or traps to prevent us from doing it again. It's not like we actually escaped Hell; we just moved down a circle."

"Yes, but by doing that, you've undermined the Inferno Games, making them almost pointless, and exposed cracks in Satan's supposedly infallible domain."

"It's not that infallible if we could get through with nothing more than a few scraps of fabric," Tate chimes in, popping a cherry tomato into her mouth. I swallow hard at the sight of her.

"Don't you see how that makes it worse?" Twila sighs. "If you had somehow passed it by fighting to the death—"

"Which you said was impossible," I remind her. "And you'll be pleased to know that I gave up on the idea of seducing it to get past."

Tate snickers from across the table.

"Anyway," I press on, trying to ignore Tate's laughter, "you were the one who told us only an angel could pass it. We just dressed Dade up in white and the beast capitulated. If you think about it, this is kind of your fault."

Twila buries her head in her hands, and I suddenly realize I might have pushed her too far when I see her shoulders shaking.

Ro looks at me as though I'm somehow to blame. I was only speaking the truth.

She reaches out and takes Twila's hand in hers.

"No one has to know you helped us. We won't tell anyone, right?" She looks around the table, and everyone nods in agreement. But it doesn't really matter. If what Twila said is true, we're all going to be toast in a few hours, anyway.

Dade clears his throat. "I have no desire to get you in trouble, Twila, but you have access to Hades. He helped us before. Is there any chance he could help us again?"

"Hades isn't a monster. He helped you last time because you saved me. Plus, one of his very own demons was plotting against the games, and he was furious. This time, he has no reason to save you. You've disobeyed his rules. He may be lenient, but I can't make any promises." She sighs. "Facing him is your only chance here. You're going to have to win him over."

"Can't you just hide us?" I ask.

"I'm pretty sure the Inferno Games leadership already knows you're here. I've come to know demons, and most of them are gossips. The concierge would have rushed down to the demon level the moment we arrived at the Brimstone Bar."

I scan the dark room for another exit, but it's so shadowy I can barely see the far walls. "We should go and hide now, then," I insist, rising to my feet. I pick up my half-eaten plate of food. I might be running for my life, but I'm not leaving food behind.

"Then what?" Twila asks.

"Then we get to survive, that's what."

Dade looks up at me, and I can tell he's about to drop some dark, profound wisdom that I probably don't want to hear. "If we hide here and Quinn and the others make it to the next circle, we're no better off than we were in Gluttony."

"Have you tasted this food?" I retort, holding up my plate.

"You won't get back to the main elevator again. Satan might have been beaten by you once, but he won't allow it to happen again."

I slump back down, placing my plate on the table and folding my arms defiantly. "So we just give up and die, then?" I pout.

"I'll take you to Hades," Twila says, "but he's not the only one you'll need to win over. There's also Ballam and..."

"Anthura," Ro finishes for her.

There's a moment of silence around the room. No one knows more than Ro how unlikely it is for Anthura to be on her side... on any of our sides. Anthura hates like it's an

Olympic sport, but she holds a special place in her cold dead heart for Rowena who dared to sleep with her plaything.

It's a somber mood when a demon waiter tries to wrestle my food away from me, only succeeding when I realize he's trying to give me dessert.

"At least when I die, I'll die happy," I muse, taking a bite out of the dessert which tastes somewhere between chocolate fudge cake and heaven.

We all eat quietly. Partly because there is nothing else to say and partly because the food is too delicious to waste by talking. Eventually, we all finish and there's nothing left for us to do. We have to go face the Leadership Team of the Inferno Games and let them decide our fates.

32

IN THE DEN OF DEMONS

ROWENA

My nerves are chattering as we enter the demon's lounge. The last demon lounge I was in, we were chained to the walls and left as demon fodder. It's clear that I'm not the only one remembering that as we follow Twila. The air is thick with a heady mix of smoke and something sweet—perhaps incense or the lingering scent of overindulgence. Dim, flickering lights cast eerie shadows across the room, revealing groups of demons lounging on opulent, crimson velvet sofas, their eyes gleaming with hunger as they glance in our direction.

"Keep your heads down and don't make eye contact," Dade murmurs, his voice low and tense. As if I need reminding. I get the feeling that it's only Twila's presence that's stopping the demons from lunging at us. I can feel Juliette's hand tighten around mine as we weave through the tables, each step making my heart race faster.

"Maybe they won't notice us," I whisper, though I know it's a futile hope. We're fresh meat in a den of predators and have a dog with three heads trailing us. Just as I say this, a demon with glittering scales and a wicked grin leans over, his eyes locking onto mine.

"Look what we have here," he says, his voice smooth like silk but dripping with malice. "A little snack for the evening."

I swallow hard, my throat dry. "We're just passing through," I stammer, my instincts screaming at me to run, but the weight of Dade's grip on my shoulder keeps me rooted in place.

"Passing through?" the demon echoes, leaning back in his seat, his laughter rumbling like distant thunder. "Where's the fun in that? We don't often get visitors down here who aren't already on the menu."

Before I can respond, Twila steps forward and places herself between me and the demon. "We're here on business," she declares, her voice steady.

The demon raises an eyebrow, clearly intrigued but not yet convinced. "Business, you say? And what business exactly would that be?"

Twila hesitates, glancing back at us before continuing. "I'm here with Hades, as you well know. If you lay a finger on me or my friends, he'll have you flayed."

The demon's grin widens, revealing rows of sharp teeth. "I don't see Hades here now."

My heart sinks, dread pooling in my stomach as the tension thickens. Cerby lets out a low growl. With a scaly finger, the demon reaches out and trails it down Twila's cheek leaving a scorch mark. She recoils from his touch, but before she can regain her composure, his hand is suddenly slapped away.

A long breath escapes my lips when I see Hades towering over the slender demon.

"Maybe you should invest in an optician, Danak," he says, his voice low and commanding.

"Yes, sorry, sir," the demon stammers, dropping from his chair into a low bow.

Hades leans closer, his expression darkening. "You will be very sorry if you even think about touching a hair on her head again."

The demon sniffles incoherently before Hades kicks him clear across the room. I cheer inwardly at the sight of the demon being sent flying, but my relief vanishes when I notice that Hades' anger is now directed at us.

"Come with me," he orders.

We all scramble to keep up as he strides toward a private room at the back of the lounge. It's dark and smoky and, though as opulent as the Brimstone Bistro, has an air of unkemptness.

"Sit!" Hades commands. The four of us sit on a plush velvet covered bench seat.

"What is the meaning of this? How did you even get here?"

"They got past Satan's Hellbeast in Gluttony and came down by way of the main elevator," Twila mutters.

Hades stares at her, his face darkening. "And you knew about this?"

Tate speaks before Twila has a chance to. "She saw us wandering about down here and I guess felt sorry for us. She took us for some food and when we told her how we got down here, she demanded that we come to you."

"She was adamant!" Juliette adds. I shoot her a look but she's too busy looking at Tate, who, in turn, is staring defiantly at Hades as if daring him to question her version of events.

"It is impossible to get past Satan's protections," Hades says.

Tate stands up and steps over to him. "Not only did we get past Satan's beast, we did it with ease."

I gawp at the balls on the woman. Hades almost seems impressed. Tate is tall for human, but Hades still towers over her.

"Did I not tell you to sit?" he growls, his voice low and menacing.

Tate holds her ground, and I fear that instead of merely feeding us to the demons, Hades might choose to devour her himself. His eyes darken, the atmosphere thickening with tension, until Juliette grabs the back of Tate's dress and yanks her back down to the bench. "Let's save it for the trial, eh?"

Hades' gaze shifts to Juliette, his expression unreadable. "Who said there was to be a trial? You broke the covenant of the Inferno Games, and for that, you will be punished."

I wince at his words. I know all too well what their idea of punishment entails—it's never a simple reprimand or a warning.

"Please don't hurt them," Twila says. "They are my friends."

"Friends or not. I cannot let them go," Hades growls. "If word got out, there would be a mutiny. These games have worked for thousands of years and I will not let them fail now because of sheer good luck on getting past a Hellbeast."

My heart plummets as Hades pulls out his Hell Cell and begins typing something into it.

"Anthura is coming down. I will let her decide your fate because I trust she knows you better than I do."

"What's that supposed to mean?" Juliette asks, her brow furrowing with confusion.

"I think it means she'll know how to torture us better than Hades can," I reply, my voice barely above a whisper.

Hades remains silent, but the look on his face confirms my suspicion. He's passing the buck. What an effing coward.

The moment Anthura steps into the room, her face lights up with pure joy. When her eyes settle on me, her grin turns malicious. "Well, well, well. If it isn't Robert, coming to fuck my boyfriend again."

Before anyone can react, Jules races across the room and stands in front of Anthura. "Call her Rowena, you fucking monster!"

Anthura raises an eyebrow at Jules, a smirk playing on her lips. "I'd have thought watching your husband brutally murdered might have cured you of your insolence, but it seems not. Maybe you should watch your friend get brutally murdered, and then you'll finally learn not to stand up to me. You always were a fucking annoyance who thought too much of herself."

In a flash of white, Tate steps in between Jules and Anthura. "You'll have to kill me before I let you get your claws into Juliette... or Rowena."

"And why the fuck do you care?" Anthura snaps, her gaze icy. "Hades. I don't know why you even asked me here. You know my thoughts on the matter. Kill them in whatever manner will hurt most. Let the demons devour them. I don't actually care, as long as I don't have to look at any of their miserable faces ever again."

She sniffs at Tate, then turns her gaze to me. "Except this one. This one is mine."

I think we've all been silenced into shock, but as

Anthura steps round Tate and Jules and grabs me by the arm, yanking me to my feet, Dade stands up and swipes at Anthura, knocking her to the floor.

"You do not treat a lady like that," he snarls. "Kill us if you will, but let us die together and let us die with dignity." He turns to Hades. "Anthura is a witch that isn't fit to lick Rowena's boots. She shouldn't be in charge of if or how we die. You are the true leader of these games. You should make the decision."

Hades narrows his eyes as he regards Dade. It's clear he's not used to being stood up to, especially by someone who is usually so quiet. The pair of them facing up to each other is breathtaking. Dade with his wings outstretched and his shirt ripped to shreds and bloody thanks to the hellbeast and Hades, who stands a head taller, looking magnificent and godlike. If I wasn't about to be murdered in the most brutal way possible, I'd almost be turned on by watching them square up to each other. "Nevertheless, I tasked the job to her," Hades answers. I notice he doesn't bother to help Anthura to her feet.

If Hades wants to do what Anthura wants, then our fates are sealed. Dade will never see Quinn again. I'll never see Felix. I hate how there's a flutter in my belly at the thought of him, but then with amazement I realize it's not my stomach that's fluttering, but the baby. Despite everything, I clap my hand to my stomach. Joy pushes out the despair. "I can feel the baby!" I say with almost a laugh. It's absurd. We'll both be dead soon, both me and my child, but here, right now, in this moment, he or she is telling me not to give up.

Jules rushes over to me and puts her hand on mine. There's a moment of utter stillness as we wait for the baby to kick again. It's like time has stood still. For the briefest of seconds it's beautiful.

You fucking disgusting bitch!" Anthura snarls, shattering my moment of hope. I instinctively step back, knowing she's about to come at me again, claws bared and ready for blood.

"What's going on? A party without me?"

Everyone turns toward the door to see a man in a sharp suit, impeccably dressed, with a slight goatee that gives him an air of smug confidence. He exudes authority, and the tension in the room shifts slightly as he strides in, his eyes gleaming with interest as they land on the chaos unfolding.

"Ah, I see we have a bit of a situation," he observes, glancing around the room, his gaze lingering on Anthura's seething form before shifting to me, curiosity glimmering in his eyes. "Care to enlighten me?"

Anthura's expression darkens, her claws retracting slightly as she realizes her chances of lashing out might be compromised by this unexpected arrival. "Stay out of this, Baal," she snaps, but there's a tremor in her voice that hints at her uncertainty. Is this finally someone that Anthura is scared of?

Baal, who I assume is the same Ballam that Twila mentioned, steps fully into the room, shutting the door behind him.

"Hades," he says smoothly, "Care to enlighten me as to what's happening in my circle?"

"I didn't want to burden you," Hades responds, his voice tight. "Twila found these contestants running through the corridors."

"Ex-contestants," Anthura interrupts, her voice sharp. "They were eliminated in the last circle."

Ballam's brow furrows in confusion. "Then explain to me how they're here if they failed. Don't tell me your demons brought them down by accident, Hades?"

Hades shifts, visibly uncomfortable. "No. They came down on their own. They got past the Hellbeast."

Ballam's eyes widen in surprise. "Past the Hellbeast? Without assistance? Remarkable. How did you manage that? I was informed that passage was... impossible."

Tate steps forward, her voice steady. "I dressed up as an angel. It let us pass."

Ballam sidles up to her, his smile curling in a way that makes the air feel colder. "And how did you know to do that?"

Tate hesitates, uncertainty flickering in her eyes for the first time. "We saw it in the Earthery," she lies smoothly. "If you don't believe us, ask the demon in Gluttony. We just copied what we saw."

"Ingenious," Ballam murmurs. He straightens, glancing between them with newfound intrigue. "So now that you're here, what do we do with you?"

Tate lifts her chin, her voice full of defiance. "You're going to let us back into the Inferno Games."

She says it as if the decision had never gone against us at all.

"Like Hell," Anthura snarls, her fury palpable. "We're going to kill the fucking nuisances."

Ballam licks his lips, his gaze traveling over Tate with obvious interest. I can't shake the feeling that her ethereal appearance is going to play in our favor. "Let's not make any hasty decisions. Weren't you telling me just this morning that half the contestants were beheaded by persons unknown? We could do with more people in the games... in case the same thing happens again."

It's clear he's needling Anthura who, I suspect, has no clue who's been murdering people.

"Not on my soul will I let you add them to the games," Anthura retorts, her voice laced with venom.

Hades bursts into laughter, a deep, booming sound. "Anthura. You have no soul. You never did. Let them in. Ballam's right. Even with the contestants from the other towers joining us, we need more people should the same unfortunate circumstances of the last trial arise again."

I let out a low breath, incredulity washing over me. That's it? It was that easy? We're actually going to get back in? I can hardly believe our luck.

But Hades' voice turns cold as he gestures dismissively. "Better let this one in too."

He shoves Twila toward Ballam, sending her stumbling to the floor.

"Hades. Why?" she cries out, panic flaring in her eyes.

Hades' voice turns cold, dark, and twisted as he glares at Twila. "I'm not the fool you think I am," he growls, his words dripping with venom. "Maybe your friends did use the Earthery, but the Earthery wouldn't have shown them an angel unless they already had that image in their minds."

He steps closer to her, his presence suffocating. "Now, I didn't tell them. And judging by the desperately pathetic look on Anthura's face, she didn't tell them either." His eyes narrow, glowing with malice. "That leaves only you."

"Hades, please!" Twila's voice breaks, trembling with fear. Tears brim in her eyes as she looks up at him, pleading. Hades steps over her, cold and uncaring. "Baal, do what you will with her. The games start in roughly two hours. I'll see you there." I hold my breath as he strides out through the door, slamming it behind him.

33

RICHES
FELIX

I'm awake long before my portal beeps. I've been awake for hours, maybe since they dumped me here. They must drug us between circles, because the last thing I remember was being in the Earthery, and then—nothing. Just darkness. Now, I'm starving, but even that's not enough to make me want to check out whatever new hellhole they've dragged me into. It's all the same—the same twisted mind games, the same psychological bullshit.

I haven't opened my eyes yet. I had a dream about Ro, and I'm not ready to let it go. Her voice, her touch, they felt so damn real. It's the first sense of peace I've had since this nightmare began, and I'm clinging to it like a lifeline. I know the second I open my eyes, it'll all disappear, leaving me with the cold, hard reality of this place.

When the Portal finally goes off, its annoying buzz drags me back, forcing me to face another day in this living nightmare. I sigh, letting the dream slip through my fingers like sand. Slowly, I start to wake up. The bed feels warm around me, softer than usual, which makes me pause. Groggy, I blink against the haze of sleep, my hands running over the sheets.

They're different. Softer, almost silky, like they belong in some fancy hotel and not... wherever the hell I am now. The air smells clean, too. Fresh linen mixed with something I don't recognize—sandalwood, maybe? Definitely not what I'm used to in Hell. This is more like I was accustomed to on Earth. My pulse picks up as I crack my eyes open. I'm not in my room. The ceiling is impossibly high; the walls gleaming with subtle hints of marble and gold accents. Panic surges through me as I push myself up. Where the fuck am I? This isn't my bed, my room, my anything. This feels all too familiar and, at the same time, not familiar at all. For a second I wonder if I'm back on Earth in one of the hundreds of swanky hotels I frequent.

"Fuck!" I run my hands through my hair, my breath catching in my throat as my eyes scan the space.

A massive window stretches across the entire far wall, flooding the room with an eerie red light. So I am still in Hell. I stand, my legs shaky, and stumble toward the edge of the bed, my bare feet sinking into the plush, cream-colored carpet. Everything feels too perfect—too pristine.

I glance around the room—opulent, untouched, like a space carved out for someone of impossible wealth or status. For me? Velvet chairs sit near a sleek, black marble coffee table, a vase of fresh white orchids perfectly centered on top, as if waiting for someone important to arrive.

"What the fuck?" The words slip out before I can stop them.

I know I've never been here before, but the vibe is

unsettlingly familiar. I've stayed in places like this before. Back when I was alive. Back when luxury penthouses were my norm. But now? Now it feels like a sick joke. Like some twisted reminder of a life I no longer have. Of a life before Ro. Ro's face flashes into my mind—her body beneath mine, the sound of her moaning when I made her come, the intoxicating scent of her skin. There's no way I could have dreamed something so vivid, so visceral. Which leaves me with one question: Where the actual fuck am I?

I glance around again. The room is as big as Anthura's penthouse, but ten times more luxurious. Where her place had been sterile, this is the pinnacle of refined decadence. I cross the room, heading for the bathroom. As I step inside, I'm momentarily gratified to see my own belongings scattered near a marble sink. So this is my room now?

Then it hits me. We're in the fourth circle. Avarice... Greed. That's why it feels so familiar. I spent my life taking everything I could, never giving back. This is the circle I should have been in right from the start. If anyone lived a life of greed, it was me. Ro and my child are somewhere above me, trapped in a circle they'll never escape. I'll never see Ro again. I'll never meet my son or daughter. The thought rips through me, and the luxury around me suddenly feels cold, empty. Worthless. All of it.

I take one last look around the room, and the hollow echo of it sinks in. The marble, the gold, the velvet—it's all a farce. It's a gilded cage, and I'm its latest occupant. And there's the rub. This is how Hell gets under your skin. The demons don't need to chase you with pitchforks and fire. They know us better than we know ourselves. Hell itself reads our minds, our desires, and it twists those dreams into something sickening.

This isn't just torture. It's personalized torment. A prison dressed up in luxury, a trap disguised as everything I ever wanted. All of it is meaningless. None of this matters when Ro is gone and my child will never know me.

I fall back on the bed, the soft duvet pooling around me like a suffocating wave. This is how they break you— by giving you everything you ever dreamed of, while taking away the only things that ever really mattered.

My portal beeps again, and this time I pick it up and read it. It's from Anthura, which almost makes me hurl it across the room, but then I see it's a group message.

WILL ALL INFERNO GAMES CONTESTANTS MEET IN THE ATRIUM AT 10AM SHARP.

I look at the time. Fifteen minutes to get dressed and haul my ass downstairs. Entering the walk-in wardrobe, I stop in my tracks when I see the rows of designer suits, all perfectly pressed and hung in neat order. Tailored jackets, silk shirts, shoes polished to a mirror shine—everything looks like it was pulled straight from the pages of a fashion magazine. The wardrobe itself is larger than my whole room in Gluttony. This is how I'm used to living. There's nothing in here that I've not owned at one point of my life or another, but now that they are here, it reminds me how shallow my old life used to be. I reach out and run my fingers over the soft fabric of a suit that probably costs more than most people's first apartment. My name is even stitched into the inside label. It's unsettling, like they've tailored everything to my exact taste and size. I pull down a charcoal suit, trying not to think too hard about who's pulling the strings here, and start getting dressed.

As I walk toward the massive windows, it becomes clear that I'm not in a penthouse after all. The curved donut shaped balcony is still there, but it's also made from chrome and glass, allowing me to see the whole tower. Every apartment has floor to ceiling windows. Finally, I get it. Everyone has everything here, but then so does everyone else. Part of the fun of being insanely rich was that I could look down on people. Everything was exclusive. Here, nothing is. I laugh silently as I pull the glass door open and step out onto the balcony. I'm in Avarice and everyone is rich. The irony doesn't escape me. This is where I should have come right at the start. I wasn't good enough to go to Heaven. I know that now. Ro and Juliette and Quinn and even Dade were there because they never really did anything wrong in their lives beyond not believing in a deity. I did everything wrong. I guess I was pulled into Purgatory somehow because of Quinn. We were both shot with the same bullet. It's not against the realm of possibility that we are linked in this hellhole. It occurs to me that Quinn is the only person I know in this circle that isn't a demon. Except Orlin and he doesn't count.

I look up and see the familiar glass-domed ceiling, the same one featured in every tower I've stayed in so far. Beyond the glass, the red clouds swirl ominously, churning like a restless sea. I wonder how far above those clouds Ro is, if she can feel me thinking about her. The ache in my chest deepens, but I push it down. No use in dwelling.

Then, because I know if I don't move, Anthura will

come pounding on my door. I round the balcony and begin to jog down the stairs.

The atrium has the same layout as the other towers, but it couldn't be more different. Gone are the wide, open spaces with modern furniture and clean lines. Instead, old leather armchairs have been placed haphazardly on the gleaming marble floors, their weathered surfaces speaking of luxury and age. The room reeks of money, with just a faint whiff of cigars lingering in the air, like a distant memory of a time when men sat in smoky lounges making deals worth millions.

My stomach growls, a reminder of just how long it's been since I've eaten anything. But checking out the food will have to wait. My eyes sweep over the canteen—or what used to be the canteen. The massive, communal dining hall with its cheap booths and giant screen is gone, replaced by a row of what look like exclusive restaurants, each one decked out in dark wood, gleaming silver, and soft lighting.

Of course, they're exclusive to everyone. I let out a dry laugh. This place is trying so hard to remind us that we're all on the same playing field now.

I sink into one of the leather armchairs, letting it swallow me up as I scope out the competition. My eyes settle on Quinn, who flashes me a half-smile. It's strange to think how Hell has leveled us. All those months ago, I was a billionaire, and she was just one step above a street urchin. Now? Now we're both just playing this same twisted game. I don't bother looking at the other contestants. I barely know them and in a few weeks, I'll be leaving most of them behind. No point in making friends down here—that only ever bites you in the ass.

My eyes shift to the leadership team. Hades is here,

but his dark little shadow isn't clinging to his side for once. Strange—she's usually glued to him. I don't dwell on Anthura, though; she's looking more furious than usual, and frankly, whatever's twisted her up today isn't my problem. I catch sight of Moloch trailing behind her, like a kicked dog, skulking back when she snaps at him. I almost feel bad for the guy. Almost. He might be spineless, but he sure didn't sign up for this circus.

Then there's the guy standing between them, notable only in his blandness. I know his type well. Hell, I used to be one of them—overconfident, money-obsessed, egotistical, the kind who measures self-worth by the number of zeroes in his account. Seeing him is like staring at an old reflection, a reminder of who I was back when boardrooms and quarterly profits defined me. No doubt he'll have the rest of the room crawling up his ass by the time he's done with his speech. Everyone but me.

"Good morning, everyone. I'm Ballam. I oversee the games here in Avarice. I trust you're finding your accommodations satisfactory?" he says, his voice dripping with polished charm. "This round will be unlike anything you've encountered so far. You've got the best of the best here—the finest rooms, the finest food. Downstairs in the Earthery, we have the most luxurious shops and the most decadent restaurants. Whatever you desire, you'll find it here."

Someone farther down the row yells, "Yeah, baby!" Ballam's mouth pulls tight, and he shoots them a cold glare before quickly smoothing it into a thin-lipped smile. I've heard spiels like this before. Hell, I've given them. Promises of the world, but there's always a catch. Always something they aren't telling you. I'm too seasoned in

Hell's games to believe for a second that all this opulence isn't just a layer of glossy deception.

"Each of you will be assigned a servant," Ballam says, his voice cold and matter-of-fact. "A personal butler, maid, aide—whatever you prefer to call it. Unlike the demons you've dealt with in other circles, these are humans. Humans here for their punishment. Each one of them has committed a grievous sin. So, spare yourself any qualms about how you choose to treat them."

I glance around the atrium, noting the people gathered here—women draped in furs, men wearing watches worth more than a typical salary. They reek of wealth, the type who flaunt it at every opportunity. The only person not looking like he was born into wealth is Orlin, but he's kinda special in that he'd look pathetic in whatever he chose to wear.

"What I don't get," I say, finally speaking up, "is why these humans look like the elite. I've known people like them. They don't work for others, don't bow down. They sure as hell aren't maids or butlers."

Ballam's smile tightens. It's clear he's not used to being questioned, but I'm not here to play nice, and he knows it. Meanwhile, some of the other contestants look all too eager at the idea of having servants.

"Let me clarify," he says, his voice a little cooler now. "They aren't servants. They're slaves. They're yours for the duration of your stay in this circle. Each one has been specifically chosen from those who have stood up to me in the past. They will obey, whether they want to or not."

In life, I had sycophants lining up to win my favor, but the idea of actually owning a slave? It makes me sick.

"Can these slaves be forced to do anything?" asks a

voice from the other end of the couches, someone I don't recognize.

Ballam barely holds back an eye-roll. "As I said, they're at your beck and call."

"So... they can't say no?"

One of the new women shakes her head slightly, her face twisted in disgust. She knows where this is going, and it's nauseating.

"They won't have the power to say no, if that's what you're asking," Ballam replies with a bored sigh. "Now, enough with the questions. You've all been through numerous trials to get here, so there isn't much left for me to explain. The tower has the same layout as the others, but rest assured, it surpasses them in both style and decadence. I suggest you take the time to explore the dining options and relax before the games start tomorrow."

I stand up, not waiting for any more of Ballam's smug instructions. I've heard enough, and the last thing I need is some forced servant. There's only one person I need, and she cowers to no one. She'd laugh in Ballam's face and tear down every illusion in this place just for the hell of it. But she isn't here. And I'm not going to find her by sitting around, listening to their twisted version of generosity. I stride toward one of the restaurants. The man who asked about the slaves falls into stride with me. "You're Felix Barclay. I recognize you from the Times Man of the Year. I'm Don Smith."

"Hmm," I mumble. I already don't give a shit.

"You're fucking awesome. I can't believe I'm now as rich as you. Look what they put in my wardrobe."

He lifts his hand and shows me a Patak Phillipe. It's the very same watch I was showing off to my friends before I was shot. The fucking irony.

"Cool about the slaves, huh? I hope I get a fucking supermodel. You get me?"

I think of all the supermodels I've known, and I've known a lot. Yes, I've slept with many of them. Not once did I have a conversation with them that wasn't about my needs, my wants. It was always about me.

"Whoever you get, treat them well. Get to know them. You might be surprised."

He gives me an odd look, as though I've lost my mind. "Nah, I'm going to fuck them senseless and get them to bring me food. I mean, what's the fucking point otherwise, huh?"

"Of course you are," I reply, my voice heavy with sarcasm. "If you'll excuse me," I don't bother to smile as I pull open a restaurant door and stride in, leaving him behind.

The inside of the restaurant doesn't disappoint, with its towering white marble columns and sparkling chandeliers. Every inch of the space oozes luxury, from the velvet-upholstered chairs to the intricate gold trim on the walls. The far wall features a fresco so exquisite it wouldn't surprise me if Michelangelo had painted it himself.

"Are you requiring a table for one, sir?" A pompous concierge asks, his nose already tilted upward. Like all the other demons here, this one is adorned in gold.

"No, actually. I want two burgers, two portions of fries, and two chocolate milkshakes to go."

The concierge raises his nose even higher, sniffing as though the air itself has offended him. "Sir?"

"You can do that, right?"

"Why, yes, but may I suggest the Wagyu beef topped with foie gras and truffles on a base of San Francisco sourdough with—"

"No," I cut him off, grinning. "I want the cheapest, greasiest meat, the cheapest bread, and normal potato fries with lots of salt."

The look of disgust that flickers across his face is carefully masked behind a professional smile. "And would sir like a seat while he is waiting?"

"Nope. I'll wait right here."

The concierge, clearly affronted but maintaining his composure, summons a demon waiter and relays my order. The waiter disappears for a moment and reappears almost instantly, balancing two burgers artfully on gold-edged porcelain plates, the milkshakes inexplicably served in champagne flutes.

I shake my head. "I don't think you understand what I want. Pretend we're in a cheap burger joint. I want my food in paper bags, and the drinks in cups with more than a sip and a half in them. And no fancy cutlery. I'll be eating these with my fingers."

His expression tightens just enough for me to know I'm getting under his skin, and that's exactly what I want.

Eventually, I have exactly what I asked for. My stomach is almost tearing itself out with hunger, but there's something I have to do. I step through to the platform and summon it.

I've been Felix Barclay, billionaire, asshole ceo for long enough. Rowena made me see who I was and I don't like it. Meeting Don only strengthened my resolve. I can't be a better man for Rowena anymore, but I sure as hell can try to be a better person for me.

I step into my room, and the first thing I notice is the cage in the corner. Inside is a young girl, no older than sixteen, dressed in the same gold material as the demon staff, but the scraps of fabric barely cover her. It's sickening, and the reality of this circle slams into me all over again. They're catering to the worst kinds of people, and until a few weeks ago, I was one of them.

The girl looks up at me, her eyes wide with shock, trembling in her cage. It's fucking disgusting. Without a second thought, I head to the wardrobe and pull out one of the robes. The lock on her cage clicks open, controlled by my portal, just like everything else in this hellhole.

I open the door and hand her the robe. "Here, put this on."

Her eyes flash gold for a moment, and she steps out of the cage with a robotic movement, taking the robe and slipping it on. Once it's wrapped around her, her eyes return to their original warm brown, but the robe itself disappears. Hell magic? Of course they want her half naked and suffering. I pull one of the sheets from the bed and drape it over her and this time it seems to stick.

"Here," I say, handing her a bag with a burger and fries. "I'm Felix. I don't give a damn what the bosses here say. You're not going to be my slave, nor my servant."

She hesitates, her eyes brightening with a flicker of hope.

"Sit on the bed," I tell her. "You won't be going back in that cage again."

Her eyes flash gold once more, and she moves mechanically toward the bed. It's as if the magic in her compels her to follow my orders. Once her eyes fade back to brown, she smiles, looking relieved as she sits down. "Thank you so much. I'm Jen." She pulls the burger from the bag, grinning wide. "I'm ravenous. This smells like heaven." Her gaze shifts, unsure. "But... I don't think I'm allowed to eat without your permission."

What the hell have they done to her? She's just a kid. "Just eat it. It's yours. I got it for you."

Her eyes flash gold again as soon as I say it, confirming what I'd already suspected. It's every time I give her a direct command, every time I say something, she has to follow. That's the magic—why she's a slave here. Thankfully, her eyes return to brown as she tears into the burger.

I sit beside her, unwrapping my own meal. She's right about one thing: it does taste amazing.

34

WHO'S IN CHARGE NOW?

QUINN

Holy shit! "Dade?"

I can barely breathe as his name leaves my lips, my heart pounding in my chest. There he is, trapped in a cage, his wings folded tightly around him in the cramped space, but his face... his face lights up with the most un-Dadelike grin I've ever seen when he spots me.

"Valentine!"

I don't think. My feet move on their own, racing across the room so fast I nearly slip on the slick marble. Nothing else matters. The world shrinks to just me and him, and I can't get to him fast enough.

"How did you get here?" My voice is breathless, almost shaking.

"My girlfriend happens to be a genius."

His words are light, teasing, but I can hear the relief behind them. I fumble with my Hell Cell, unlocking the cage with trembling hands. The second it clicks open, I don't hesitate—I throw myself into him, crashing against his body with a force that knocks the wind out of both of us.

Our lips meet in a desperate collision. It's not soft, not gentle. It's raw and hungry, every emotion we've buried, every fear and hope crashing together in that kiss. His hands are in my hair, pulling me closer, as if he's afraid I'll disappear. I feel the warmth of his wings as they unfold, wrapping around us like a shield from the rest of the world.

"Fuck," I whisper against his lips, pulling back just enough to look at him. My fingers trace the line of his jaw, memorizing every inch of him, like I'm trying to convince myself he's really here. "I thought I lost you."

Dade's eyes soften, his thumb brushing across my cheek. "You didn't. You never will. I will always come for you, Valentine."

His words are a promise, but there's something more —something deeper. I kiss him again, softer this time, the taste of him grounding me in a way nothing else ever could. Each kiss is like a lifeline, tethering me back to reality, to him.

I pull him closer, my body melting into his as our kiss deepens. It's fierce, burning with everything we've been through—survival, fear, love—and it makes my heart ache in the best way. The world around us fades, and for a moment, it's just him and me, tangled in a kiss that says everything words can't.

"I love you," I whisper against his lips, feeling the truth of it down to my bones.

"Let's get out of this cage and you can show me just how much," he teases.

"I don't know," I say, looking him up and down. He's

wearing nothing but a gold cloth. Beneath the pair of us is a gold cushion.

"I think I want you to fuck me in here."

The moment I say it, his eyes turn gold and his face slackens. "As you wish."

He starts pawing at my clothes with no finesse. It's almost robotic in his movements.

It's not sexy. He rips away my shirt, exposing my bra. "Dade! Stop!"

His eyes flash again before settling into a deep, familiar black-brown, the wild intensity gone as quickly as it appeared. I push myself up and stumble out of the cage, clutching the torn remnants of my shirt around my shoulders. I can't stop staring at him, barely able to reconcile the person I thought I knew with this altered version of him.

"Sorry, my Valentine," he says softly, a grimace flickering across his face. "They've cursed me. I'm compelled to do whatever you say. I have no control over myself when you give me directions. It's... my punishment for coming to find you." He pulls himself from the cage and stands before me. His aura is dark, but warm. "It is my curse to bear, not yours. I shall leave and find somewhere else to be until I can control myself around you."

"Don't even think about it, Dade Angelis. I've never been able to control myself around you. Not once, not ever. It's about time you saw what it's like to be so completely under another's spell."

Dade's eyes flicker with lust. "I have always been under your spell, Valentine. You have always enslaved my heart." His voice deepens into a growl. "It's just that this..."

"Could actually be fun?" I interject, a teasing smile playing on my lips.

This time when Dade kisses me, it's tender, his lips soft and apologetic against mine. The shift in him is immediate, and I can feel the difference in every brush of his fingers along my skin. His kiss isn't rushed or desperate now; it's slow, reverent, like he's trying to pour everything he feels into it—his regret, his longing, his love.

He looks down and notices a scratch on my breast where he was too heavy handed with ripping my shirt.

"I'm so sorry," he whispers against my lips, his forehead resting against mine. "I didn't mean to hurt you." He leans down and plants a soft kiss on my breast where the faint lines of his fingernails scratched me.

"I know," I interrupt softly, pulling him up. I cup his face in my hands, forcing him to look at me. "You don't have to apologize. None of this is your fault."

"I don't want to hurt you," he murmurs, his voice raw. "But I can't control this."

For a moment, we just stand there, wrapped in each other. His arms come around me, protective and warm, and for the first time since stepping into this tower, I feel safe. He presses his lips to my forehead, then pulls back just enough to look at me.

"So you're saying you have to do whatever I say?" I say with a sly grin.

"Valentine," he warns, but there's no anger in it.

"If I told you to lie on the bed, you'd have to do it?"

"I guess there's only one way to find out."

I lick my lips. This is going to be interesting.

"Dade?"

"Valentine?"

"Go and lie on the bed. And while you're at it, take that stupid gold loin cloth off."

His eyes flash gold and he does exactly as I say, albeit in a mechanical way. The end result is the same, though. He's naked and in my bed. Exactly where I want him.

"I could have some fun with this," I giggle, inspecting his erect penis. I climb on top of him, noting his black-brown eyes. "Just kiss me."

I lean down to kiss him, but the moment my lips touch his, I feel the tension beneath his skin. It's not the heated anticipation I'm used to—it's something different. His hands move up to my hips, but the way they grip me feels forced, mechanical. The gold flash in his eyes from a moment ago still lingers, and it unsettles me.

I pull back slightly, hovering over him. "Dade?"

His gaze softens, but there's an edge there, like he's fighting against something. "Valentine, I want you—always—but this isn't me. It's the curse. I can't be what you need when I have no control. You need to stop telling me what to do. Trust that I want to do it, anyway. You have no idea."

The raw honesty in his voice cuts through my playful mood, and I can feel the weight of his words settle between us. I was teasing, thinking we could have fun with this, but now it feels wrong. Like the curse is trying to strip away what makes us, us.

I brush a hand through his hair, sighing as I shift off him. "I want you, Dade. Not this curse. Not some puppet controlled by Hell."

His hands slide up to my waist, this time gentle, real, and he pulls me back down to him, his lips brushing against my forehead. "There's nothing in this infernal curse that means I can't command you though, he says playfully, lifting me up and gently lowering me onto him. I let out a long sigh that turns into a moan as he thrusts his hips up, catching me off guard.

"Who's in charge now?" he asks, gripping my waist. I couldn't get away from him even if I wanted to, which I most definitely don't.

"You are," I whisper, leaning into him. I'm more than happy to let him lead and as he shifts us round so that he's on top, I know I prefer it this way. Dade's hands tighten around my waist as he moves us effortlessly, shifting his weight to hover above me. His breath is hot against my neck as he whispers, "That's right. I'm in charge now." There's a playful growl in his voice, but it's laced with desire, and it sends a shiver down my spine.

His hips press into me with a slow, deliberate rhythm, each movement drawing out a gasp from my lips. I reach up, fingers tangling in his hair as I pull him closer, needing more of him, needing to feel the connection we've fought so hard for. Every thrust pulls me deeper into the moment, the heat between us building until it's all I can focus on.

Dade's gaze locks onto mine, and I can see the intensity there, but it's no longer forced. This is us—no curse, no commands—just pure, unfiltered desire. His lips find mine, and the kiss is hungry, full of passion, his hands exploring every inch of me as if he's trying to memorize me.

"I've got you," he murmurs against my lips, his voice low and full of promise. And he does. Completely.

Afterwards, breathless and sweaty, with me cocooned in his arms, I listen to him tell me how he got past the hellbeast in the exact way I told Tate. Tears fill my eyes when I find out that my best friends are here and are back in the games, albeit as slaves like Dade.

"I need to go find them. I'd like you to come with me, But I'm not going to ask you to."

He kisses my nose and slips out of bed. "You don't have to command me to do the right thing, Valentine. I wouldn't be here without them. We also need to get you some food. Your stomach gurgling almost put me off my stride earlier."

"I've not eaten," I admit. I'm starving.

I head to the wardrobe and find a dress that I'm pretty sure I've seen on the cover of a fashion magazine before now. When I look for something for Dade, I come up empty. "There are no clothes in here for you. Didn't they give you anything to wear?" I peek around the door to find Dade holding up the hideous gold loin cloth. "I think they expect me to wear this. It's a mark of a slave."

I laugh before realizing he's being serious. "You can't wear that. You'll have to wear one of the suits in here. They are all my size, so they'll be a squeeze, but anything is better than that."

I throw him the biggest pair of pants I can find, but the second he tries stepping into them, they disappear in his hands. I throw him another pair and the same thing happens. I find both pairs hanging back up in my closet as though neither of us had touched them.

"It's this infernal slave curse they've got me under," Dade growls as a shirt of mine disappears into thin air and somehow finds itself back on a hanger in my closet. Reluctantly, he puts the loincloth back on.

With his long dark hair and his black wings, not to mention the dark expression on his face, he does look sexy as all hell. If he was planning to stay in my room all day, it would be fine, but out in public. Dade is the most private person I know and this will kill him.

"How about I go out on my own and get us both some food? I'll see what I can do about the clothes situation too."

Dade looks murderous, but he nods his head. Being on his own in a room isn't the problem. Dade has always liked his own company, but being forced to do it, is not something he's going to cope with.

Downstairs, I'm once again struck by awe at the grandeur around me. In life, I cleaned the houses of the rich, but this place makes those look like hovels. It's palatial, every detail dripping with wealth. Under any other circumstances, I'd be floored to be in a place like this. But here, it's just a façade—a pretty shell over the ugly truth. In these games, it doesn't matter how luxurious the surroundings are. A jewel-encrusted knife can kill you just as easily as a rusty one.

I don't know where Juliette, Rowena, or Tate have been assigned, so I head toward the row of restaurants to see if they're inside. I try a few places before I hear shouting behind me. I pause, listening closely, and there it is—that voice I'd recognize anywhere. Felix. Probably in another screaming match with Anthura. My stomach growls, a sharp reminder that I came here to get food. I've never been this hungry in my life. But something in Felix's tone gives me pause. It's raw, more heated than usual.

I shouldn't care. After everything he did—what happened to Jenny, the way he treated all of us—I should walk away. But he could've killed me in the Labyrinth, and he didn't. That complicates things.

With a heavy sigh, I turn and follow the sound of Felix's voice, cursing myself for caring. It's coming from near the platform entrance and the back stairs. I ease the door open slightly and peek through. My blood boils instantly at what I see.

One of the male contestants is standing there holding a leash—a leash attached to a choker around Rowena's neck. She's dressed in a ridiculous gold bikini, shivering in the cold. Without her usual floaty dresses, the swell of her pregnant belly is painfully obvious. It's disgusting, humiliating, and infuriating all at once.

I gasp, then clasp my hand to my mouth. I know I should storm in, rip that leash from the bastard's hand and beat him to a pulp. But something holds me back. Felix's voice, sharp and full of anger, cuts through the air again, and I realize he must be just out of my view.

"Let her go or I swear to God I'll rip your windpipe from your throat and strangle you with it." I've never cheered for Felix in anything, but I'm cheering silently now.

The man doesn't even flinch. "You've got your own hot piece of ass," he says, nodding to someone just out of view. "Leave me to do what I will with mine."

Felix is like a blur as he barrels into the man, knocking them both to the floor. Both men seem evenly matched, but it's weird to see Felix fist fighting. He spent his entire life having staff to fight his fights for him so he could keep his hands clean. His hands aren't clean now. He's like a man unhinged as he pummels the other man. But the other man is fighting back. I grit my teeth as I watch the pair. Felix gets him in a chokehold.

"Rowena. Go jump off the first flight of stairs," The man manages to grit out.

Almost as soon as the words leave his mouth, Rowena turns towards the stairs, her eyes a gleaming gold. The sound of the leash hits each step as she starts upwards.

"Shit!" I barrel fully through the door and race up the stairs after her, passing someone next to the stairs.

"Rowena stop!" I cry out, but her eyes remain gold and she continues on. I try holding her back, but she's stronger than I am. "Stop!" I cry, pulling on her arm. Tears roll down my face as she drags me from step to step.

"Command her to stop!" Felix yells out and I'm not sure if he's talking to me or the lunatic he's holding by the throat.

"I can't!" I yell back.

"Command her to stop or I will fucking end you. Do you hear me?"

The lunatic laughs, a strange high-pitched laugh, but doesn't say the words to make Ro stop. We're almost at the top of the first landing. It's about twenty feet from the ground. If she falls, she might survive, but it's unlikely. I grip onto her with all my might, forcing myself between Ro and the edge. Her eyes glisten unnaturally, but I know she sees me despite the compulsion. If she takes a step forward now, we're both going over the edge.

"Rowena!" I plead, my face wet with tears. "Please don't do this. You'll be killing your baby!"

A solitary tear streaks down her face, but she presses forward. First I go over the edge, then right after, she follows.

There's an almighty scream.

Half a second later, I fall on something soft and it takes a few seconds to realize Dade has me in his arm. Ro is holding onto his other arm, sobbing loudly now that the spell is broken.

"I heard you yelling stop," Dade explains as he flies us both back up to the landing we'd fallen from.

"You are fucking dead meat!"

I glance down to see Felix pound his fist into the man's nose. Blood spurts everywhere, but Felix doesn't stop.

"Felix!" Ro shouts out, causing him to momentarily pause.

"Don't kill him. You'll be out of the games."

Felix looks insane with madness, but there's something in his voice that lets the man go. The man's head drops to the side. He's not dead, but he's unconscious, which means Ro is safe for now.

"We need to get him to a hospital," Ro whispers.

I look at her incredulously. "He tried to kill you."

Before she can respond, Felix charges up the stairs, positioning himself protectively between us.

"Ro. You nearly fucking died. I almost lost you."

"But you didn't."

Felix's hands tremble, and I can see the storm brewing in his eyes. His chest rises and falls rapidly as he takes in Ro, making sure she's still standing, still breathing.

"That monster doesn't deserve our mercy," Felix growls, glancing back at the unconscious man. "What if he wakes up? What if he comes after you again?"

"And what if they throw you out of the games?"

"I would relinquish my place in the games if it meant keeping you safe. I will not let him touch you again." Felix clenches his jaw. The fire in his eyes flickers as he grapples with her words. "I'd rather burn this whole fucking place down than see you hurt."

"I know," she replies softly, reaching out to place a hand on his arm, grounding him.

I grip onto Dade as Felix leans in and takes Ro in his arms and kisses her.

I want to feel happy that Felix has finally got his shit

together where Rowena is concerned, but I can never forgive him for what he did to Jenny.

Ignoring the stab of pain in my heart watching them, I glance back down to the unconscious man and finally get a good look at the person Felix was with. The one I raced past in my desperation to get to Rowena before she threw herself off the landing.

My heart tightens and I can't breathe. Standing on the floor below me, staring up at me, tears in her eyes, is the one person I came to Hell for. The other half of my soul.

"Jenny?" I say in a hoarse whisper. I've heard her voice before in Hell, but it wasn't real. Maybe this isn't real either.

But then she starts to run up the stairs, her long red hair bouncing behind her.

"Quinn!" She throws herself into my arms and grips me tightly. Tears pour from my face as I hug her. I've found her. I've finally found my baby sister.

"I thought you were in the seventh circle?" I finally manage to say I pull back and look at her sweet fifteen year old face, covered in tears and snot and the most beautiful smile I've ever seen.

"I was, but yesterday they brought me here and put me in a cage in Felix's room."

"You're Felix's slave?" I glance over at Felix and my stare hardens.

"Don't worry. I'm not going to hurt her. There's only one woman I want, and I've finally got her." Felix turns back to Rowena, a smile spreading across his face, and that's when the anger in my chest ignites.

"That's all well and good, but she's the reason we all ended up here. You fucking raped her!"

"I literally met her for the first time about twenty

minutes ago, Snowflake. I gave her a fucking burger. Does that sound like the act of a rapist to you?"

Anger boils though my chest. "I saw a photo of you and her together so don't lie to me." I pull Jenny to me and wrap her protectively in my arms. She's wearing nothing but a gold bikini like Rowena. Whoever came up with this shit had some perverse Princess Leia fantasy.

"I. Have. Never. Met. Her. Before." Felix nods towards Jenny. "Ask her if you don't believe me."

I know he's lying. Maybe everything messes with my mind in Hell, but I saw the photo of them before I was shot. I turn to Jenny, hate how I'm exposing her to this. "Jenny. You know Felix right? Did he ever... hurt you?"

Jenny looks terrified. Slowly she turns her eyes to Felix then back to me. She lowers her head, nodding almost imperceptibly.

I point a finger at Felix. "Don't you dare come near my sister or me ever again." My voice shakes, and angry tears stream down my face as I turn to Rowena.

"And if you even think about dating this disgusting asshole after everything he's done, don't expect us to be friends."

With that, I take Jenny's hand and lead her up the stairs back to my room.

FREE COLORING BOOK!

Grab a free Inferno Games Coloring book here
https://dl.bookfunnel.com/dgn11s6xmo

ABOUT THE AUTHOR

Elise Knight is the secret pen name of a USA Today bestselling author. In this guise, she reads by candlelight while eating dark chocolate and wearing slippers. Her books contain fearless women and men you'll either want to kiss or kill (sometimes at the same time!)

You can find out more about her by checking out her Facebook page or signing up to her newsletter

https://www.eliseknight.com/newsletter

www.facebook.com/eliseknightsdreamers

Other Books by Elise Knight

INFERNO GAMES

Inferno Games

Lust

Insatiable

Greed

REALM OF NIGHT SERIES

Dream King

Nightmare King

Queen of Darkness

BLIND SIN DUET

Sinful

Blind Sin